The Aussie Sinner

by

Lynn Shurr

A Sinner's Legacy, Book 7

The Aussie Sinner

Cover Art by *Diana Carlile*

The Wild Rose Press, Inc.
PO Box 708
Adams Basin, NY 14410-0708
Visit us at www.thewildrosepress.com

Publishing History
First Champagne Rose Edition, 2021
Trade Paperback ISBN 978-1-5092-3417-2
Digital ISBN 978-1-5092-3418-9

A Sinner's Legacy, Book 7
Published in the United States of America

"I'm sorry. What I did was cruel—but no more so than making a fool of me in front of my friends."

"Not my doing. Angus blurted out what I wanted to tell you and didn't get the time—that I did want to meet the great Joe Billodeaux and have a go at the Sinners, but that wasn't all. Didn't you hear me say you were more important to me than that?"

"I did, but believed you lied."

"No, I wanted to court you like a princess and ran out of time. Then you were on your way home and without giving me a chance to speak. I thought you didn't mean the things you said to me about quitting and going back to Australia. I suppose because even the worse situations have always turned out well for me in the end. Cockeyed optimist." He gave her one of his irresistible grins. Only this one did not reach full-blown and skewed to one side.

"I believe you now. A girl who loves tiny penguins and platypuses wouldn't hurt any creature she cared for. I can't marry you, Lori, but I can give you what you want. I called the agent and told him I wouldn't sign the contract. I'm going back to Australia, my team, my mates, my brothers. I was willing to leave them all behind for you."

"That's insane!"

Praise for Lynn Shurr

"Shurr is a wonderful storyteller."

~The Romance Studio

~*~

"Lynn Shurr's delightful New Orleans Sinners series is sure to please both non-sports fans and sports fans alike. Do yourself a favor and dive into the world of the Sinners."

~Farrah Rochon, USA Today best-selling author
of the New York Sabers football series

~*~

"The author has created a family full of surprises with the Billodeaux bunch. After reading just one book, I am eager to read more about this colorful family."

~Rachel's Willful Thoughts, The Romance Reviews

~*~

"Very easy reads, well written, combined with conflict, believable plots and secondary characters that make the plot come alive."

~Jane Lange, Romances, Reads and Reviews

~*~

"I love how deep and well-written the characters are."

~Juliette Brandt, Blogger

Dedication

To my intrepid Australian guides,
Ngaire Douglas and Peter Burns,
who informed me about Australian Rules Football.
Any mistakes are definitely my own.

Author's Note

A few years ago, I was privileged to travel to Australia, a place full of wonders and wonderful people. While touring Melbourne, the plot to *The Aussie Sinner* came to me, but with other books in the works, I began the story a year later. Before I was able to finish it, along came the devastating fires that turned the Sydney skyline red and then the COVID-19 epidemic that rocked the world. Personally, I underwent some serious surgery and painful physical therapy not conducive to spending hours at the computer. Having started in September 2019, I typed the final words in May 2020 during my last week of seclusion from the virus.

I want to say this is a pre-fire, pre-epidemic story with Australia and the world as it used to be before these events. I hope it will take the reader's mind off such dire problems for at least a short time. My apologies if I got any of my Australian facts wrong, because I know I have a few fans on that continent. As I always promise, the book does have a happily ever after, and I wish the same to all of you.

~Lynn Shurr

A SINNER'S LEGACY
The Children of Joe and Nell Billodeaux
who fulfilled the prophecy that they would have
twelve offspring, this way, that way, all ways.

1. Dean Joseph Billodeaux — Joe's illegitimate son by a one-night stand with a woman who planned to shake him down for money. He is adopted by Nell who believes she cannot have children of her own. Current Sinners quarterback. (*Wish for a Sinner* and *Son of a Sinner*)

2. Thomas Cassidy Billodeaux — a redheaded son who enters the family through an open adoption with a teenage mother. His birth father is Joe's no-good cousin. He is a kicker for the Sinners. *(Wish for a Sinner. Kicks for a Sinner, She's a Sinner)*

3. Jude Emily Billodeaux — twin of Ann, conceived by in vitro fertilization using eggs purchased from Nell's sister, Emily. (*Wish for a Sinner*)

4. Ann Marie Billodeaux (Annie) — Jude's quiet twin. (*Wish for a Sinner* and *The Heart of a Sinner*)

5. Lorena Renee Billodeaux (Lori) — First of Nell's little frozen babies to be born, one of the triplets. (*Kicks for a Sinner* and *The Aussie Sinner*)

6. Mack Coy Christopher Billodeaux — Second of the triplets to be born. (*Kicks for a Sinner)*

7. Trinity Billodeaux — Youngest of the triplets and named for the Father, Son, and Holy Ghost, smallest of the three and in need of a powerful saintly help to survive. (*Kicks for a Sinner, Dream for a Sinner, Goals for a Sinner*)

8. Xochi Maria Billodeaux — child of Joe's no-good cousin by a young Mexican woman. She is Tom's half-

sister and is adopted into the family after the terrifying deaths of her parents. Her name means "blossom" in Aztec. (*Kicks for a Sinner* and *Sister of a Sinner*)

9. Teddy Wilkes Billodeaux — a child with spina bifida abandoned by his mother at Nell's health care center and adopted by the family. He believed himself to be Joe's natural son. (*Paradise for a Sinner* and *Never A Sinner*)

10. Anastasia Marya Polasky (Stacy) — daughter of Nell's sister, Emily, and a bogus Polish prince. She becomes a ward of the Billodeauxs upon her parents' deaths but is never adopted by her own wish. She arrives on their doorstep the same day as Teddy. (*Paradise for a Sinner* and *Son of a Sinner*)

11. Edith Patricia Billodeaux (Edie) — a normally conceived child, twin of Rex. (*Love Letter for a Sinner*)

12. Rex Worthy Billodeaux (T-Rex) — Edie's twin brother and future Sinner's quarterback, maybe. (*Love Letter for a Sinner*)

Chapter One

March and the hot, sweaty palm of Australia's summer had yet to lift itself in favor of the cooler hand of Melbourne's autumn. The heat rested heavily on the shoulders of Jock Brown. He did not care. In a few weeks, he'd either be training for Australian Rules Football or, if his plans went well, be on his way to the States to have a go at the NFL. Meanwhile, he and one of his footy teammates sat blistering their behinds in the stands watching the Amazing Maisie Morton and her partner crush their opponents in beach volleyball.

"We're sitting here burning our arses because you want to see if Maisie still has enough left in her for another go at the Olympics, is that it? Personally, I think the new girl is propping her up a bit after having two kids—or do you have something else in mind?" Angus McCall remarked to his best mate.

Jock's gaze never left the sandy court or Maisie's partner. "Would you look at the way that long, black braid whips back and forth like the tail of a tiger snake," he said of the tall and lean young woman returning a volley.

"Snakes are mostly tail, right?"

"Yup." But he wasn't imaging that kind of tail. The player he had his eyes on fell to her knees to make a ferocious dig that sent the ball high into the air before it hit the ground, a perfect setup for short-haired, blonde

Maisie to smash it across the net into the faces of the other pair and score a point. As her partner rose on those fantastic legs, she tugged her bikini up to cover a tiny exposure of crack.

He envisioned hooking his fingers on either side of that bottom and drawing it all the way down to her ankles, then stripping off the tight athletic bra that flattened what he believed to be a fair-sized set of breasts, maybe deeply tanned like the rest of her body. Probably, she had a wax job like most female athletes, but what kind? So much to discover and enjoy. A sharp elbow caught him in the ribs.

"Now I got it. You want to shag Maisie's girl. Wouldn't waste my time on that. She turned me down flat the other night when I went over to her table at a bar and asked her if she wanted to give it a go. She said, 'no,' not even a no thanks, just went back to her beer and her hen party. I meant have a dance, but she seemed to take it another way. Maybe she's a lesbian. Lots of them are. I mean, who turns down this." Angus cocked a freckled arm and raised an impressive bicep.

The women taking a water break failed to notice. After a few swigs, the brunette upended her bottle and let the stream flow down her neck and into her cleavage. Jock followed every drop to its destination while still tweaking Angus. "Could be she didn't care for that enormous ego you carry between your legs, or maybe she doesn't like gingers."

"What? All the girls love gingers." Angus raked his thick mop of red hair between his fingers, making it stand on end. "It's the Prince Harry effect, but that one is a lot darker than Duchess Meaghan. Think she's got abo blood?"

Jock took a turn giving his teammate an elbow rougher than the one he'd received earlier. "Indigenous peoples. Don't be so crude. You're aggro with her because she turned you down. What you're looking at there is a Cajun gal. They take a tan well, unlike you, who peels like an orange the first few weeks of the playing season. And she is royalty, American royalty."

"Huh? Like a film star?"

He enjoyed his mate's gob smacked expression for a moment before moving on. "Nope, sports royalty. She's one of Joe Billodeaux's daughters. You know, the NFL quarterback who won five Super Bowls and is still a big name in the game despite being retired. You don't treat her like any female you want to root. A woman like that needs to be wooed."

"Good luck, mate. Her eyes might be that inviting deep dark brown, but the 'get lost' stare she gave me nearly froze my nads."

"I'd guess she's used to being hit on by athletes, but I have a plan." He called up a list on his phone entitled *Ten Most Romantic Places in Melbourne and Vicinity* and showed it to Angus.

"Really? Punting at the botanical garden. That I'd like to see. I beg you to take me along."

"Won't be enough room in the boat for your over-sized carcass."

"I don't see it. Women throw themselves at a footy ruckman. Why bother?"

"Because I have an itch to go to the States and try out for the New Orleans Sinners. Lorena Billodeaux might help me out with a few introductions." Not all he had in mind, but no sense wasting his time explaining to Angus.

Angus McCall went breathless for a minute and then let his words spew. "Are you mad? Aussie Rules is the best game in the world. Non-stop action, no padding like those soft Yanks wear—and you. I forgot about your thigh and knee pads. Maybe you'd fit right in."

Jock rose, all six feet six of him, a mountain of muscle, and he knew it. "You saying I'm soft. You play ruckman just once, bashing into another man the same size to tip the ball, and you'd understand why I wear pads."

"Sit down. Sit down. You know I'm too short for a ruckman. I can't believe you'd desert Collingwood and all your mates on the team. You holding out for more money?"

Jock shook his head. Unlike Angus of the wild locks, he kept his sandy hair clipped close, less to get in the way when playing. "It's not the money. I haven't signed my contract yet. I'd like to see the world, try other options while I still can. I've had to care for my brothers since I was fourteen with mum dead and pop on the dole and the grog. He drank up the money as soon as it came into his hands if I didn't meet him at the bank and shake some out of him. Good for us I was taller than him by fifteen. Now, the boys are settled. Mick is finishing his EMT training, and Nick is studying medicine same as I wanted. He might find a cure for the cancer that killed our mum. I'm leaving them my unit now that they're responsible enough not to use it for partying."

"Like you never did."

"Not when the boys were around. I shipped them to boarding school to get them off Brunswick Street as soon as I had the money. Tried to get Pop to move, but he didn't want to leave the mates he drank with and the pubs who would let him run a tab. He passed away from liver disease in the same sorry house where we grew up with a prostitute on one corner and a drug dealer on the next. He kept saying the place was bought and paid for by his time in the mines, and he wasn't leaving."

"Yeah, tough neighborhood, Collingwood. That's why it turns out the best footy players." Angus watched another volley cross the net. Again, Maisie scored a kill thanks to a nice assist from her partner.

"Funny thing, those old hovels are being gentrified now. I got a wad of cash for it when I put it up for sale. The bistros are pushing out the tattoo parlors. One more point, and I'm going to chat her up. You coming?"

"Wouldn't miss seeing you go down in flames. Maybe then you'll think twice about deserting your teammates for American football." Angus managed to infuse those last two words with all the scorn he could muster.

"Match point. And Amazing Maisie and Lovely Lorena do it again. Only fitting we get down there and congratulate them." Jock took the steps to the sand two at a time, easy to do with his long legs. He jumped a barrier and made nice with a guard, explaining who he was and his desire to congratulate the winners. Turned out the man was a Collingwood fan who waved him through. Angus tagged along to watch the show.

****

Lorena followed Maisie, thanking their opponents for a good game. They toweled off, drank more water, and picked up their kits to head to the locker room and a refreshing shower. "Here they come, Lori. You've attracted a pair of footy lads. They've eyed you the entire game."

"You think they're for real? Anyone can buy a black and white striped Collingwood jersey."

"They're for real, even wearing their own numbers on their guernseys. Lord knows I've seen those two beat my Roos more than once."

"Why do you think they're interested in me?"

"They aren't looking to root these ancient bones. I have stretch marks from my babies older than them." Maisie gave her slightly rounded belly a rueful glance. Otherwise lean as Lorena, athletic tape covered her old injuries.

"Not true. Your children are five and seven, and you're still in great shape."

"Speaking of which, we have to talk." Maisie avoided her partner's dark brown eyes.

Lorena tried to make light of it. "Are we breaking up?"

"Let's get showered and go carbo-load on Lygon Street. How about Piccolo Mondo? I'm paying."

Worse and worse, this sounded like taking a date to a public place to give her the bad news. Usually, Maisie wanted to get home to her kids while her superb husband made a dinner worth eating, often on the proverbial barbie. What could she do but say, "Sure, I'm always up for Italian, and Piccolo Mondo is one of the best. Maybe we can take something home and give Augie a break on slaving over your cooker."

He'd arrived, a sandy-haired giant with green eyes brought out by his tan, and all over muscles. "How ya goin', Maisie? I'd say you were amazing again today."

His accent was pure Melbourne, which is to say he

didn't draw out his vowels like many Australians and pronounced his native town as Mel-bun, which Lorena learned soon after her arrival. Many people considered the residents of this fine city built on the profits from gold mining, full of beautiful parks, Victorian buildings, and wonderful museums, to be guilty of snobbery. Lorena thought they had reason to be proud.

He held out a hand big enough to engulf a football, tuck, and carry it across the field. "Jock Brown, ruckman for the Magpies, and this is Angus McCall, only a humble rover." The two men engaged in more of the elbowing she'd noticed earlier. "But the best in the game. When I need a target, I can't miss that flaming red hair. Are you a Collingwood fan by any chance?"

Maisie's usually cordial face fell into a frown. "ABC," she said. "Anything *but* Collingwood."

"I do get tired of hearing that." He turned to Lorena. "You're a Yank, I hear. We're like the New England Patriots. Everyone hates us because we're great. I hope that doesn't extend to you." The hand he'd offered to Maisie now came her way.

She shook, noting that he didn't try to crush her fingers as some men that big might. "Lorena Billodeaux. Since I come from Louisiana, I might take exception at being called a Yank. I'm Cajun through and through."

Jock snapped his fingers as if something had just occurred to him. "Any relation to the great quarterback, Joe Billodeaux?"

"Otherwise known as my dad. You follow American football?"

"Avidly."

The redhaired rover, who'd said nothing, snorted.

"Not as good as what we've got here."

"Certainly not as rough and tumble as footy," she agreed. She'd long since learned not to get into debates over which sport was superior.

"You've been to our games, then? I'll fix you up with tickets when the season starts," the irrepressible Jock Brown said.

Before he could go any farther, Masie cut him off. "We have only a shower and lunch in our near future. If you'd just step aside."

He did, but not without an exit line. "Pleasure to meet you, Lorena. Let us take you for that lunch."

"We'll be a while. Why don't you move along?" Maisie nodded for Lorena to precede her to the locker room and guarded her back as they went.

It really wasn't like Maisie to be so short with people. Once inside the cool, tiled interior of the locker room, Lori questioned her attitude. "I thought he was quite polite and sort of charming."

"They all are. You shouldn't get mixed up with a footy player."

Lorena laughed. "My mother might give the same advice—yet she married a football player as did three of my sisters. They aren't all tossers." She used the local term for jerk. Having little to strip off, she padded toward the showers.

"I made an offer of the partnership, took you away from home. You're part of my family now. I stand in her stead. Be careful, Lorena."

Chapter Two

Electing not to sit outside, Lorena and Maisie entered the cool interior of Piccolo Mondo, its walls rustic brick and tables topped with red cloths. Greeting them with a smile, the hostess led the way to one of the many four tops. A huge hand waving in the air stopped their progress.

"Why not share a table with us, ladies?" Jock Brown asked, offering them the two extra seats.

"Sorry," Maisie countered. "We have details of today's game to discuss. You'd be bored." She gave the waitress a curt nod to seat them elsewhere, which she did.

"I think they're stalking us," she told Lorena.

"Maisie, they were here first. Maybe they think we're stalking them. I'll bet women do." Still a little dehydrated from the game, Lori asked for water rather than a drink. Maisie did the same. A basket of hot bread arrived with the beverage, and they settled in, ordering linguine accompanied by prawns and gnocchi gorgonzola. Two tables over loud enough for them to hear, the men they'd rejected asked for the barbecued calamari, and the inky linguine also made with squid.

Lori wrinkled her very straight nose. "I don't know how they can eat that stuff. I mean fried calamari is okay, but served in its own ink? I don't think so."

"They're showing off their manliness is my guess,

still trying to get our attention. Ignore them. Have some bread."

Waiting for whatever was to come, Lori did that. They discussed today's game until the last remains of the meal sat on their plates. Maisie ordered a large lasagna to take home—which gave them more time to talk. She placed her wide, tanned hand over Lori's and looked her in the eye.

She'd been here before, but back in the States, way back in college when Stuart took her to a fancy restaurant, not their usual hangouts, and grasped her hand in exactly the same way. While she'd majored in physical education and kinesics, mostly because she only wanted to play volleyball on a top team, she'd avoided jocks and other athletes. The last item on the Lorena Billodeaux agenda was marriage to a football player. She'd seen enough of them with two of her brothers in the game, plus most of the family friends.

On a whim, she'd taken an elective in philosophy for a change of pace. *Cogito, ergo sum*; I think therefore I am, about all she had retained from that class. But there she'd met Stuart Fogler, tall, skinny, long-haired, and bearded. Stu, so full of idealism for mankind that his plans to save the world simply burst from his mouth on any occasion. This included post-coital conversation on the mattress laid on the floor of his messy apartment. Deep, very deep, and so unlike the blunt come-ons from athletes. He had awed her.

Maybe taking him home to meet the family had been a poor idea. Not that the Billodeauxs didn't do marvelous good deeds through their charities. Her mother worked for free as a psychologist at the local health clinic. Her dad made numerous appearances at events for worthy causes. Plus, their large family ran Camp Love Letter for seriously ill children every summer on the ranch. They did immediate good for those nearby. Voltaire: "Take care of your own garden, and the world will take care of itself" should be their motto. Ah, she'd soaked in more philosophy than she'd thought.

Stuart's idealism was of a different sort. He wanted to end world hunger and stop nuclear proliferation, lofty goals with murky solutions. Still, she'd been impressed. The girls on the volleyball team did not understand the enchantment and would have preferred one of her hunky brothers. Sexually, he'd been better than her high school boyfriend, all hands and tongue, and eager to get to the main event. Stu had endless patience, but in hindsight, she'd done most of the work, suspecting his mind traveled to loftier realms while she concentrated on the physical.

Needless to say, he hadn't been a good fit at Lorena Ranch. To him, dragon boat races for the camp kids seemed frivolous as did pizza parties. What of children starving in Africa? We give to those causes as well, her parents said. Here we offer one week of joy to those who have little. Her dad had given Stuart one of his backslaps that nearly propelled her boyfriend into the bayou and pretty much avoided Stu thereafter. Not that anyone had been mean to the guy, but even her nerdy brother, Trinity, gave computer lessons to camp kids and worked on the newsletter. Stuart contributed nothing but criticism.

At the end of junior year, they broke up in a place like this in a scene like this. He'd joined the Peace Corps without telling her. Going to college wasn't saving the world. Well, yeah, he'd majored in philosophy. She should do the same, quit school, quit volleyball, and her goal to play in the Olympics one day. Maybe they could get dual assignments in Africa. He didn't mention marriage. Just as well since her reply had been what were her qualifications—the ability to teach volleyball to girls who often weren't allowed to go to school. Some good that would do them. She'd split with him in a temper, not in tears. Right now, she felt more like crying as Maisie covered her hand.

A motion at the other table caught her eye. Jock Brown held up a fork spooled with black spaghetti, nodded to show her how tasty it was, and downed his final bite while his friend mopped up the last of his barbecue sauce with a roll and made a whispered comment, probably snide. Lorena slid her hand away. "Just say it, Maisie. It's you, not me. We don't suit as partners after two years of playing together."

"No, oh, no. I'm preggers again. You know how we don't get our periods often when we're doing heavy training. I can't keep track. Augie got frisky one night, and now I'm up the duff, over three months along. The doc says I need a break if I want to carry this one to term. Not as young as I used to be. I'll do what I did the other two times, take a year off, then come roaring back in time for the Olympics. Meanwhile, you go home but stay in shape. I wouldn't have anyone else when I return. I love my little rippers but hope this one will be a girl. I'd like to name her after you."

Relieved and touched, Lorena dabbed at her eyes with the corner of a napkin. "I'd be honored, and I am happy for you. I'll need time to send word home and get my stuff together, but I've missed two family weddings already. One of my triplet brothers is getting married in May. I want to be home for that."

"The gorgeous one who plays for Dallas? I guess I've missed my chance with him, but you stay with us as long as you need. You're family now."

"I don't think Augie would let you go. No, not Mack, my geek brother. He's marrying Josee Riley."

"Sweet as! The supermodel? And you didn't tell me. How did that come about?"

"Thought you'd know by now. It's been in all the celebrity magazines."

"As if I have time for reading anything at all."

The waitress returned with a large aluminum pan of lasagna covered in foil. Maisie handed over a credit card and said, "It's what's for dinner. You coming along now?"

Lorena shook her head. "No, I think I'll stay downtown for a while. Maybe do some souvenir shopping. After being gone two years, I'd better bring something home for the clan. Don't worry. I'll find my way to your place in time to share that."

She waited until Maisie passed from sight, balancing the container of lasagna on her fingertips, before summoning the waitress and ordering a glass of Yarra Valley pinot noir. She dabbed at her eyes again. Glad for Maisie, yes. Certain she hadn't just thrown away two years of her life and Olympic dreams, no. All might turn out, as Maisie said, but sports careers had no certainty. What could she do for the next year except train on her own?

The waitress returned with double servings of tiramisu, two glasses, and a bottle of red wine. Right behind her, Jock Brown settled himself in Maisie's former seat. "Seemed like you could use something sweet and more than one glass of wine."

Had she looked that miserable and distraught? "Thanks, but I really don't want company now. Why don't you take that dessert back to your table and share it with your mate? He doesn't appear very happy either. But you can leave the bottle."

"I'd be irresponsible if I let you drink all that alone. Tell me your worries. I'm a good listener," he claimed.

She raised her dark brows, doubting that. At his former table, Angus rolled his blue eyes. "I'll keep it brief, then you can go. Maisie is pregnant again, so I'm going back to the States soon. I don't know if I'll return."

"Tough, like getting cut from a team, but she might bounce back, our Maisie. When are you leaving?" He filled both glasses, offered her one.

"Maisie says no hurry. I might take time to see sights I've missed while I've been here, always training."

"I do know. Let me show you some of my favorite places. Ever been punting on the Yarra River? We can rent a boat at the Royal Botanic Gardens tomorrow."

Lorena sipped her wine, a more expensive vintage than she'd ordered. It paired nicely with the tiramisu she discovered at first bite. What the hell, she wouldn't be here much longer and could shake free of Jock Brown before she left. "Okay, I've gone running there. Beautiful place, but I've never been on the river. You do know how to punt?"

"I'm sure I'll be a natural at it. Or did you mean the American football term for kicking the ball as far as it will go when you lost your chance to score."

"Maybe both."

"I'd be good at that, too. Ever seen my drop punt? I'm brilliant at the torpedo and the banana kick as well."

"Not to mention your colossal modesty. I'm not sure American football would have any use for them as Aussie rules uses kicks to score. We only use kicks for field goals and extra points."

He shrugged his huge shoulders. "I have other skills. Lots of them. So meet you at the dock at half two—or stop by Maisie's place?"

Considering how aggressive and conceited the man seemed, he'd given her a choice to make her feel comfortable. Surprising. "I'll meet you there at three."

"Grand. We can have tea afterward. Now, what are your plans for this arvo?"

She had no trouble translating it into this afternoon. She'd heard it often enough. Should she tell him and risk having him follow her around for the rest of the day?

At the other table, Angus rapped his fingers against the tabletop and looked at his huge sports watch. "Half a mo'. My mate is getting restless."

Jock rose, grabbed a clean wine glass from another table, filled it from their bottle, and carried the offering to his impatient teammate. After a bit of a confab, the redheaded man tossed the wine down as if it were water, slammed the empty glass on the table, and walked out.

"Is there a problem?" Lorena asked.

"No worries. He's jealous because I'm sitting with a beautiful woman."

"Flattery will get you nowhere."

"A man can try." He upended the last of the wine into his glass since hers was still half full.

How had they emptied the bottle so quickly? She did feel better, almost giddy, not a good sign. Had he gotten her liquored up for seduction? Still, she answered his question. "Souvenir shopping for my family. For all the time I've been here, I haven't bought a thing for them. Talk about last minute."

"Queen Victoria Market has tons of souvenirs, but mostly made in China. Now, if you want high class, try the National Gallery gift shop. Let me take you there. I've been meaning to see the aboriginal art exhibit."

"Really?" He certainly didn't seem the type to spend an afternoon in an art gallery.

"Haven't seen it, now have I? I'll bring you back to your car after."

"Actually, I'd like to see that, too, but I'm not driving. I planned to take a taxi to Maisie's house."

"I can do that, free of charge." Jock helped her out of her chair and offered her his arm.

She wasn't that drunk, but she laid her bare arm on top of his anyway. A warm feeling swept over her body. Probably just the wine. A laugh bubbled out of her. Off to see native art with a jock named Jock.

Chapter Three

Mothering her again, Maisie dropped Lorena at the park gate nearest the dock. "If you need a ride home, call me."

"I'm sure I'll be fine. Jock was a complete gentleman yesterday."

Maybe too complete, but she'd decided to take her chances. They had toured the aboriginal art collection from its primitive beginnings to modern works, some done with neon lights. Inspired by what she'd learned, she scooped up items in the gift shop: a pile of bright tea towels in native patterns covered in emu tracks, signs for water, and women sitting in a circle, a stack of wooden bowls with similar motifs burned into their sides, and a sack of boomerangs crafted by locals that she believed her brothers would get a kick out of throwing. The tab ran a little high, but she'd put it on her credit card after rejecting an offer by Jock to foot the bill. Afterward, they went for coffee at a nearby café and simply talked about what they'd seen and what she'd purchased.

"Huge family. I need a lot of stuff."

"Probably could have gotten it cheaper elsewhere."

"My mother always said the money spent at a museum goes back to support it. I try to follow in her footsteps—although my feet are a great deal larger than hers."

Jock eyed her polished toenails shown to advantage by sandals. "They seem fine to me. Goes with the rest of you really well. Sounds like you have quite a family."

"Don't pretend you don't know about the Billodeauxs."

"Only what I read in celebrity mags. Are they really that solid, that giving?" He spoke as if he couldn't imagine it being true.

"Yes, but we are also competitive and in each other's business. Coming to Australia with Maisie was me getting away from all that for a while, but I miss them. I hope the offer to be in Trinity's wedding still stands since he's my triplet brother."

"To the supermodel. Lucky man."

"I doubt luck had much to do with it. Trinity always tries too hard to succeed in other ways because he can't compete athletically. Josee has lots of good sense, though. They'll do well together. Now, tell me you've never dated a supermodel."

He didn't deny it. "Some of the Aussie ones. Beautiful but somehow lacking, in what I couldn't tell you."

Soon after, he'd driven her home in his Toyota HiLux Predator, white with a black hood and a magpie decal on the rear, a vehicle her brothers would approve. Jock had gotten down to help her out as if she were a delicate outback flower with a short blooming season when she was perfectly capable of jumping from the cab of any truck with her long legs. Still, this old-fashioned courtesy had a nice feel about it. She half expected him to cage her against the now closed door for a kiss, and he might have if Maisie hadn't come bounding out to save her whether she wanted her to or not. Now Maisie cautioned her again at the gate into the lavish gardens.

Lorena said, "Yes, Mom, I'll be careful of big, bad Jock," and slammed the door to Maisie's car. She set off on the winding path lush with eucalypts of many varieties along with foreign specimens. A flock of lorikeets, heard but not seen in the heavy foliage, chattered as she passed. Two kookaburras sitting on opposing branches released their insane laughter at each other or possibly her. Was she foolish to go on this oddly archaic date? She began to hum the children's song about a kookaburra sitting in a gum tree, a favorite of the kids that came to Camp Love Letter. They loved that the bird mistook them for monkeys. The shaded path opened to the sunny dock, tearoom, and gift shop.

She didn't see any sign of Jock. Jilted? Maybe simply late. Checking her watch, she took a seat on a bench. No, she was the late one by fifteen minutes. Maisie had made a leisurely drive of it. No worries, as the Aussies said so often. If he didn't show, she'd simply enjoy the afternoon and walk the paths reading the signs instead of running past all the attractions. She continued to hum the song to herself, waiting, waiting. She'd give him fifteen minutes.

A pair of large hands covered her eyes. Jock didn't say, "Guess who?" but in that wonderful Melbourne accent replied, "You aren't certainly a monkey, but you are late." Jock dropped his hands, rounded the bench, and joined her. "If you're ready, I've already rented a boat, even got a short lesson in punting. All you have to do is enjoy the ride."

He offered a hand to pull her up and didn't release

it until they stood on the dock where the fellow who rented the punts helped her into the boat to rest on cushions in the bow. As Jock stepped into the stern, the small craft wobbled under his weight. He steadied it with the pole that reached the bottom of the shallow, tea-colored waters and pushed off. "Don't worry, I won't dunk you, but you do swim just in case?"

"Like an otter. I grew up with a pool, and I have my lifeguard certification."

"Good, then you can save me. I surf, but I'm no otter."

A shark, perhaps, she wondered.

He regarded their surroundings as he propelled the boat forward. "Not the prettiest river in the world, the Yarra, all silty and brown."

That made her laugh. "You've never seen a Louisiana bayou then. So full of mud, you can't see the bottom. Still, people do swim and fish in them."

"I'd like to do that someday. Never got farther than San Francisco."

"You don't travel much?"

"No, I had to look out for my two brothers since my parents died. Didn't think I could be away too long and leave them unattended."

She started to question him about that subject, but a bird striding on large yellow feet over the lily pads caught her eye. "Look, a purple gallinule. We have them in our marshes."

"You a bird watcher, then?" He steadied the boat again as it had canted when he turned toward the bird. Otherwise, Jock appeared to pole along without effort, his muscles hardly straining. She'd chosen a white sundress and borrowed a large straw hat with a silk rose in the pink headband, which made her feel like a Victorian lady being courted by her swain, fitting for Melbourne founded in that era.

"Not really, but we have so many species in our state a person can't help but learn the names of a few."

"Tell me more about Louisiana."

She would rather have pursued his comment about his brothers but had no chance. Another unexpected sight got her attention. "I believe we have company. Isn't that Angus coming up behind us?" Being a weekday, they'd had the waters pretty much to themselves until now.

Jock chanced a glance over his shoulder. "Yeah, and Willie Taylor, the other rover for the Magpies." He dug in the push pole and sent the boat surging forward.

"Looks like they're trying to catch up to us." While Jock had dressed in practical khaki shorts and a deep green polo shirt that spanned across his chest and enhanced his eyes, Angus and his friend wore whites like the officials at the footy games and straw boaters. Willie lolled on the cushions, a grand dame being escorted by a servant.

Jock hadn't gotten enough of a head start to outdistance them. Bends in the river had obscured the other craft until now in a straightaway. Angus poled mightily to draw abreast.

"I say, old chap, excellent day for punting." His friend aped a British accent. Willie guffawed.

"What are you now, Angus, a bloody Pom? Bugger off." Jock executed another hard shove and drew ahead.

Angus matched him, coming close to their boat, almost bumping it. He'd switched the pole to the same side as well. Lorena sat up. She'd seen her brothers duel in pirogues to upset each other, not to mention tangling oars in the dragon boat races, which sometimes became heated. She prepared herself as Angus crossed poles with Jock preventing him from drawing away again. They sparred as if dueling with staffs, each one trying to push the other away. The boats rocked dangerously. Lorena leaned forward and shot out one of her strong, tanned hands that had delivered many a crushing blow over a volleyball net. She jerked their rival's pole from his grip and plowed it into the side of his punt. The boat heeled over enough take on water. With Willie jerking up and Angus wheeling his arms like a red pinwheel, the craft overturned and dumped them in the muddy waters.

Jock grinned, maybe shark-like, certainly white enough in the sunshine. "You can play on my team any day, Lori."

"As I said, I have lots of brothers. I'm able to play rough when I must."

He pulled ahead and executed a rather awkward turn. "Almost teatime. We have to go back."

"Aren't you going to help them out?"

"Throw them the pole as we pass. It's plenty shallow. They won't drown."

She did as he asked. Angus caught it with the hand not clinging to the overturned punt. With their whites no longer pristine, Willie watched his straw hat drift away on the sluggish current. Jock laughed so hard she thought they might tip, too. They left the men sputtering in the water. Tea awaited.

In the small restaurant with wide windows overlooking the river, a table covered with a white cloth sat already bearing a tiered tray of cucumber sandwiches, lox and cream cheese on rye, a whole layer of scones, and a topping of iced cakes and chocolate-covered strawberries. Jock pulled out a chair for her and motioned the waitress to bring the pot of tea, piping hot. She poured a cup for each. Though they started properly with the sandwiches, Lorena couldn't wait for the scones. She'd developed a taste for them, better than any she'd had in the States.

In Jock's big hands, the dainty wedges of crustless bread seemed ridiculous. Certainly, a man that size could devour the entire tray of goodies and still be hungry. Yet he split the sandwiches between them before reaching for a warm scone and breaking it open. Lorena hurried to catch up. She'd learned to pronounce the word as scon with no long e on the end to avoid ridicule, but when she loaded hers with strawberry jam from a little pot, Jock said, "Here now, it's the clotted cream first, then the jam. Didn't Maisie teach you that?"

"Let's say we rarely had time for fancy teas, though I've been to some at home when the women of the family were invited to a charity event. At the ranch, we're more barbecue and pig roast people."

"Sounds like an Aussie would fit right in."

"If you mean eating huge amounts of meat with a beer chaser, yes."

He grinned wide as the Cheshire cat. "That's exactly what I meant. Throw some kangaroo steaks on the barbie, and it's all a man could wish for, except for sharing it with a bonzer girl."

She ignored the compliment. "I know kangaroo tastes like beef. I've had it a few times. People say the tail is the best, exactly like alligator, but I can't say I've tried it."

"Why not? You can find the tail in the frozen food section."

A commotion at the entry cut off their discussion of strange foods. Their waitress, her gray hair bundled into a net, and practical white nurse's shoes on her feet trundled toward the door. "Here, now. You boys can't come in like that, all wet and muddy."

Angus pointed toward their table. "We're meeting friends."

"No, you aren't. That's tea for two. I know a crasher when I see one—or a couple." She gave the miserable, dripping Willie the evil eye as well. "Sit yourself down on the bench out there, and I'll bring out what you want. I doubt it's girlish tucker."

Willie, his dark hair plastered on his forehead, dripping down his chin and off his short goatee, said, "A roast beef sandwich would be right on the spot. Hot coffee to go with it."

"Make that for two." Angus plodded toward the sunny bench leaving a wake of muddy footprints behind.

Totally without sympathy, Jock finished his second scone, licked a bit of jam off his big thumb, and scarfed up a petit four topped with a candied violet. Lorena selected a chocolate-covered strawberry and bit off the end. They watched each other's gestures as if they were foreplay. Could be it was. Her mind roved in that direction, but Jock broke the spell by asking where she'd been in Australia.

"Oh, up to Sydney, Bondi Beach. I played a few friendly volleyball games, but had to hold back and let others have a chance to win."

"Did they?"

"No. I couldn't help myself, but I didn't make them eat sand very often. I took surfing lessons, too. We have more swamp than beaches in Louisiana."

"Bet you were good at it."

"So the instructor said, but he believed in a lot of hands on instruction, a little too much hands on for my taste."

By the intensity of his green eyes, Jock appeared to be making mental notes in a book with her name on the cover. Flattering if he meant to please her. He picked up a tiny macaron and ate it in one bite, just as he might do to her. She shivered.

"The air-conditioning too cold in here for you? Have another cuppa. It will warm you."

She already felt warm. The A/C had nothing to do with it.

"Where else have you gone?"

"Out to the Great Barrier Reef for some snorkeling. Amazing place. Do you snorkel?"

"Can't say that I do. You'll have to teach me—hands on."

"I'd be willing," slipped from her lips before she could stop herself.

"Another day. How about the Penguin Parade on Phillip Island? It's a nice day's outing. We can stop at a wildlife sanctuary. I know you like Italian food. There's a great place by the bay. The birds don't come out of the ocean until dusk. I can book tickets for tomorrow."

"I'd love to do that, but don't you have training for footy season right now?"

"I train all the time. They only give us the months off around Christmas. I can spare a few days for you."

Obviously, he did not lie. Every part of his body appeared toned and chiseled. "Fine, let's do the Penguin Parade tomorrow."

The waitress hustled by with two large roast beef sandwiches and mugs of hot coffee, delivering her burden to the two soaking men on the bench.

"Finished?" Jock asked. "I prepaid. We can leave any time."

"Really full, but I'm taking that last scone with me." Lorena wrapped it in a napkin and stuffed it into the small purse she'd brought along. Again, Jock helped with her chair. He led her past his two wet mates without a glance their way.

"Shall we stroll in the garden?" He offered his arm, turned, and said to his teammates, "Ta-ta for now," instead of the usual Australian hooroo.

Angus shouted, "Who's the Pom now?"

As they entered another leafy pathway, Lorena asked, "I know you call the British Poms with no great regard, but why?"

"Some say it comes from Prisoner of his Majesty from the old penal colony days when petty thieves and troublemakers were dumped here to live or die under harsh conditions after the American colonies won their revolution, and they couldn't take their trash there anymore. I don't think anyone really knows."

She considered that statement. "Are you descended from convicts?"

"My family didn't go in for genealogy, but judging by my pop, a real wanker, probably. He was a miner who took to the drink when his back gave out. We lived on the dole."

"Still, you shouldn't talk about your father that

way."

"S'truth. Heavy-handed when he was on the grog to both my mum and brothers until I got big enough to protect them. I'm glad he's dead and gone. You'll never have to meet him. What about your pop?"

"Oh, he's great, a little larger than life and very protective of his daughters, but great."

"He comes across that way in interviews and such. I'd like to meet him."

"If you ever come to the States, we can arrange that."

"It's now considered wonderful to have the original convicts in the family tree. People used to hide the fact."

"That's too bad. You shouldn't be ashamed of who you are."

"Glad you feel that way."

Could his lower-class background truly bother a man who'd made a fortune as a football player and had a life of luxury now? Deeper than the Yarra was Jock Brown, she thought.

They circled the park where ibis in the bushes were as common as seagulls and arrived back at Jock's truck parked on the street nearby. Time had slipped away, days being longer so far south on the continent but shortening with the coming of autumn. Lorena checked her watch, glad it hadn't taken a dunk in the river. "I told Maisie I'd be home around five, and here it is five-thirty."

"Is she your mum?"

"In absentia. I don't want to worry her."

"Righty-O. I'll get you there by six."

He did. Helping her down again, Jock walked her

to the door of Maisie's modest suburban home set on a hilltop and surrounded by lush foliage. His lips barely brushed her cheek with a soft kiss when the door flew open, and Maisie and her two little boys tumbled out.

Before Maisie could get a word in, Christopher, the elder with his mother's blonde hair and a spray of freckles across his nose, piped up. "Mum says you're a famous footy player. Are you?"

"Some say."

The shyer little brother, dark of hair and eye like his dad, poked Jock's rock-hard thigh. "Can I feel your muscles?"

Jock squatted down and popped up an impressive bicep for the boy who gave it a squeeze. "Wow."

Augie, the stay at home dad who worked an online job to be there when the boys returned from school, appeared with a meat fork in hand. If that had been her own father, a threat might have been implied, but not from gentle Augie with his short, dark, professorial beard, wire-rimmed glasses, and mild demeanor. "I'm grilling tonight. I can always throw another steak on the barbie. They were already thawed when Maisie got here with the lasagna."

"Thanks, but I should probably spend my evening mending fences with my mates. Lori, eight tomorrow for our penguin trek. I'll stop by for you."

The boys jumped up and down. "Penguins, can we go along?"

Jock ruffled both heads, one blond, one dark. "Not this time. School night, right?"

Two small faces fell. "But definitely another day." He walked back to his vehicle and roared off, which also impressed the boys.

"Maybe I want to be a footy player and never go to school," Chris remarked.

Jock Brown, good with children. Who would have believed it? Not Lori.

Chapter Four

Jock found his teammates right where he thought they'd be—in their favorite pub dining on bangers and mash, a pint in easy reach. He took a chair at their table and signaled the waitress he'd have the same. They did not welcome him.

"Hey, bugger off. If we're not welcome at your tea party, you can't come to ours," Angus sulked.

"Just why were you mucking about on the river? Trying to ruin my time with Lorena?"

"He claimed we'd have a bit of fun with you, and I got sucked in. Now I have to take those whites to a dry cleaner before returning to the official I borrowed them from. That joke cost me. But now that Angus told me what you plan to do, it's you who deserved to end up in the muck." Willie had slicked back his dark hair, still wet, probably from a thorough shower to get Eau-de-Yarra River out of it. "You're running after Lorena Billodeaux because you're deserting Collingwood and scouting for a place in American football."

"See here, I talked to Coach about my plans. My contract is coming up for renewal, and I'd want more. It's as good a time as any to try my luck elsewhere, but I made a promise. If it doesn't work out in America, I'll come back and won't play for anyone but Collingwood if I'm still wanted. As for Lorena, you've seen her. I'd have a go at her without the connection to her dad. You know that song about walking five hundred miles for a woman. I'd do it for Lorena Billodeaux—in the outback during dry season."

"Oh, right. You're courting her, not just looking for a shag," Angus mocked. "Where to tomorrow, Prince Charming?"

"As if I'd tell you. Don't try to follow us." Jock's hands gripped the edge of the table. He suppressed a strong urge to overturn it and see his mates covered in mashed potatoes. Not a bright idea. He hadn't been in a brawl for years off the field, not since his brothers grew big enough to defend themselves, and certainly not with teammates who were more often like family.

The waitress approached with his plate circled by plump sausages, a mound of mash in the middle. "Make that to take away and give these blokes another round on me." He peeled off some bills and went to the entry to await his dinner. How much nicer it would have been sitting with Lori, beers in hand waiting for Maisie's husband to finish grilling a steak, or maybe playing footy with those cute kids. He had a longing he couldn't explain, now that his brothers were well on their way, for a life that included his own children and a special woman by his side. He had the house, the Ute, and as many easy women as he wanted. He could tell that wasn't enough. What business was it of his cobbers whether he wanted to have a crack at something new anyhow?

Not to forget, he needed to make reservations for the Penguin Parade. He pulled out his mobile and took care of it.

****

Lorena waited for him right on time. He approved

her slim jeans and long-sleeved red T-shirt that hugged her body but sent her inside to retrieve a windbreaker since the air could be cold by the beach this time of year, and the penguins marched whether it rained or not. He'd read all the directions and made sure she wore sneakers, not thongs as directed. Nothing could go wrong this time. Once she passed inspection, they were off, leaving two wistful little boys waving goodbye.

They sped up the Yarra Valley with Lori remarking on the beauty of the farms, the rolling hills, and the mountain ranges in the distance. "Remind you of home?" he asked.

"Cairns is more like south Louisiana, warm and steamy with sugarcane fields galore. No mountains, though until you get around Arkansas.

"The Yarra range will have snow on its peaks come July."

"Pretty rare for us to have snow in Louisiana, but it happens from time to time. Then everything shuts down, and we go crazy, making tiny snowmen on the hoods of our cars and rolling snowballs in one inch of the white stuff."

"Sounds like fun."

"Oh, it is because it's so rare. We probably have as many hurricanes as Cairns, not so much fun."

The many vineyards they passed showed leaves with the first hint of autumn color. "These vines will all be naked by winter. Workers might be out harvesting tonight while we're watching penguins. It keeps the sugar content of the grapes stable."

With a bit of surprise in her voice, Lorena said, "You seem very knowledgeable about grapes."

"Tomorrow, we'll do a wine tasting. Right now, I

want to get to Healesville Sanctuary. We don't want to miss the bird show or the platypus experience."

"I guess you've been there before."

"Nope, my pop didn't do family excursions. We never left our part of the city. It's just what the guidebook said." His app said a great deal more, like let her pet a platypus, and she'll want to pet yours. He had high hopes this might be true.

Upon arrival, he shelled out an extra twelve dollars to allow Lori to feed the pushy and voracious emus, maybe not the best experience. He'd planned to soften her heart toward footy players with beautiful birds and cute, furry animals. The scrum of aggressive emus was no help. Afterward, they strolled the tree-shaded paths edged with native bushes looking for dingoes and kangaroos and koalas, which mostly appeared to be brown lumps dozing high in the trees. The wombats stayed in their burrows as did many of the nocturnal animals, and she said she'd seen kangaroos before.

No help for romance that cutouts of Crapman kept popping up, dressed in a green superhero costume with a red cape, a large CM on his belt, and a roll of toilet paper in his hand his motto: Saving Wildlife one toilet at a time. "What's that all about," Lori asked.

"Oh, biodegradable toilet tissue. We should all use it. The ad campaign is rather crude, though. I know Americans use the word crap, but doubt they'd make a hero out of it."

"I'm not immune to it myself when I miss a setup, but you are right. The character would have to be Heine Man. And before you make any jokes, I know you Aussies call Americans Septics."

"That's only rhyming slang for Yank, but I never

would."

"Go over there and put your head in the hole. I've got to have a picture of this."

Jock did it to please her, crunching up his big body to fit behind the cutout and thrusting his face through the hole. He gave her a bright, cheeky grin and prayed she wouldn't remember him as Crapman. Lori chuckled as she clicked the photo.

He feared the trip might be a bust until they reached the Land of Parrots and entered a large flight cage with birds from large to small flying free. He snapped a picture of Lori holding a stunning red-tailed black cockatoo on one shoulder, and her braid draped over the other. They did a quick walkthrough of the reptile house displaying Australia's deadliest snakes, which reminded him of his comment about that braid, the way it whipped around when she played. How he'd like to unravel it and let her long hair cloak his body.

Pushing that thought aside, saving it for tonight, he hustled them over to the Spirits of the Sky show featuring birds of prey and parrots. A magnificent wedge-tailed eagle soared over their heads along with a variety of other raptors. The star of the show, a black-breasted buzzard, broke open a simulated egg with a stone to get at the food inside. The performance ended with a laugh as a cunning parrot dropped a sign featuring a chubby wombat holding a roll of toilet paper and urging the audience to Wipe for Wildlife. Ah, Lorena's laugh, not giggly and girlish, but hearty, all in, and not afraid to show her amusement.

"If we were birds, you'd be that black cockatoo, and I'd be the eagle," Jock told her, striving to say something romantic.

Lorena answered back, teasing, "That cockatoo was a male. Mating between them would be impossible."

"We'll both have to be eagles then." Jock checked his watch. "We must get a move on if we want to see the platypus act."

"Wouldn't want to miss it. I've never seen a real one."

"Me, neither."

As it turned out, the platypus was as charming as advertised. Small and adorable, the young female swooped through the tank leaving a trail of bubbles from its fur behind its beaver-like tail. She rose for a treat and a tickle from her trainer who explained all about this shy creature. The delight on Lori's face said it all. Just wait until she found out he'd arranged for the $199 Wade with a Platypus option.

Instead of leaving when the show ended, he steered her to the front, where the handler took them inside the inner sanctum of the platypus. They donned waders and got into the water where the little critter swam around their feet, accepted tidbits from their hands, allowed its sleek fur to be petted, and its rubbery bill touched. No worries, the handler said, about being spurred. Only the males had poison sacks and rarely attacked anything but another male getting into their territory. Lori demanded another picture of him cradling the small animal in his hands, better than being recalled as Crapman. Once the experience ended, Lori hugged him hard, her warm breasts pushing against his chest. "That was unbelievable."

He held her a moment longer than he should have before letting go. "Yes, incredible. How about a snapshot on the carved platypus by the entrance to remember this?" She posed for him like a delighted child with her long legs drawn up and hugged by her arms as she peered over them. Though hungry for only one thing, he suggested lunch.

They ate in the Sanctuary Harvest Café, specializing in regional fare. Jock downed two of the meat pies mounded with chips and a cold beer. Lori settled on a fresh wrap with crisps and cider. "I could stay here all day," she sighed.

He ran his hand down the length of her braid and gave it a slight tug to get her going. "Sorry, we have to backtrack to get to Phillip Island and our date with the penguins, but we can come back another time."

Her richly colored lips bowed downward in her tanned face. "I don't have much time left here in Oz. I fly out on Qantas for Dallas on Sunday at six p.m., leaving from Sidney and must catch the noon flight from Melbourne to make the connection. Then on to Lafayette, another two or three hours before I get home."

"So soon. I thought we'd have more time together—but we'll always have the Penguin Parade, baby," he tried in such a poor Bogart impersonation it did bring out her laugh again. He'd have to make his reservation tomorrow if he wanted to be on the same flight. Telling her he needed to use the toilet on the way out, he suggested she do so too. Knowing women always took longer, he had enough time to detour into the gift shop and buy a plush platypus for a souvenir. The way she gushed over it you'd think a guy had never given her such a gift before. "First stuffed toy?" he questioned.

"No, my high school boyfriend liked to show off at street fairs and win them for me. He pitched for the baseball team. But I've never had a platypus. I love that they didn't make it fuzzy, but sleek like the real thing, and the bill is all rubbery. Every time I look at this, I'll think of Australia and what a time I had here." She rubbed the artificial fur against her cheek, and he felt a twinge of jealousy.

"You won't think of Jock?"

"Oh, I'm naming it Jock."

Satisfied with that, they headed for his Ute.

A long drive brought them to Mario's Bayside Bistro in San Remo for dinner because he knew she liked Italian. With its view of the water and interesting old motorcycles parked outside, it offered them both a little something extra. More in the mood for red meat, he ordered the grain-fed steak, the usual chips, and a tad of salad. Lorena didn't go for the pasta after all and got fish, barramundi. He asked for a glass of pinot noir and a sauvignon blanc for her. Again, she seemed impressed by his knowledge of wine, figuring, he supposed, that footy players only downed huge amounts of beer. They topped off the meal with cheesecake for dessert before heading to the island as the sun dipped toward the sea.

Lori pointed out the small kangaroos, wallabies, in the bush who sat up and took note of their passing. When she saw the hawks soaring in the sky, she feared they were also waiting for the Penguin Parade, looking for a meal of the tiny creatures. "Afraid so" he had to answer, hoping again it didn't spoil the romance of the moment. He suspected Maisie saw him that way, a bird of prey swooping down on her penguin chick.

They parked at the visitor's center and began the

long walk to the Penguin Plus Experience bleachers. The seats were crowded with Chinese visitors who came by the busload, but they managed to find a place to sit. A volunteer explained the rules: no noise, no photography of any kind, no standing on the bleachers, no pushing or shoving to view the penguins from the railings—and no dangling of feet over the edge. Anything could startle the tiny birds and send them back to the ocean for safety instead of seeking their burrows in the hillside.

"Keep your eyes on the sea. When a dark spot appears to be moving toward us, that is a raft of penguins coming ashore. They practice safety in numbers. Once on land they will move as quickly as possible to their nests for the night. Quiet now."

As the birds began to emerge, body surfing onto the rocky beach, standing up, and making haste for their burrows, Lori squeezed his bicep in excitement. He wished she'd show that much enthusiasm for him. A teenager, taller than the average Asian, stood up in front of them, his mobile in hand. Jock growled a low warning. The boy turned to give a cheeky response, but simply seeing his size solved the problem. The kid sat and pocketed the phone.

Lori murmured to him, "Great game face. Scared the hell out of him." Was that a good or bad thing?

"I should have gotten the VIP tickets instead of the Premium Plus," he grumbled.

Lorena placed a hand on his arm and whispered, "It's wonderful. Enjoy the moment. Look, some penguins are tired and are lying down on their bellies for rest."

The other penguins merely waddled around the

small lumps of resting birds. A second and third raft came in before the march petered out to a few stragglers. The penguins turned off onto narrow side paths to find the burrows they'd made themselves or to a convenient box built for their use.

"Sort of a shame we have to exploit the penguins to protect them, but then all the money paid to see them goes toward their good," Jock said as they pushed forward in the retreating mob far thicker than the avian parade.

"I was thinking the same but didn't want to offend you after paying for the tickets and bringing me here," Lorena admitted.

"No worries. You can always speak your mind with me." If she doubted that, she didn't say so, but he'd meant it truly.

Like the penguins, the crowd disbursed, traveling in their own version of the rafts toward the buses. Lorena insisted on a stop at the gift shop to purchase plush penguins for Maisie's boys, also buying each a little jacket made of natural fibers by volunteers for use on sick penguins. She threw in a third for her youngest sister, Edie.

"Aren't you going to get something for your brothers?"

That coaxed a laugh out of him. "They've outgrown fuzzy animals."

Walking back to the Predator, a cold, misty rain began to fall. Lorena zipped her windbreaker and put up the hood, that braid of hers secure beneath it.

"Nice of you to remember the boys and your sister with a gift," he said.

"I've lived with the Mortons for two years. I'm like

a sister or an aunt to Chris and Kyle. As for Edie, she's taking care of my dog, Brody, while I'm gone. The Australian quarantine rules are too tough to bring him here. I'd like to meet your brothers before I leave."

"Saturday they'll be hanging about. I guess we can work that in."

"Tell me a little about them."

"Michael and Nicolas, Mick and Nick we call them. I had the care of them since I turned fourteen, promised my mum before she died. Mick is four years younger than me, and Nick two years younger than him. Well, you'll see them tomorrow."

He helped her into the Predator and turned on the heat and the wipers. He wanted to make her as snug as a penguin in its burrow on the long drive around the bay and back to the lights of Melbourne across the water. Lorena was tough enough to be Maisie's partner and a strong woman, yet he felt a tenderness for her excitement over the birds and the platypus. Tenderness, a man wasn't supposed to have any. His father had never shown any sign of it. Good on him, then. He didn't want to be like his pop.

"Thanks for this day. It was truly special, even more so if I don't return."

"Don't give up. Maisie isn't called amazing for nothing." He hoped the old doll still had enough left in her to bring Lorena back to Australia if he failed at becoming an NFL player. He'd be back with the Magpies and staying put.

The rhythm of the wipers sluicing away the now much more torrential rain, the warmth of the cab lulled Lori to sleep like an over-excited child who'd finally wound down after a long day of fun. Her head nodded and settled against his shoulder. Nice, except he guessed, there would be no passionate snogging session in the car when they got to Maisie's house. Sure enough, a porch light burned for Lorena, who awakened when he stopped. Before he could get down, Augie rushed out with an umbrella to see her inside. Part of the family, indeed.

Chapter Five

Jock showed up at eight sharp for their Saturday together. She'd dressed up in a sunny yellow dress that hit above the knees, a white cardigan against the early cold, and white flats, though with a man his size, she'd never have to worry about being taller than him. He'd planned a little sightseeing, a wine tasting, an elegant lunch, a leisurely afternoon, he told her, but since she insisted, they'd stop by to see his brothers.

Jock drove to the area around the University of Melbourne, a top-notch school, and pulled into parking reserved for the tenants of a multistoried building, judging by its doorman, too expensive for students. They crossed a vast lobby full of tropical plants and blooms to the elevator, which opened onto a foyer giving access to a single apartment.

"This is my unit," he said as he unlocked the door. "And these specimens are my brothers." They stood up on cue, rising from a black leather sofa. "Mick is the big one, and Nick is the baby. This is Lorena Billodeaux, a cracker volleyball player. Don't know why she wanted to meet you bludgers."

A very big baby, Lorena thought. As Jock went to stand beside them, they could have been a set of nesting dolls with him as the largest, then Mick who had to be six-three, and Nick coming in around her height, an even six-footer. All of them had sandy hair, though worn longer than Jock's, but neither his green eyes. Mick's were twinkling and blue, and Nick's a serious brown. They shared the same cheeky grin, toothy and white. All dressed in khakis and knit shirts. A hint of tattoos showed below Mick's short sleeves, but otherwise, they seemed to be in uniform.

Nick was the first to suggest they sit down around a glass and steel coffee table. All three men crowded onto the sofa that normally seated four lesser men while she took one of two white leather bucket chairs opposite. She sat with her back to a tall set of windows, offering a wonderful view of the campus buildings shaded here and there with eucalypts. Bedrooms down the hall, she assumed. If there were three, the cost in Melbourne must be terrific. Beyond the living area, a dining table, again steel and glass surrounded by six matching black-cushioned chairs atop a black and white tile floor that led into a spotless kitchen far fancier than the one in Maisie's house if you counted the espresso machine and lots of stainless steel appliances unmarred by kiddie fingerprints, and as far as she could tell, either unused for cooking or used by incredibly tidy men. None of them seemed the type to spend their days polishing kitchenware.

Stiff with formality, Mick gestured to a tray holding a teapot in a knitted cozy vaguely resembling a black and white bird, an insulated carafe of coffee, sugar and cream for both, and a centerpiece of Lamingtons, those Australian delicacies made of sponge cake rolled in chocolate and covered with coconut.

"Would you care for a cuppa or maybe coffee? Help yourself to the Lamingtons, fresh from the bakery this morning. You won't get those back in the States, will you?"

"No, this might be my last for a long time. Thank you, I'll have tea with a little milk."

Mick prepared the cup with hands nearly as big as his eldest brother's and handed it over. He took coffee as did Jock with only the youngest fixing his own tea. They each had a cake. For some reason, she'd thought they'd be teenage boys like her brother, T-Rex, not these large men who appeared to be as tongue-tied as any adolescent around a girl. She fished for a topic of conversation. "Are you attending the university?"

Mick answered. "I was, but academics didn't suit. I switched to EMT training. Nearly done with it. I like the action. Nick is the one studying to be a doctor."

"One of us had to, considering Jock gave up his scholarship to play footy and get us through uni. He was the one who wanted to find a cure for our mum's cancer when he started. Now that's on me. Least I can do to repay him. Without Jock, we'd both be selling drugs on Brunswick Street." Nick, stirring his tea, gave credit where it was due.

"Not me. I'd rather have been a pimp." Mick grinned, and those blue eyes sparkled. The ice in the room cracked wide open as Jock shot him a laser-like glare. "We're supposed to be on our best behavior this morning, not move a thing the cleaning lady put to rights yesterday, don't eat all the Lamingtons, watch our language. I guess I buggered that last one."

Lorena answered with a smile. "I have six brothers and have seen and heard worse. They get in my face and get in my way, but I miss them. You can be yourselves around me."

"Oh, you don't want that." They began elbowing each other the way her brothers did when they acted out in the back of the family van. It made her homesick to watch them. Well, she'd soon be back at the ranch again.

"Are those brothers big fellows?" Mick asked, still with a teasing glint to his eyes.

"Some of them, but one is in a wheelchair, and another is a computer geek. I do have two enormous brothers-in-law, however. Most play football, even one sister-in-law."

"We've heard. Maybe Jock can take on the handicapped one if they start punching on each other," Mick said, still grinning.

"He doesn't know them well enough to punch one."

"Not yet," Nick added, possibly to stay in the conversation. He appeared to be the quiet one.

"That's enough. Lori, we have to go." Leaving his coffee mug half full, Jock stood.

"One last question, Lorena. Are there any more like you at home?" Mick asked, his grin growing even wider at irritating his big brother.

"My sisters are mostly married. One is studying medicine like Nick and has no time for men. The other is underage. Sorry." She appreciated the compliment, though she'd heard it a million times.

"Just so you know, I'm available if you ditch Jock."

"I'm returning to the States, not dumping your brother—just so you know."

Jock rose, came behind her, and tugged her braid. "You've seen the monkeys in the zoo. Let's go."

She would have liked to explore his family dynamics more but gave in to the insistent tug. "Nice to have met you."

"Hooroo," Mick said with a wave. "Don't let him show you his snake. But don't do anything I wouldn't do. That gives you lots of room for mischief."

"Ignore him. Jock is the best of us," Nick spoke up as they went out the door.

In the elevator, Jock said nothing at first as if embarrassed by his kin. Lori fell back on the usual Aussie reassurance. "No worries. They didn't offend me. In fact, I enjoyed them."

"I'm not the best of them," he muttered. "That would be Nick. He'll save people's lives one day when I'm knackered from playing footy. So will Mick for that matter, though he fancies himself a ladies' man."

"He does have a sort of crude charm and beautiful eyes."

"Yeah, my old man used to black them from time to time. I have green eyes and looked exactly like him but bigger. Nick has my mum's brown eyes, beautiful like yours, so Pop suspected Mick didn't belong to him. We had grandparents on both sides with blue eyes, Mum would tell him, not that he listened until I put an end to him beating on Mick and all the rest of them." His large fists clenched and unclenched.

Lorena placed her hand on his arm. "It sounds as if you made their future possible."

"Lori, don't give me too much credit. I do what I have to do."

The elevator doors opened silently, releasing them into the maze of plants and flowers again and out into a bright, brisk day. Jock reclaimed his truck and steered it to the grounds of the Shrine of Remembrance, originally a monument to the Anzac dead of World War I. Now, it served to honor all Australians and New Zealanders who gave their lives for their countries. Lorena knew that much about it. She thought the huge building appeared as if it had started out to be a Greek temple but become encased in Victorian add-ons. Tons of symbolic statues adorned its stately walls.

"Ever been inside?" Jock asked.

"No, but I've gone running on the parklands. Beautiful and so well-kept."

"Have you run in all the parks?"

"Yes. It was a great way to learn parts of the city. How about you?"

"We run round and round the cricket pitch. Not as interesting. Did you notice the absence of statues on the lawns? They're not allowed to honor any one man. I've often considered they didn't think much of their generals."

They walked along up the hill toward the monument. "What about this one? It's a statue." She paused by a figure of a man with a donkey.

"That honors the stretcher-bearers from the First World War. The actual man was John Simpson, who hauled a bunch of wounded from the field using a donkey. He did die in a later battle. Turned out he was a Pommy, born in England to Scottish parents. Simpson jumped ship here and enlisted. But the statue honors all the stretcher-bearers. We have more to see."

Interesting, even if he had learned it from a guidebook, she supposed.

Passing the Eternal Flame and entering a red alcove, they moved into the cool granite building itself and went to stand before a marble a plaque in the floor, which proclaimed a verse from the Bible, John 15:13. "Greater love hath no man." As they stood in contemplation, a ray of light moved across the words and came to rest on the word Love. Standing behind her, Jock locked his arms around her waist. He gave her a light hug when the phenomenon occurred. Was he sending her a message, or simply as moved by the spectacle as she?

"On Anzac Day in November, the light falls on that word naturally from a hole in the roof, but now it's recreated daily for the tourists."

"Natural or not, it did bring tears to my eyes. Have you seen it before or only read about it?" She'd begun to suspect he'd studied up on all the places he took her, more effort than most men would bother to impress her.

"Seen it. One of the few places my pop took us, usually after he'd had a few. We'd get a lecture on how he had no damn money for university, so we'd better enlist like he did, not that the army improved him. Rather ruined the message for us, but I think you've restored it for me." As if uncomfortable with this revelation, Jock added, "Ready for some wine? I am."

They set off along the Yarra Valley, but this time turned into one of the many wineries along the road. Brownlowe Valley Vintages a rustic hand-carved sign read. They drove up a hill to a very modern visitor's center. Behind the wide glass windows offering a view over the vines, a party appeared to be taking place inside while the parking lot held two tour buses. "Looks like business is good," she remarked.

"Wasn't always. Not until we got the visitor's center built and started doing publicity."

"We?" she questioned.

Jock cleared his throat. "I'm a part owner. It's an investment. The Lowes, an old Italian family here in the valley, had a small business, mostly bottling for other companies. Luca Lowe wanted to develop his own brand and had no capital."

"Lowe doesn't seem very Italian to me."

"They changed it to fit in better from something more complicated. So me and my mates came here for a tasting, and he approached me about a deal. He'd take care of everything if I'd put up money, lend my name to the business, do appearances, that sort of thing. Said I could build a country house here, keep horses if I wanted." He snorted. "As if anyone from Collingwood rode to the hounds. I had my lawyer and business agent check it over. They thought it a sound idea."

Not such a dumb jock at all, but a man who planned ahead. More like her father with fingers in many tasty pies from quarter horse breeding to minor movie roles, television ads, and a hot sauce brand. She was more and more impressed by Jock Brown. "Did you build your house?"

"I did. We'll have lunch there after the tasting."

He led her through a lavish gift shop with hand-painted wine glasses and pricey tea towels for sale, as Lori noted when she turned up the corner of one, always looking for more items to carry home. Of course, racks of their wines filled the walls. Maybe she'd take a bottle or two back for the Mortons. Too much trouble to drag onto a plane.

Luca Lowe, himself, greeted them. He possessed dark southern European good looks, far more Italian than his last name implied. Lori imagined his luminous black eyes sold as much wine to women as the quality of the actual product. He escorted the pair into the tasting room already occupied by a group of older American tourists eyeing their spit buckets and joking about them.

"Here's the last couple to join our group today. We have celebrities among us—one of our most famous Australian Rules Football players, Jock Brown, a co-owner of the vineyards." Tepid applause ensued. An elderly man, whose facial folds had settled into a permanent scowl, muttered, "Never heard of him," and received a flabby poke in the ribs from his wife who'd gone in the opposite direction, a pleasant full moon face that plumped out all her wrinkles. She softened the insult by saying, "He can spit in my wine bucket any day."

Jock gave her a wink. "I might take you up on that."

"Oh, honey, sit next to me. My old man can move over."

That set a tone of conviviality, although Luca carefully steered his co-owner to a safe spot on his right-hand side far from the spunky old lady. "We also are honored by the presence of Miss Lorena Billodeaux, an American women's beach volleyball champion, and partner to our own Maisie Morton."

"Heard of her," the same cantankerous old man said. "Why aren't you playing for the US team?"

Another phrase she'd heard a hundred times. Lorena put on her best smile. "America has lots of great players already, but I was approached personally by Maisie to be her partner, a signal honor. I've learned a lot from her. If we take a medal in the Olympics, I feel I will be honoring both countries." There, the same thing she'd told *Sports Illustrated*. She took the remaining seat next to Jock, filling out the table.

"We begin with our signature chardonnay. The volcanic and clay soil of our district makes these vines flourish." She noted Luca lacked an Australian accent as if he'd been educated in a British boarding school.

A discreet assistant who'd stood in the background poured from a towel-wrapped bottle, just a few swallows into each glass. Luca sniffed his, swirled the wine, sipped, and spit as elegantly as she'd ever seen a man expectorate. The class followed his actions, but she noticed most of the Americans drank all of theirs and did not use the buckets, either out of a waste not, want not mentality, or simply because they did not want to spit. Jock didn't appear to care about delicate. He spit with gusto like the athlete he was. As for herself, she swallowed only a small amount and managed a half-decent dainty spit. Maisie had gotten up and prepared her a full Australian fry up of eggs, sausage, fatty bacon, tomatoes, mushrooms, and toast, urging her to eat it all because she didn't want her to be tipsy and taken advantage of by Jock Brown. Maybe, that's what she did want, more and more.

The wines progressed through a sauvignon blanc, a pinot gris, and on to the reds with notable pinot noir, a hearty sangiovese, and lastly, the sweet gewurztraminer made from frost-bitten grapes.

"Usually, a tasting starts with sparkling wine if one is available. We will end with one, a new vintage for Brownlowe not yet on the market. Let us fill your glasses, and give me your valued opinion, too sweet, too dry, or *perfecto*. Cleanse your pallets with a bit of water first," the charming Luca directed. The well-lubricated tourists clinked glasses and cheered. "*Perfecto!*" they cried. Arising wobblier than most elderly, the group awaited instructions at the direction of their totally sober guide who had not partaken.

"Toilets on the right on the way out. Lunch is waiting on the veranda—plenty of good bread already on the table. Lamb today or fish if you prefer," the guide said.

The moon-faced woman rolled toward Jock and held out a napkin for him to autograph. He glanced at the name tag laying on her broad bosom. "To Sheila, right?"

She laughed so loud she turned heads. "I am a sheila, and my name *is* Sheila. How Australian is that? My, you're a lovely piece of beefsteak. Plant one right here." She offered a plump cheek. Jock gave her a light peck. Then the other women began to line up, all demanding autographs with benefits. He handled that well, Lori thought. A few held out their napkins for Lorena to sign as an afterthought.

Eventually, their guide herded them in the right direction. "Lively bunch for their age," she apologized. "Like herding roos. No worries. They'll be fine by the time we've eaten."

As the last of them vanished, mostly into the restroom, Jock asked, "How about you?"

"Very nice for champagne," Lorena acknowledged. "I'd send some for my brother's wedding, but the liquor has already been taken care of by a friend."

"Sparkling wine," he corrected. "Only wine from Champagne can be called champagne." He offered her an arm to stand. "But I meant, are you good with walking to the house, or should we drive?"

"I'm in better shape than our drinking buddies. I'd like to walk. It's a glorious day outside." She felt only mildly buzzed. Indeed, she had spit out most of the wine, but that last full glass had perhaps taken her over the top. Thank heaven for her choice of flats as footwear.

In one room of the restaurant, the bachelorette party, judging by one of the women wearing a cheap, short veil with a plastic tiara, roared on. She'd been to several types of Australian hen parties, even a baby shower, where the drinking ran heavy for all but the expectant mother. Women here could keep up with their men and partied hard. She felt a tiny pang that she wouldn't be around for Maisie's baby shower.

The bride to be shouted out, "There he is, Jock Brown. Jocko, how about my last shag before the wedding day?" Her friends hooted. Jock smiled, waved, and guided Lori outside as fast as possible.

She didn't need his help strolling along a pebbled path but leaned into his arm anyhow. Sturdy like a branch of a live oak back home, able to withstand hurricanes and hold a complete set of triplets safely as they played. His house—also modern like the visitors' center with grand views and an open floor plan that flowed into outdoor living space—appeared lightly used and decorated professionally. Nothing much personal about the interior, again a black and white color scheme, red accents here and there in pillows, and a single vase on an ebony end table. A long sofa upholstered in broad black and white stripes faced a low gas fireplace topped by a single slab of black marble veined with white. Plenty of black leather chairs filled the space in small groupings, one of them a set of loungers before a big-screen TV on the opposite wall.

"Oh, I get it now. Magpie colors," she said. "But no trophies, no framed jerseys on the walls?"

"Not yet, but I was thinking some modern Australian art eventually like we saw at the museum. I had my teammates out to warm the place up, but they broke most of the lamps and knickknacks the decorator sat around when things got a bit out of hand. That red vase is the sole survivor. Here, they didn't get the chandelier in the dining room, just a few broken bulbs easily replaced." He flipped a switch to illuminate the area with a fixture made of wrought iron.

A table waited already set with plates and cutlery, glasses filled with water, and others with the pinot from the resting bottle on the table made from native woods. She noticed a waiter lurked in the open kitchen, waiting to serve them. They were not dining alone—a pity.

Jock held her chair and seated himself next to her. He summoned the waiter who brought the salads and then beckoned him again. "Antonio, bring the entree and dessert now. We'll serve ourselves. I think Luca might need your help with that party."

The young man with the pretty face and a foreign accent rolled his eyes. "I'd rather stay here than be pinched and pecked by that mob, but you are the boss, no?" He brought the dishes, and back braced, headed to the center.

"Luca's boyfriend. Brought him back from his last trip to Europe. Good waiter, but I don't want his company, only yours."

Ah, there it was. Alone at last. "Women must be really impressed by this place."

"You're the first to come here."

That revelation made her tongue-tied as if she bore the burden or pleasure of breaking in a beautiful virgin house. She groped for conversation. "Is this the same wine we had at Piccolo Mondo? I recognize the label, those artistic autumn grape leaves." She picked at her salad of field greens with walnuts and crumbled goat cheese already coated with a tangy basil dressing.

"Yes, it was."

"Why didn't you tell me?"

"You were all broken up over Maisie."

"Yes." Her sorrow returned at the memory. She drank the pinot and started on her lamb, which lay in a tart red sauce, fingerling potatoes, and an interesting assortment of veggies to the side.

"Native berries, that red stuff," Jock informed her.

"Are you a gourmet, too?"

"Nope. The chef told me beforehand."

"Tell him it's delicious. The lamb is tender and mild, not gamey like we sometimes get in the States."

"Trying to pass mutton off as lamb, most probably."

"I think so." Was he mutton or lamb, strong or tender, false, or genuine? She gazed out at the landscape, this time through the window that brought light into the dining area. "You do have room for horses. I saw plenty of them in the pastures coming here."

"And what would I do with them?"

"Ride these lovely valleys. Use the manure for your garden."

"Don't have a garden. It'll be a rare day when you see Jock Brown on a horse."

Laughter bubbled out of her at the vision of his large body astride one of the ranch ponies, his over-sized feet dragging on the ground, a sign she'd had too much wine. She needed to cut back.

"Think that's funny, do you? We'll have to see who rides." He leaned over, cupped the back of her head, licked the residue of tart berries from her lips, and nudged inside for a long and powerful kiss. He'd been drinking, too.

"Do you really want dessert? Flourless chocolate cake with a raspberry coulis. We can save it for later." He offered his hand.

"Chocolate cake is hard to resist," she said but accepted his hand.

Hadn't they been working up to this for days? Their destination, the master bedroom up a flight of open stairs and down a short hall. He flung open the door to reveal his king-sized bed. She didn't notice much else at first, but he hadn't thrown her down on the silky black duvet accented with a wooly white sheepskin, simply seated her there.

Jock sat down behind her. "May I?" he asked as he pulled the tie from the end of her braid. "I've dreamed of doing this, unraveling your hair, running my fingers through it." He paused. "Seeing if it's as sleek as the fur on a platypus."

Perhaps, he could see her smile in the mirror of the dresser opposite. "In that case, by all means, enjoy yourself."

"I plan to." He took his time separating the three hanks of the braids, then raking each strand with his blunt fingertips, burying his face into their depth. She watched him in that same mirror, watched her nipples peak beneath her thin, yellow dress, and her lips part, ready for more.

An insistent doorbell rang, twice, three times. "What the frickin' hell!" he said. "Be right back." Jock thundered down the stairs. "What?" he asked, loud and annoyed.

Lorena emerged from the bedroom, still fully dressed, but hair flowing down her back, to stand at the balcony rail like a dark-haired Rapunzel, not really caring if the waiter noticed.

"Please come, sir. Those women will not leave until they meet you. I believe they might riot. Luca, he says, this is part of your contract to meet the guests when you are here. Come quickly," Antonio begged with his hands making imploring Italian gestures.

"Bugger all!" He turned to see Lori above. "I'll be back as soon as I can. Make yourself comfortable." He followed Antonio from the house.

Make yourself comfortable. She believed she would.

Lori returned to the bedroom. When a woman wanted a man, she should be able to show it. She realized she'd left her cardigan at the center and had no intention of retrieving it. She'd selected this dress, easy to step out of with no zippers or buttons, and did so. Though she'd chosen sexy, nearly transparent underwear, oh well, why not dispose of that, too, and save a little time. Her private striptease revealed a fresh Brazilian wax and full breasts unsuppressed by a bra in the mirror.

She knew she ran too long, lean muscle with little body fat due to her training, but her breasts were shapely if not particularly large. Large just got in the way. Since they played in bikinis, Jock would already have figured that out. She hoped he enjoyed what she had to offer because she planned to enjoy him. After all, this was *her* last Australian shag before she went home, and there hadn't been but a couple in the last two years, not living with Mother Maisie.

The sheepskin beckoned, promising soft warmth. Lorena spread herself out on it, selected one of the six red pillows at the head of the bed, a black leather headboard of course, and tucked it under her head. Wine always made her drowsy. She closed her eyes.

"Lori,' he said softly. She woke to find Jock standing at the end of the bed, simply drinking her in with green eyes like cool, deep water. He appeared disheveled. Even his short, sandy hair seemed ruffled. His shirt hung out partially untucked, and its breast pocket ripped off. She wasn't sure if he knew his fly was half-unzipped. Where had his belt gone?

"What happened to you?"

"I've been pawed by a rampaging bunch of women. We had to call the police to get them back onto their bus and out of here. Me Too movement, huh. Now I know how you must feel if someone gropes you."

Lori sat up. "No one gropes Lorena Billodeaux without getting hit in the balls. Keep that in mind."

"Groping is not my intent. Over an hour to get that settled, and I return here to have my fantasy fulfilled, you, lying on my bed, tanned from top to bottom, with that Brazilian fringe between your legs and your hair loose on my pillow. You restore my faith in women."

"Now restore my faith in men. Off with your clothes."

His signature grin returned. "Righty-O."

Shirt off, pants down. He'd gone commando, probably regretting that now after the intimate melee. Loafers without socks kicked off in a second. All that remained was an impressive erection throbbing against a taut belly. He rummaged in the night table drawer, retrieved a condom, and ripped it open with his teeth.

"Very masculine," she said as she lay down again on the sheepskin. "Thank you for doing that without being asked."

"The only valuable thing my pop taught me was not to put a bun in anyone's oven—because you'd have that bun for the rest of your life no matter how stale it got. I often wonder if I was the bun that caused my mother to marry that wanker. Can't fathom any other reason why she would." He smoothed on the condom, rolling it tight against his crotch, no leaks allowed.

"You don't want children, then?"

"I do at the right time with the right woman, only not today. Though maybe I've found the right woman."

Lori didn't give him a right man validation. Men mouthed this kind of thing without meaning it. Guys in a bar asked her to have their baby. This was a fling, her last in Australia. She'd leave it at that no matter how much Jock Brown intrigued her. By the time she returned, if she returned, he might be baking buns with someone else. She intended to enjoy this chance.

Jock lay down beside her, not rushing to mount up. He began with the kind of deep kiss they'd shared earlier, long, satisfying. His hands, big and slightly callused, massaged her breasts. She gave herself over to waves of sensation, not thinking about leaving on a jet plane tomorrow. Nope, her mind was on Jock and how she was falling for him so fast.

The tingling began between her legs, increased when he moved a hand to cover her there, banishing all thought. He found her hot spot, rubbed with a thumb. She pushed her hips upward, pressure building inside her. He sent her over the top.

Not until then did he move over her, keeping his weight on his arms, though she was no frail blossom but an athlete like him. He entered large and fulfilling, brought her up again and over the jump, an expert rider, but not of horses.

In the last few days, he'd done everything right. Romanced and wooed her like no other man. Why did she have to find a man this great just before going home? She felt his shudder as he emptied into her and his release of tension as he fell to her side.

"Next time you can be the rider," he said, twining a strand from her loosened braid around a finger. "I want to lie beneath a curtain of your hair as we do it. But first, we clean up a bit and eat chocolate cake naked in front of the fireplace downstairs. You could stay the night. I'll see you get on your flight in time."

"Yes, to the first, but no naked cake eating or anything else. I mean, I am tempted, but Maisie is throwing me a surprise going-away party at six. You are invited. I have to get back by then, and your adoring fans took up a lot of our time."

"The bride stole my belt and got into my trousers. Don't I deserve pity sex?"

"Poor baby, of course, you do, but I cannot tarry."

"How do you know about your own surprise party, anyhow?" His voice held distrust as if he thought she'd made an excuse to leave.

"Augie told me. He said I might get too distracted

by you and not come home in time. That would hurt Maisie's feelings."

"How about mine?"

"I think you will survive and go on to shag many other women."

"Not women like you, Lori."

She ignored him, wanting to believe him but unwilling to show it. She rolled off her side of the bed and sauntered into the master bath with its double black marble sinks and a huge glass box shower with so many interesting jets. Sigh, no time for a shower with Jock or to dry her long hair, which was sometimes a nuisance. A basket of guest soaps and red hand towels sat nearby. She turned on the tap and waited for the hot water to spew before wetting the towel.

"Too bad you don't have a huge tub, too."

He opened a set of louvered doors she'd assumed held a linen closet, but no, a huge, free-standing bathtub sat on a pedestal. And yes, made for two. A window above it sat low for the bather to enjoy the landscape, but not so low that anyone could peek. "Tempted?" he asked. "No one has used it yet. We could christen it together."

"Very tempted. I'm always taking showers, but do enjoy a good long soak when I can get one. No time for it now."

Jock again came behind her and removed the washcloth from her hands. "Allow me." He took the time to wash her thighs with the lemon-scented soap, went higher and got into all the cracks, teased her clit until he had her leaning back against him moaning.

"You should stop, or we'll be right back where we started from."

"Nothing wrong with that. I have observed extra orgasms never hurt a lady."

He had a point. She rested against that broad, warm chest with just a light covering of sandy hair, relaxed, and let it happen. She remained there until her legs could support her again.

"Want me to help you clean up?" It seemed only fair.

He released her, the penis that had been pressing against her at half-staff. "He wants you to believe he's ready to go again, but he'd be lying. He desires chocolate cake to recover. Go on. Get dressed. I'll be along in a mo'."

She didn't take much time getting back into her clothes. Finding the tie for her braid in the thick carpet took longer. Jock returned, still naked, she drew her hair up into a high ponytail and knotted it once around the tie before she let it flow downward again. "Sometimes, I think I should get rid of all this. It's a nuisance to wash and dry and braid, but Maisie says it's my trademark and not to cut it until I have children that start grabbing at it and getting it gunky."

"You shouldn't cut it then, either. I tell you men dream about that braid, especially this man. I think I could learn to do a braid."

Oh, that made her laugh, the thought of tough Jock Brown's strong fingers doing her hair. She suspected they'd have sex before he halfway finished the job. Perfect, just so perfect.

"If I get back to Australia, I'll let you have a try at it."

"Righty-O, I'll look forward to that."

He rummaged in the dresser drawer, giving her

time to admire his firm, rounded glutes. He discovered a pair of black briefs, found a clean shirt in another drawer, and pressed khakis in a closet as big as her bedroom back home. Dressing progressively as he went, he soon stood oh so tall in his Italian loafers and ready to go. Jock took down a garment bag. "Might as well take this back with me—custom made suit. I'm hard to fit."

"No kidding." He must buy his clothes from a men's biggest and tallest shop. A shame this was her last time with Jock Brown. If she'd stayed, she knew it would grow into more than a fling, but the start of something as large as Australia.

Chapter Six

They roared down the highway with Lori's cardigan, his garment bag, and two bottles of Brownlowe wine to contribute to the party. They'd had the chocolate cake, a little soggy in the now sticky raspberry coulis, to fortify themselves for the drive. He ate his with a cold glass of milk, which he actually preferred to sparkling wine. That gave Lori a laugh. Her brothers would do the same, only out of the carton, to the ire of their housekeeper.

Time, he needed more time to tell her his plans to accompany her to America. He tried to find the best way to express this, but it didn't come easy. He'd left behind the sham sophisticate at the winery.

"I'd like to meet your family," Jock began.

"Whenever you're in the States, give me a call. You can stop by if you're near the ranch." Lori gazed out the window at the passing scenery, not at him, as if, too, harboring a secret.

"Near New Orleans, are you?"

"Why does everyone assume every place in Louisiana is near New Orleans? No, it's a three-hour drive because a huge swamp is in the way. Can't go over it, can't go under it, have to go around it. That isn't quite true. At some point, you must cross the Atchafalaya Basin on one of the causeways. The scenery is interesting, especially the section of logged out cypress, jagged stumps, and young trees growing up, water hyacinths blooming at the right time of year."

"Sounds as if you love it."

"Louisiana has its own beauty, just like this valley. Look at those wonderful horses."

Horses again. Was she obsessed with horses? Fine, he'd buy her a horse if she wanted one, anything she desired—a thoroughbred, a huge opal like the one her brother had given the supermodel for their engagement, a real platypus. The last made him smile, but these thoughts got him nowhere.

"Won't your playing season be starting soon? That will tie you down. It's the offseason for my brothers. They get some months to relax, and in the case of my brother-in-law, Junior, gain weight he'll have to take off in camp." She smiled at the recollection. "He owns a restaurant like you."

"Don't own it. The chef leases the space. He's very good."

"No argument there, and a lot less work for you. Junior loves to create new dishes, but his lasagna is to die for."

He'd almost had an opening. Now, they were discussing restaurants. He gave it another try. "I've sometimes thought I want a crack at American football."

She seemed surprised. "Why would you? You own a beautiful house, a winery, a great condo in beautiful Melbourne, women mob you, probably you earn a good salary. Your brothers are here. Cajuns tend to stay close to home. Besides me—I broke the pattern—all my siblings live within a few hours of my parents. Well, Mack is in Dallas, a little farther, but easily drivable.

I've missed a couple of weddings and the births of several nieces and nephews. I'll be home in time for the Easter egg hunt, and that will be fun with new little ones. My parents are up to nine grandchildren of their own and one honorary now."

"Are you religious, then?"

"Egg hunts aren't religious, but I'm not particularly. Religion in our family is so complicated. My dad is Catholic, and after a Vegas wedding to my mom, Mawmaw Nadine, that's my iron-willed grandmother, insisted they marry in The Church."

"Catholic, eh?"

"It's the first thing she'd ask if you meet. You Cat'lic, boy?" she imitated.

He answered without thinking. "Bloody hell, no! My mum baptized all of us in The Church, but I won't be a part of any organization that tells an abused woman she has to stay in a terrible marriage or be cut off from their holy rites. No communion or last rites for her if she gets a divorce. I believe the new pope has changed that up a bit, but too late for my mother. Mum paid high for her holy wafers."

God damn it all, he'd fallen into the morass of religion, not to be discussed on what, a third date? To his mind, it shouldn't be brought up until the very verge of marriage when a couple decided on a civil or religious ceremony. But he might as well find out. Weren't most Cajuns Catholic? "Sorry about that. I'm guessing you are."

"Oh, no. My equally strong-willed mother wouldn't let her daughters be raised Catholic. She feels The Church has too much non-compassionate control over women when it comes to birth control, abortion rights, and divorce, that even nuns are treated shabbily. No women priests allowed, ridiculous. She reached a compromise with Mawmaw. Dad and the boys go to the Catholic church, and she takes the girls to the Episcopal. That worked well until my parents adopted Xochi and Teddy. She'd been raised Catholic, and Teddy's mom was a Baptist They switched out those two, six each. Frankly, the men don't care much, which means the grandchildren are raised every which way. Despite having some doubts about a Mexican grandchild, Xochi has turned out to be Mawmaw's favorite, but the family now skews Protestant. By the way, should you meet either my mom or Mawmaw, the correct answer is a simple yes or no. I'd leave off the bloody hell."

He tried to process all this valuable information. "Episcopal—that's like Anglican?"

"Mostly, but we don't answer to the Archbishop of Canterbury, not since the Revolution, about the same time the colonies stopped accepting prisoners from England. I guess that's why your family ended up here and mine in America."

"Big world." Tomorrow, he embarked on an eighteen-hour flight and then some, showing exactly how true that was. He needed a change of subject.

"It's true I make good money, 1.2 million a season, but that's Aussie dollars, so not as much as it would be in the States." Did he subconsciously want to impress her? That wouldn't do the trick as her father and quarterback brother made far more. He'd checked.

"Most American football players don't earn that. Good for you." She wasn't impressed but didn't say it in a sarcastic way either. Yes, good on him. He could have added he was one of the top paid players in his league.

The scenery turned from rural into suburban Melbourne. They approached Maisie's home. He still hadn't made his points: he wanted to give American football a go, meet her family, and see much, much more of Lorena, not necessarily in that order.

A suspicious number of cars lined the quiet street. As Jock pulled up the drive, two small faces peering out the window disappeared. He inhaled the scent of snags dripping their grease onto the coals of the barbie and probably a pile of hamburgers, too, as he opened the door for her and walked Lori to the house. She might as well have set off an alarm as she inserted her key in the lock because of the blast of noise that greeted them. Shouts of *Surprise*, and *Bon Voyage, Lori*, filled the air of a very crowded living room. Some of the slogans made it onto signs and a long banner declaring *Come Back Soon*. Jock swore he'd been deafened in one ear by a vuvuzela, the bloody horns so popular at soccer games. Her teammates and other friends acquired in Australia loved her as much as he did.

Lori did a terrific job of feigning surprise and delight with the two little boys dancing at her feet, holding up their toy penguins. The crowd moved her toward the bottleneck of the patio doors and spilled outside to where Augie did indeed turn sausages and burgers on the grill. He took a moment to welcome Jock. "Have a good day?" he asked with a knowing smile and a twinkle of the eyes behind his professorial glasses. Might be Lori's unbound hair gave him a clue.

"Wish it had been longer. I brought wine." He held up a Brownlowe Vintages bag.

"Put it in the Esky. We have soda, Fosters, and Fourex in there already. Take what you like. Put this platter on the table for me while I start another batch."

Jock accepted a tray piled high with meat, set it in the only open place on the table between stacks of buns and plates of dressings: fatty bacon rashers, tomato, lettuce, onions, rings of pineapple, and the indispensable canned beetroot for Aussie burgers. A dessert table held a cake decorated to resemble a volleyball, two huge meringue rings encasing pudding and a topping of fresh berries—the popular pavlova, and of course, a plate of Lamingtons. By the time he'd stowed the wine, Lorena had been seated, engulfed by friends, in a place of honor with a paper crown on her head. No place for him, even at her feet.

He did what Augie suggested, seized a Fourex, and built a burger with everything on it, remembering that his mum always cautioned to put the beetroot on top of the lettuce to prevent a soggy bun. Adding a snag topped with mustard and grilled onions and a pile of potato salad to his plate, he went to sit on a low wall for lack of a seat. Women closed in around him.

An attractive, cheeky redhead sat to his right. "Jock Brown, right? I heard you were stepping out with Lorena. Sad, she'll be gone soon, might never return. Got your mobile on you?"

His mouth stuffed with a burger, he simply nodded and tilted his head toward his pants pocket. She accepted that as in invitation and dug it out, showing no shame, giving his thigh a squeeze along the way to adding her name to his contacts list. "There you go, in case you get lonely, Arlene, right there in the A's."

"Give it over," demanded the girl on his left, her

dark hair sliced at odd angles, her cheekbones sharp. "I'm Xenia. You have to scroll way down, but I'm worth the trouble."

He nodded, still trying to consume his burger. He had a list full of names he couldn't associate with any one woman and rarely called them. More likely, he'd take one home from a party if he fancied her, but still trying to set a good example for his brothers, rarely did.

Across the way, Lorena seemed to be laughing at his predicament as she opened small gifts that might fit in her suitcase. Chris and Kyle, rather lost in the crowd, came to sit at his feet as if he provided protection from being trampled. Their toy penguins engaged in a terrific battle over a rock, one claiming it, then the other. Maybe the boys would keep the women off him as they swarmed like flies on raw meat. He'd have to stay to the very end to get another word with Lori. He shoveled down the potato salad and bit into his snag.

The doorbell rang. Must be latecomers, though where the Mortons would put them, he didn't know. Two fit, lean girls, more teammates, arrived with brightly colored gift bags, and their male companions. They sidled toward Lorena to deliver their offerings. He caught a flash of red hair not belonging to a woman, bloody Angus with Willie Taylor in tow again. How had they gotten invited? By latching on to the real partygoers, of course. They followed along until they reached Lori, who made much over small tubes of expensive sun cream. Then Angus raised his loud voice, more often heard on the playing field beckoning for the ball.

"I've got a better present for you, Lori. The truth about why Jock Brown is trying to seduce you—or maybe has."

Jock stood. Lorena's joy vanished to be replaced by puzzlement. The tiny penguins pecked his toes oblivious to the charge in the air.

"All he wants is an intro to your father, so he can get a tryout with the Sinners football team. He'd abandon the Magpies for American dollars. You are only a way to the means. S'truth."

Puzzlement turned to anger in her large, dark eyes, all of it directed toward him. "Shut your gob, Angus, before I come over there and shut it for you," Jock yelled too late.

"Like to see you try," replied the man half his size but totally full of shit.

Aware of the children at his feet, Jock used the initials for what he wanted to say, "GFY." He stepped carefully over Chris and Kyle and their toys. One piped up, "When are we going to see the penguins?"

"Someday," he answered. "Someday."

The mass of celebrating people shoved back and made an aisle for him as if they'd relish a good brawl. He started forward only to be intercepted by the previously friendly Augie, who brandished a greasy spatula and a pair of tongs. "Out of here, the three of you. Start anything on my lawn, and I'll call the cops, understood?"

"Lori," Jock shouted over his head. "You're more important to me than that. Believe me."

She shook her head and sent that high ponytail swishing hard, bringing back sharp memories of unbraiding it strand by strand, not likely to happen again the way she glared at him. "No big deal. Men have tried to use me that way before—and failed. I thought here in Australia…Please, go."

Willie Taylor accepted the order not really meant for him. A smirk on his face, Angus followed. Jock moved forward only to have the tongs point the way out. No big deal for her, but for him a huge deal, a high stakes games for a place with the Sinners and the heart of Lorena Billodeaux. He'd do what he had to do to win both—get on that plane tomorrow and follow her home.

Chapter Seven

Feeling like a stalker, Jock took a later flight out of
Melbourne but easily found Lorena in a shop selling
Australian goods near their gate to Dallas. By the
delighted expression of the salesgirl, the purchase had
been large, though it all fit into a fairly small bag. He
hung back until she returned to the waiting area around
a corner, then chatted up the clerk who rearranged the
few jewelry boxes left in the case.

"Big sale, eh?" he asked.

"Ten opal drop pendants and one larger piece for
her mum. Nearly cleaned us out. Says she's buying for
bridesmaids at a wedding. I'd like an invite to that one."

She wasn't a particularly pretty girl, a bit pudgy
with freckles across her nose and natural red hair, not of
the attractive sort, very carroty. All day, she sold tourist
items in an airport, not the worst job or the best. Why
not make her day?

"I hear those opals are for the wedding of Josee
Riley to Trinity Billodeaux. That woman is his sister."

"Sweet as!" Her jaw dropped open, not making her
any more beautiful, but she'd have a great story to tell
on her tea break. He was about to make it even better.

"Can you recommend some gifts for me to take to
the people I'm visiting in the States."

She pondered. "Our T-shirts are buy one, get one
free."

"Don't know their sizes. Something else. Maybe for children."

"Well, Easter is coming. We have a nice stock of chocolate bilbies and a lovely storybook about the Easter bilby."

He tried to recall the number of Billodeaux grandchildren. Only "a lot" came to mind. Everyone liked chocolate, right? Even better in the shape of a cute marsupial with big ears. "Give me twelve of those and the book."

He glanced over the shop for something more adult and settled on a large tin of Anzac biscuits made famous during World War One, nutritious and a good conversation starter. And Vegemite, four jars. Who knew if they had it over there? His mum insisted her sons have some on their butter bread every day for its vitamin content. He still started his morning by spreading a thin layer of the yeasty brown stuff that looked like shit on his toast. Didn't want to be without it, but he would share. He braced himself for the reaction as he presented his credit card.

The blue eyes that were her best feature widened. "*The* Jock Brown, the footy player?"

He pressed a finger to his lips. "Yes, but don't tell."

"Oh, I won't. You look much bigger up close and personal. Autograph please, or people won't believe me." She offered a sales slip and a pen. "To Audra."

He wrote, "Pleasure meeting you, Audra. Jock Brown."

She accepted it with a sigh before carefully wrapping his purchases with the Vegemite on the bottom and bilbies on top. With a shy wave, she handed over the goods.

Shouldering his garment bag, Jock moved away to find a place to hide like a bilby during daylight. No sense in starting a row in the terminal if Lorena spotted him. He'd board last, probably pass her in the first-class compartment. He'd booked too late to get one of those cherished seats and had gone for business class. At least, he'd have a roomy seat that folded down into a bed.

He emerged from the dark, crowded bar where he'd had nothing but coffee when the announcement for tourist class came over the air. Garment and shopping bags gathered, he crept forward at the end of the line, finally breaking free of the masses when the boarding tunnel split into two, one path leading to the upper level of the large plane and other down into its bowels. He ducked his head and moved between the luxury pods of first class: no Lorena, no Lorena, no Lorena.

Entering business class, he noted lots of spacious seats mostly unoccupied. No Lorena. Finding his seat, he stowed his bags but didn't buckle up at once. A curtain separated his area from the enhanced tourist class. No harm in taking a quick peek. There she sat, second-row center, aisle seat, sipping the orange juice one of the flight attendants offered. She flipped idly through the flight magazine. He ducked back. A tap on his shoulder by another flight attendant indicated he needed to be in his seat for takeoff. Satisfied, he complied. He accepted the champagne option for a drink and settled in for a long, long flight—plenty of time to execute his plan.

A couple of hours later, dinner arrived, pretty much the same meal as first class and fairly decent tucker.

The flight attendant, taking in his size, asked if he'd like another. Why not? He accepted the second option of pasta and had a glass of red wine. Still, he waited. He might run into Lori in the curtained-off toilet area sometime during the night. Not a good idea to startle her like that. Once the trash was cleared and most passengers settled in with a selection on the telly screens buried in the armrest, he made a request of the attendant who seemed quite taken with him, though she ran toward middle-aged in a well-preserved sort of way.

"Would it be possible for me to move to the bulkhead area in tourist class where I could stretch out a bit more?" If he'd asked for first class, that might have been a problem, but no one downgraded.

"Certainly, if you'd be more comfortable. Would you like a second blanket to cover those long legs?"

"I would, thank you."

She followed him, blanket in hand. The lights had been turned down, encouraging passengers to sleep away the many hours until landing. Not many did. Some fiddled with iPads, a few read books, others had put on the silky eye masks provided in a little comfort bag along with socks and dental necessities. Lori was among the last, curled sideways in her seat, blanket up to her chin, pillow tucked under her head, eyes covered. Debatable whether she slept or not, but when he selected the seat directly in front of her and dropped it all the way back into her lap, she muttered, "What the hell. How rude." She'd see only the top of his head and the tips of his toes from back there.

Jock spread his second blanket over his knees, splayed out his legs, and imagined how lovely it would be to have his head truly resting on Lori's warm crotch with no headrest between them. At the thought, his snake wanted out of its cage. Worse things than hard-ons happened on airlines, but he quelled his urge by repeating the NFL rules he attempted to memorize. That put him out for several hours. Around three a.m., he awakened to a kick aimed at the back of his seat.

"Let me out! Let me out. I have to pee." Lori landed another swift kick to his seat.

"Righty-O." He popped his seat upright. She raced off, showing urgency without a second glance at him. It might not be a bad idea since the men's room indicator light showed unoccupied. The cubicle sat on the other side of the ladies'. Pity they weren't both in there together. He heard the flush from the additional bathroom, gave her a few minutes to wash and escape its cramped confines. Sauntering back to resume his seat, she'd already curled up again, mask down. He resumed his position, too, and lowered his seat into a little bit of her paradise. She swore but refrained from landing another kick. What Lori did after that, he had no idea, having dozed off, but hunger rumbled in his stomach around six a.m. He summoned his attendant.

"Might you have a cheese plate or a spare apple for a starving man unless we're due for brekky."

"No brekky for another two hours, but I could heat an empanada for you."

"That would be a bonzer treat. And another for the lady behind me. I know I take up a lot of space." He thickened his Aussie accent, keeping up the ruse, and put his seat upright.

"You certainly do," Lori huffed. Awake then.

The empanadas came steaming on a small plate. He wrapped one in a napkin, turned, and offered it to her.

"G'day, Lori."

"Thank…You! I thought I recognized that Righty-O. What are you doing here, Jock? Go back where you came from."

"Hmmm, it's an Australian plane, and I'm an Australian. You're the one going back where you came from." He expected a seething hot empanada to the face at any moment and prepared to duck.

"I mean, how did you get on this flight, the same as mine?"

"Paid for it. Couldn't get first class as I booked too late. Expected to see you in there right up front. I settled for business class, but I noticed you here and wanted to be closer to you, maybe explain a few things I didn't get a chance to say."

"Closer. Because of you, I have leg cramps and nearly wet myself."

"Lori, I mean to try out for the Sinners whether I have your father's endorsement or not."

She answered with a choice Aussie phrase. "Get stuffed!"

Not open to reason right now, having a bit of a tantrum, he thought. Retreat might be the wisest choice. He gathered his blankets and his snack and headed back to business class. "Enjoy that empanada." Until he slipped behind the curtain, he wasn't entirely sure he wouldn't be wearing it on the back of his shirt, suspecting her aim to be very accurate with a strong arm behind it.

The flight attendant hustled up to ask him if he had a problem. "I do. Can I get a glass of milk to wash this down?"

About four more hours to go. Dawn would soon

catch up and poke her rosy fingers around the window shades as if trying to pry them open. Best he behave, get off first, and lose himself in the long customs lines. He'd not been to Dallas but expected the airport to be big like all things Texan. Hell, those cowboys hadn't ventured into the endless outback and didn't know what huge meant. Hiding out would be harder in the boarding area where the flights to small airports embarked. He'd better work on explaining why he landed in Lafayette, Louisiana, and not New Orleans. Whatever he said, she'd despise it.

Bloody oath, he did want to meet her old man. Who wouldn't? But he had enough talent to impress the Sinners' coach on his own. Mostly, he hoped to immerse himself in all things Lori, her entire family, the ranch, Lori herself. Jock checked his final ticket. Yeah, he'd be back by the toilets. Appropriate since everything appeared to be going shithouse.

Chapter Eight

He'd followed her home, all the frickin' way home to Lafayette. She thought she'd lost him in Dallas, that he'd go to New Orleans on a larger plane, but no. Sitting on the left side of the small aircraft with only single seats, Lori knew exactly when Jock Brown entered the cabin, the very last passenger to board, bent over to avoid hitting his head, moving sideways with a large shopping bag similar to her own, his garment bag turned over to the stewardess. The other women on the flight certainly took notice as he bumbled down the narrow aisle, saying, "Excuse me" every few seconds, but in her case, "Lori." She turned her gaze toward the dark tarmac and the night sky. He went to sit in the last seat by the restrooms, the worst on the plane. That gave her some satisfaction and the fact that he'd have no leg room or chance to recline his seat after what he'd put her through on the Qantas flight.

She kept her anger fueled with the weak coffee she needed to stay awake until they landed at the small airport. Far from pushing forward when the door opened, Jock allowed all to go before him, either very polite or trying to establish a buffer zone against a potential explosion of her temper. Well ahead, she descended the escalator into the mob scene below, her mob, her scene. The Billodeaux clan had turned out en masse, complete with babies she'd yet to meet, a brother-in-law that had to be Matt Keaton by his size with sister Annie tucked under his arm and Jude, her twin standing nearby. Jessie, the new sister-in-law, sat in her wheelchair with one of those children in her lap, Teddy, behind her on his crutches. Red-headed Tom and his tall blonde wife added color to a mostly dark-haired crowd. A lopsided banner proclaimed, "Welcome home, Lori." Tall, teenaged T-Rex held one end while his height-challenged twin, Edie, held the other.

So good to see them all, so many she couldn't tell who was missing. Her mom and dad pushed forward to engulf her in hugs. "Good to have you home. Sorry about things not working out with Maisie," her mother said, whether she meant it or not.

"Oh, it still might."

They stepped aside to let her siblings have a moment. Even Mack, her triplet brother, and usually sullen rebel made an effort to greet her, dwarfing her other womb mate, Trinity. Both gave her hugs. The eldest grandchildren, who hardly remembered her, split off toward the allure of the escalator, followed by a very quick little girl with a head of dark curls who had to be Teddy's adopted daughter. Stacy, Dean's wife, herded them back to the group. The buzzer for the baggage carousel sounded and had them heading in the other direction to watch the show. The kids' father and Sinners quarterback, Dean, charged after them, shouting over his shoulder, "How many bags, Lori?"

"Two big ones, both red."

Other passengers, who'd simply gotten out of the way, followed the alert. She remained determined not to look behind her for any sight of Jock Brown. Made no difference. He stepped up to her father standing nearby and offered a hand.

"G'day. How ya going?"

Her Hall of Fame quarterback dad, never one to turn down a handshake, accepted the offer with a slightly perplexed look on his face. "We did bring the family van if you need a lift somewhere."

"I meant to rent a car, but I see all the booths are closed. I'm on my way to New Orleans."

"That's a long drive from here. Australian, right? Friend of Lori's?"

"I couldn't be anything else. Jock Brown, ruckman for the Melbourne Magpies."

Her father remained puzzled. Seething, Lori pulled her mother aside. "Mom, he followed me home. He knows damn well where New Orleans is because I told him."

"Language," her mother said absently, her gaze on Jock. "What exactly is going on here?"

"We had a very short relationship. He only wanted to use me to meet Dad and get an in with the Sinners because he plays footy."

"Footy?" Her mom's dark, and very perceptive eyes, turned her way.

"Australian rules football—and he is very good at it, but he took advantage of me."

"Did you sleep with him?"

"Once, only once. I thought he was tender as lamb, but it turns out he stinks like mutton. I told him to get lost, yet here he is sucking up to Dad." Though they whispered, her father's voice boomed out.

"A fellow athlete then." He guessed. "Since you're a friend of Lori's, why don't you spend the night with us at the ranch? We have plenty of room. We'll set you on the right path tomorrow."

Lori shook her mom's arm, "No, no. Drop him at a motel."

"I can't rescind your father's offer. Do you expect this man to assault you in the night at our home?"

"Of course not. He's not a rapist. In fact, he's very good in…never mind. As long as he's gone in the morning."

Mama Nell began rearranging sleeping quarters. "We can put him in Dean's old room, move Dean and Stacy to Stacy's former room across from yours. Tom and Alix will be next to him, then Mack and Trinity. You'll be surrounded by family if he tries anything."

"I'm not worried about that. I simply don't want him using Dad or me to get a tryout with the Sinners."

Her mom studied Jock Brown again. "By the size of him, I doubt he'll have trouble getting a tryout on his own. Well, let's make the best of it and get this circus on the road." Small but mighty, her mother began moving people toward the parking lot. T-Rex and Edie folded their banner and followed to a large white van. They took the seats in the back. Lori did the same to be as far away from Jock as possible. Of course, he made the best impression by helping her mother inside, though her dad assigned the shotgun seat to his new Aussie friend. Dean stowed Lori's bags and Jock's single, sleek but enormous suitcase made of some metallic substance in the rear and trotted off to his SUV to buckle up his children.

"Kids, this is Jock Brown from Australia, a friend of Lori's. He's staying the night." Her dad rolled down the window and shouted in a voice used to giving audibles or controlling twelve children. "Anyone else riding in the van? Okay, then, we're heading for the ranch." He shut the window and flicked the air-conditioning on low. Off they went at the head of a procession worthy of a wedding or a funeral since most of her siblings had brought their own cars: Teddy's red handicapped van next, Dean's big SUV, the same type carrying Annie and her husband and sister Jude, Mack's Jaguar, then Trinity's Tesla.

"The standard joke on the ranch is that you can tell who is visiting by the cars parked at the barn," her mom said for Jock's benefit.

"That was quite the reception," Jock agreed.

Mama Nell got right down to finding out all about him. "Yes, and that wasn't all of the family. You'll meet more tomorrow. How about you? Brothers, sisters?'

"Two younger brothers, grown. My parents are deceased."

"So early in your life," her psychologist mom commiserated.

"Mum's been gone a while, cancer. Pop recently from the drink."

In the darkness in the back of the van, Lori tried very hard not to have pity or admiration for a man who'd raised his brothers under such circumstances and was as charmed as she by tiny penguins and platypuses. No, he was a lying, lowdown venomous snake.

Edie's voice piped up. "Did you grow up on a cattle station and attend the School of the Air?

Jock's deep chuckle resonated inside the van. "No, I'm a city boy. Only time I've been to the outback, I went to see the big red rock, Uluru. Most of us live along the coast."

"Do you surf?" asked T-Rex. "I have a few times in Hawaii and Samoa. We really don't have the waves for it here."

"I can surf, but only learned recently up on Bondi Beach. I'd guess you are better at it than I am."

Her mother's voice sounded. "Lorena just got home. Don't you have any questions for her?"

"Sure," Edie said. "How did you meet Jock?

She refused to answer that one, but Jock did. "I introduced myself after one of her matches. We've been together ever since then."

"That would be three days, four or five if you count the airplane ride home."

"I do. I fell asleep in her lap," he had the Aussie audacity to say.

"It wasn't like that at all," she denied. "He put his seat all the way back and..." Lori stopped when she heard Jock's low chuckle. He'd gotten a rise out of her. "It doesn't matter."

Her mom picked up the fumbled ball of the conversation and ran with it. "Xo and Junior will be over tomorrow. She didn't want to take her babies out so late at night. Josee is driving up from New Orleans in the morning. Since it's so close to Easter, everyone is going to hang around until Sunday night. You can get acquainted with the new family members and enjoy the old ones."

"Sounds like a bonzer family. I'd like to meet them, too." The nerve of Jock Brown to invite himself to their family celebration.

Her mother hesitated, but her oblivious dad said, "Unless you have plans in New Orleans, why don't you stay with us for the holiday?"

"My plan was to check into a hotel and arrange a tryout for a place on the Sinners team."

"Walk-ons usually try out in May. Won't be many of the Sinners staff around this weekend anyhow. My boys and I will give you a workout this weekend and tell you if you have a chance. No sense wasting your time if you don't."

"Sounds fair enough. Thank you for inviting me to stay."

"No trouble, we always have room for one more at Lorena Ranch."

"Your daughter is named for the place, right?"

"After an ancestor. The ranch bears her name."

Weren't they just so cozy? Edie and T-Rex had dozed off as her watch showed midnight. If she weren't so angry, she'd be asleep, too, as the van moved through the night past the neon signs of mini-casinos promising "Loose and Easy" or "Big Payouts." The monotonous fields of sugar cane, still young and low to the ground, slipped by in a blur. As she finally settled and began to nod, the sharp turn off the highway onto the backroad into Chapelle woke her again. The potholes made her head bounce against the window. In the front seat, Jock snored lightly with his big head lolling next to her dad, but her mom behind them stayed alert for any hazard that might imperil her family be it an armadillo in the road, a drunk Cajun driver—or a Jock.

They passed through the sleeping town of Chapelle, by the Catholic church with three illuminated crosses, one draped in purple, planted on its lawn defining the holy season, then on to another backroad worse than the first. At last, the gates of the ranch swung open like wide arms welcoming her home. The sensors in the live oaks activated the lights along the long alley. Teddy's vehicle peeled off on the lane to his house on the property. The others followed the van and went to park by the barn. Her dad rolled up to the side door to the kitchen and began opening doors and gathering baggage. She was home at last after nearly two days on the road.

Those still sleeping awoke groggy. Her mom got down to direct the flow of traffic. "Dean, I'm moving you and Stacy to her old bedroom. Put the children in Xochi's room. Go get your things. I want to get Jock settled. He must be dead on his feet."

If they were surprised, they were accustomed to obeying Mama Nell. The couple gathered their nodding children and went ahead to vacate the room. Jock, totting his suitcase, garment bag, and shopping sack followed his hostess to the grand staircase at the front of the house where a dimly shining chandelier lit their way. Despite his burdens, he mounted the steps with ease, Lori noticed.

"Lorena, if you want to take the elevator since it's closer to your room, go ahead. You need to rest." Her mom put space between her daughter and the Aussie, though he wouldn't know that.

However, Annie and Matt, just behind her and unaware of any tension, put that plan awry. "Oh, I want you to see my babies, Lori, just for a minute. They're sleeping in the nursery. Matt, carry her suitcases up. We'll only take a peek."

Of course, the old nursery sat across the hall from Jock's room. Still, Lori couldn't deny this small request when she heard the joy in Annie's voice. "Sure, I'd love that."

While her mom steered Jock toward his guestroom, even opened the door for him and explained the attached bath shared with the room beside it, Annie led her sister into the nursery where a young woman in her late teens dozed in the rocker near the nightlight shaped like a teddy bear. A white noise machine hissed softly, lulling the occupants, not babies but toddlers: a tow-headed boy sleeping on his back with one thumb corked into his mouth, another boy, dark-haired and sturdy, with his rump in the air, and another, also brunette whose blue eyes opened for just a second and closed again after seeing his adoptive mom.

"Don't tell me. Let me guess." Lori pointed with her finger. "Drew, Gabe, and Danny." She knew them well from the photos and messages Annie sent, proud of all of them, though she'd adopted Matt's son, Daniel, a preemie she'd cared for in the hospital, Gabriel, their own son, and Andrew, who belonged to the girl with the cap of blonde hair, Dre. To Annie, who cared for them, they all belonged to her and always would. "They are beautiful, Annie."

Figured Jock, towering over the women, would steal a glance and say, "I'd like my nursery to be filled with little boys exactly like them someday." Of course, Annie beamed at him.

Dre awoke and took in Annie and two people she didn't know. "Sorry, sleeping on the job."

"You were here if they needed you. Go to bed. I believe Mom put you in Teddy's old room at the very end of the hall by the elevator by Lori. Matt and I will take the monitor in our room. We'll be right across from the nursery."

Great, her well-meaning sister had given Jock directions to her sleeping quarters—though her mother had put a running back and a quarterback between them, plus a wide receiver if Mack slept in his old space. Trin, the third of the triplets, would be nearby, too, small but scrappy, he'd claimed ever since participating in a bar fight and shooting his fiancée's stalker. If she gave the word, Trin might shoot Jock for her.

Dre nodded. "I'll get the introductions in the morning. Night." She wandered down the hall, a tall, slim girl already a mother. Jock watched her go into the last room on the right and shut the door.

Again, her mom attempted to put Jock into his own bed. "I hope the little ones don't wake you too early." She again pointed to his room.

"No worries. I sleep like a wombat in a log. G'night." At last, he and his damned charm had been contained. With that, her mom felt free to rest and moved toward her suite.

Annie claimed the baby monitor, shut the nursery door with the softest of clicks, and slipped into her room across the hall where Matt waited. The rest of the family staying in the big house must have come up in the elevator and avoided the group in the hall. Their doors were closed, with no lights showing around the frames. Only Edie and T-Rex still trailed. Rex gave them a tired wave and went to his bed. Edie opened her door cautiously, which did not prevent the white pouf of a dog from charging out, jumping into Lorena's arms, and lavishing kisses on her face.

"Oh, Brody, you remember me." She shifted her

bichon frise onto one arm. "I'm so sorry I couldn't take you to Australia with me. Want to sleep with me tonight?"

"He's stayed with me while you've been gone," Edie said, a trifle sad as if something wonderful had come to an end.

"We can share while I'm home. Tonight, I'd like to keep him in my room. But hey, I've got something for you. Come with me for a sec."

Her suitcases lay on the bed in her lavender and lace bedroom with its wisteria trim high on the walls, a place more feminine than she'd ever been. Still, she adored the place her loving mother had created for her when separation from the boys became necessary. She opened the case containing mostly souvenirs and gifts. "Here, a replica of the fairy penguins. Volunteers make little jackets for them when they are ill. I only thought it looked cute. It won't replace Brody, but you can snuggle with it tonight."

"I'll do that. Tomorrow, I want to hear every detail about Australia. Maybe I can visit you there someday." Edie gave Brody a goodnight kiss and moved along to her room.

Lorena started to close the suitcase, but there on the top lay the plush platypus Jock had given her. She should let Edie have that, too, but for some dumb reason, she threw it into the back of her closet. It landed on top of a pile of stuffed animals left over from high school, things from the past. Let it stay there.

So tired. Too much trouble to unpack. She placed the suitcases on the floor, and locking her door, she simply stripped off her travel grungy clothes and went to bed naked between the cool, clean sheets. Brody curled up on the duvet at her feet, a bedmate who would never betray her.

Chapter Nine

Lorena intended to sleep late, very late, figuring Jock with all the rest he'd gotten on the plane, would be up and out earlier. Maybe her mom told her dad how Jock had played her, and he'd already revoked the invitation to stay and driven their guest back to the airport for a rental car. But a love-starved mockingbird sang his incessant, discordant song outside her window, and Brody whined by the door wanting out. She washed her face, smoothed her braid, dug out a clean sports bra and bottom, and a tracksuit—no need to be made up and fancy at home. As soon as she passed into the hall, the scent of blueberry pancakes, her favorite, lured her to the kitchen.

Jock sat behind a tall stack of them. Blueberry syrup cascaded down the sides of the tower while a fat pat of butter melted in the middle. Small sausages adorned its base, and three cups with orange juice, milk, and coffee surrounded it like pillars holding up the entire construction. He sliced through the heap clear to a piece of sausage, engulfed the whole into his mouth, and after swallowing, said, "Best I've ever eaten, dear." The "dear" had been directed to their beloved housekeeper and now relative by marriage, Corazon, who beamed at him as she poured more batter on the griddle. "G'day, Lori," he added.

"Fresh and hot for you, my Lorena," she said. Jock

had appropriated the entire previous batch without a doubt.

"That's fine." She opened the door for Brody, who went to do his business and meet with Lil, the black Lab mix, who could have slept inside but seemed to prefer a nest of straw in the barn most nights. "I'll have my juice and coffee while I wait." Pointedly, she sat at the far end of the long table away from Jock after she poured her beverages from carafes that sat right beside him.

"Going for a run? I need to work out the kinks in my legs after that flight." Jock had bulldozed through half his breakfast. "Won't take me but a mo' to get ready while you eat."

Really, he had kinks in his legs when he'd spent the whole flight sprawled out in what should have been her leg space while she'd been curled in her seat.

Corazon placed two large pancakes on a warm plate with a couple of sausages and sat them in front of Lorena. "Enjoy," she said but bent way over to whisper in Lori's ear. "It is rude to sit so far from our guest." A second mother always ready to correct the behavior of the Billodeaux kids, that was Corazon.

Jock had finished his meal. He stood, stretched, and kissed Corazon on the cheek as she passed. "*Magnifico*, you and the pancakes. Better than Aussie pikelets," he said.

"Yes, they are," Lori answered as if she sucked on a lemon rather than sugary sweet blueberry syrup.

Corazon shooed him away as he carried his dishes to the sink, but Lori could tell she'd already been seduced by his Aussie charm and good manners. As soon as Jock left the kitchen, she bolted the rest of her breakfast. She'd planned on a long, hot shower and a thorough wash of her hair. The day appeared warm enough to lie by the pool, which would still be chilly, and let it dry on its own. Now, however, she wanted to be gone before Jock returned. Busing her own dishes and kissing Corazon's other cheek, not the one he had polluted, she went outside, did a scant few stretches, and called the dogs. "Who wants to run?"

Lil and Brody came along eagerly even though Corazon shouted after her, "You not wait for Mr. Jock?"

No, she would not wait for Mr. Jock, who was ruining her homecoming. Just let him try to find her in the maze of paths around the ranch.

****

He hadn't been gone that long since he'd showered and shaved before going down for his brekky, and a great brekky it was, but Lorena had taken off without him. However, another shift of Billodeauxs now sat at the kitchen table, the rest of the triplets, one an athlete, muscular with flowing black hair around his shoulders, the other a dag, the brainy, near-sighted one with black-framed glasses and curls hanging in his face.

"G'day. Any idea which way Lorena went? She had her tracky daks on, so I assume she's out running."

Hostility as hot as Corazon's griddle wafted off of them. "No idea. It's a big ranch," the small guy said. He had a scar over one eye that made him look a little less of a wimp.

"Yeah, big ranch," the fit one, Mack, agreed as he tucked into a stack nearly as big as the one Jock had consumed earlier. "No telling where she'll go."

"Oh, she take off with the dogs, probably past the

pool, then into the palm grove, make a big loop, and come back to the pool for a swim or shower," Corazon offered. She pointed to her left. "Around the house, then to the pool."

Trin, the computer genius about to marry a supermodel, glared at her as if she were a corrupted file.

"Thanks, Corazon. I'll do a few stretches, then see if I can find her." Jock stationed himself just outside the slightly cracked kitchen door. He kept his ears open as he bent his legs this way and that, and his eyes on the panes of glass, noting the family dynamics. It soon paid off.

"We don't know if we like this guy for Lori," Trinity said. "We'll have to see."

"Humpf, he better than that other one she bring home who looked down on me for being a housekeeper. I should be back in Mexico helping my own people, he say."

"Yeah, one weekend, and he managed to offend nearly everyone in the family."

"He told me I probably didn't have the brains to do anything but play football," Mack added as he stuffed an uncut sausage into his mouth.

"You have brains. You just don't use them much," Trin answered and got an elbow in the ribs. Trin elbowed his brother even harder and caused the expectoration of half a sausage. "Don't make me Heimlich you again."

"I wasn't choking."

So brothers who loved each other yet couldn't stand the other at times. Too bad, they seemed united against him. He'd work on that. Enough with the stretching. After that huge feed, he should take it easy on Lorena's trail.

He found the pool easily enough and passed through its two gates. He ran through a palm grove right out of the South Pacific and past a sand volleyball court, but no Lorena. The curving path brought him out to a more open area overlooking pastures. The serene eyes of white cows turned his way. The bull in their midst seemed more hostile, kind of like Lori's brothers. Horses and ponies kicked their heels closer to a river that was indeed a deeper brown than the Yarra. A path ran alongside the grazing areas. Perhaps, she'd gone that way.

He paused by a low wall that set off a patio in the back of a fairly new home more modern in design than the fake antebellum mansion they called the ranch house. A small pixie face full of mischief peered over its edge. "Hi, Aussie man. Stay outta the bullpen," the little girl said, her eyes wide and blue, her hair, wild black curls. "Come see. We making Easter eggs." She leaned further toward him.

"Lizzie, away from the wall," her wheelchair-bound mother cautioned. "You'll tip over."

Which is precisely what the child did with every confidence that the strange man would catch her. Jock tossed her into the air and tucked her under an arm. He walked around to the patio entry. "Appears I have something of yours."

"Yes, that one is Lizzie. May is in the playpen. She's happy there as long as I'm near, but Liz figured out how to escape at nine months. I'm Jesse in case you didn't remember from all that chaos last night."

"Oh, I never forget a pretty face or an active child." He placed the delighted Lizzie on the bench where her mum had laid out cups full of bright dye and crayons that the child could use to decorate the shells of the eggs in a bowl nearby.

"I'm sure the wheelchair helped your memory."

"And the child escaping toward the escalator."

Lizzie plucked an egg from the bowl and drew a crude round circle with two big ears and maybe two eyes and a nose with a yellow crayon. She dumped it into a cup and sloshed green dye on the wooden picnic table. "You see why we're out here. Less of a mess to clean up."

A minute later, her mother fished it out to dry. "See, I drewed the Easter bunny. Now, you." Lizzie offered him her crayon.

Well, he guessed he had the time since Lori was nowhere in sight, and the view from the patio should have exposed her. He selected an egg and attempted to sketch a bilby, the big-eared but tiny Australian Easter bunny. When it came out of the blue dye, Lizzie pondered it and asked, "Wazzit?"

"The Aussie Easter bunny," he told her. "On Easter, I'll tell you a story about it."

"I like stories. It's a funny bunny because it comes from down under."

"That's right. Smart child."

"Oh, I showed her Australia on the globe this morning and said it was down under. This one forgets nothing."

The toddler in the pen began pleading, "I want egg."

Jessie said, "I'll hold it, and you draw." She rotated the egg until a wiggly abstract emerged. "What color do you want?"

"Red."

Actually, the design turned out to be very pleasing. "I can see you are all better artists than I am. I'd better give it up. Has Lorena passed this way on a run?"

"Haven't seen her. Maybe she turned around rather than be ambushed into dying Easter eggs."

Hmm, turned around. He considered for a moment. "See you later, Lizzie, May, and Jessie." Repeating names helped him remember them though he'd studied this tribe well before coming here through magazines and computer searches. He even knew the names of their dogs beforehand. Yes, he wanted a place on the Sinners team, and Lorena more than that, but he also suspected he desired to be part of this supportive clan who did good deeds and looked out for one another no matter how irritating that might be. In studying the Billodeauxs, he'd found the family he'd always craved.

Jesse and the girls waved him off with good cheer. He'd track Lorena down if it took all morning. Reentering the palm grove, he jogged along slowly, watching the trail until he saw a footprint entrenched deep in the sand as if someone had leaped aside into the bushes. He followed lighter prints and the paw marks of the dogs deep into the grove to a hidey-hole surrounded by low palms, a great place to make love outdoors, he calculated. So she'd squatted here until he passed and doubled back to the big house. In no hurry now, he returned to the trail and the pool. He stopped at the gate. Lorena found.

There she lay, her long brown body spread out, basking in the mild spring sunshine on a lounger. She wore an athletic bra and bikini bottom as if she prepared for a match. Her hair spread out loose and wet, her brown eyes were closed, and a small smile sat upon her lips. The little white dog curled at her feet, and the black one nested in a towel by her side. He could have studied her all day in exactly that pose, better if she'd been nude, but the animals gave him away. Brody sat up and yipped. Lil emitted one sharp bark.

Lorena sprang upright with her long legs straddling the lounger. "You!"

"Decided on a swim rather than a run? Wish you'd told me."

"Dad only took the tarp off last week. The water is still too cold. Don't you understand I'm trying to get rid of you?"

"I doubt that will happen since I've been invited to spend Easter with your family. He entered the pool area and swished his hand in the crystal-clear water. "Chilly, all right, but nothing I can't handle. You?"

"Go swimming with you? No, thanks. I just took a quick shower in the pool house. I'm waiting for my hair to dry."

Stripping off his gray sweatshirt, he shucked the bottoms along with his running shoes. Beneath, he wore a Speedo low-slung on his hips. A banana hammock, the Aussies called it, and he knew he wore it well. He watched Lori's glance slide down his torso like sun cream straight to the zebra-striped pouch.

"Go into that water, and your banana will turn into a peanut," she sneered.

"Won't know until we try." He covered the space between them so fast she was unprepared to be gripped by the wrists, hauled upward, and slung over his shoulder. They entered the water together with one huge splash. The black dog, showing its Labrador heritage, plunged in joyously. The poufy dog wisely stayed on the lounger observing, head cocked with interest. All three swam rapidly to the side and climbed out. Lil shook herself free of excess water and went back to her towel.

Jock made his own observation. "Not the size of a peanut, but it could use some warming up if you're willing. That place in the palm grove where you hid…"

"Willing? No, I am not willing. Never again, you liar, you user." As quickly as he'd dunked her in the icy water, she darted for the pool house and locked the door.

She'd cornered herself and had to hear him out now. He rapped on the door as if paying a polite visit. "Lori, I didn't lie to you. My bloody oath on that."

The barking dogs drew an audience, the last thing he wanted right now. The male contingent of the triplets came running through the gate and lined up side by side.

"I think we can take him, Mack, if you go high and I go low. You have the muscle, but I'm scrappy," Trinity Billodeaux exclaimed.

"Trin, look at the size of him. He could kill you. You've had one bar fight. I've had many. Let me handle this." Mack stepped forward, prepared to defend his sister.

Lori opened the door a crack. "No fighting. Jock, that means no pounding on my brothers if you need to hear it in Aussie. All three of you go away and let me alone." She snapped the door shut and clicked the lock.

"Okay, Sis." Mack sidled next to Jock, so close his body heat might have evaporated the water droplets on his body. "After you," Mack said, his famous receiving arm pointing the way.

Not much choice but to pull on his sweats and shove on his shoes for a return to the house as her bigger brother continued to guard the door. "I only wanted a chat with her," he said as he passed Trinity at the gate.

"Funny way to achieve that by dumping her in an icy pool. Now she's madder than a wet hen. Understand my meaning."

"I do, but sometimes, you have to get a woman's attention first before she listens."

"Been there," Trin conceded. "Let's get moving. Dad wanted to know if you'd like to ride along to pick up the crawfish for dinner. We found you exactly when you dunked Lori in the pool. Not cool, man."

"Cold, freezing even." He thought he'd gotten a half-smile from the smaller brother, but they fell in behind him like a police escort. "So we're having crayfish tonight."

"Sure, it's what Cajuns do on Good Friday. Finish up Lent with a big crawfish boil. Dad knows a special place to buy them." Trin continued to answer him, but Mack played the strong, silent, and intimidating type. Didn't bother Jock. Wide receivers ran away while he'd been in the heart of many a scrum.

"Do we have to catch them?"

"Nope, but it is fun when you do."

"I'll put on dry clothes, and I'm good to go." Exactly what he wanted, to spend the morning with three Billodeaux men instead of Lori.

Chapter Ten

Good Friday, the day Christ died, did not weep on Cajun Country. The morning remained mild with a cloudless blue sky above and low humidity below. Jock gathered it to be miraculously perfect for a huge sacrifice of crawfish.

They loaded into a more gray than silver ranch truck with a double cab that showed its age and utility in dings and scratches and worn upholstery. Mack called shotgun and stretched out his long legs in the front seat. Trinity settled in comfortably in the rear seat next to Jock, whose knees rested under his chin. The place to get the best crawfish, he might as well use the Cajun term, apparently was not right down the road.

They bumped along country lanes full of potholes, and the equally annoying repairs that roughened the ride like speed bumps and made his teeth clash together. Joe breezed through small towns possessing short main streets having the incredibly low limits of speed traps with the confidence of a celebrity who would be waved along in exchange for an autograph.

Once clear of these small traces of civilization, they emerged to an area of flooded rice paddies with bobbers marking the locations of crawfish traps, and more than one pool owning a contraption to do the harvest. "Dual-purpose dry land rice farming," Joe Billodeaux explained to Jock. "The seed is sown by airplanes into the water. While the paddies are flooded, the farmers harvest a second crop in crawfish. Later, they drain the fields and let the rice ripen to be harvested by combines. Louisiana rice is sold all over the world, but our crawfish stay right here. If you haven't preordered for Good Friday, you are out of luck."

Interesting, he supposed. A boom shook the air and sent a flock of white egrets into flight. "What was that?"

"Oh, a noisemaker to startle the birds away from the mudbugs. They like to eat them, too. These paddies attract migrating geese and ducks in the winter. Great hunting, but most of them have gone north by now. If you're still around in the fall, I'll let you use my duck blind."

"That's very kind of you, but umm, I don't hunt."

The deep brown eyes of all three men turned toward him. Joe's thankfully gazing in the rearview mirror to stare. "You're one of those animal rights people?" Mack questioned. He sensed this issue was as sticky as the one about religion that Lori had brought up.

"Not at all. You see, gun laws are quite strict in Australia. You may have as many guns as you want but can only use them on your property. Of course, they must be licensed. In the city, we haven't much use for them, but the men on the cattle stations in the outback need their weapons to put down animals, take care of vermin or predators like the dingoes. Kangaroos are fair game as they compete for grass with the sheep and steers. Carry a gun in your car, and the fine is fairly stiff."

Trin looked up at last from the latest iPhone he'd been perusing for most of the ride. "Oh, good, Josee is almost at the ranch. You ever eat kangaroo?"

"Tastes like beefsteak. People say the tail is the best. You can find it in the freezer section of the grocery stores. I'd bet Lori has had it several times."

"Probably. She's the one who took the dare to eat a worm when we were kids. She claimed it tasted like bacon."

"The grubs the indigenous people eat do, or so I'm told."

The conversation on weird foods ended as Joe steered the truck to a stop in front of a shack on the edge of one of the paddies. They were expected. A grizzled man with enough lines in his face to compete with a plowed brown field emerged. He wore overalls and white rubber boots, topped the whole with a red ball cap.

"Dare you are Joe Dean." He pumped the hand of the hall-of-famer with fingers knotted by farm work. "I got your order ready. Purged dem yesterday. Nice and clean. So glad to see you and your boys, me."

"Mack and Trin, load the sacks into the truck for Mr. Poo-yie. He always gives us the best."

"I sorted out the big ones for you myself. Dat'll be…"

Joe Billodeaux peeled off an amazing amount of money for creatures that lived in the mud and ate whatever filtered down to them. Jock helped in hefting four large net bags full of living, snapping crustaceans, enough to feed a crowd, into the truck bed. Dinner would be an experience.

"You come inside for coffee before you leave, no?"

Mr. Poo-yie asked.

"Not today, we need to get these mudbugs home to the boiling pot. Next time I come out here to hunt, we'll sit down and have a nice long talk. I know you'll have my blind in great shape."

"Dat I will, Joe."

The transaction took little time considering the length of the trip to get their cargo, but Jock was glad of a chance to stretch his cramped legs. Maybe Lori had a point about his hogging her space on the airplane. They loaded up again and started back along the same rutted roads with the sacks bumping in the back. The sun stood overhead, and he wouldn't admit to being hungry after that superb brekky, but Joe must have felt the same way. In one of the small towns, he pulled up in front of a cinderblock building unpretentiously called Mom's. The checkered oilcloth-covered tables were greasy, and the napkins consisted of a roll of paper towels sitting by a selection of hot sauces. They took a table by a window.

"We're in luck. Mom must be a Baptist. A lot of places close on Good Friday." Joe examined the pepper sauces and held up a bottle. "Joe's Hot and Spicy, my own brand. Use it lightly," he cautioned Jock.

His sons snickered, "As if you do."

"A man has to build his resistance to it to get the full flavor."

"Right. He's being kind to you by giving a warning, Jock."

"Keep an eye on the truck, boys. Holiest time of the year and some *couillon* will steal your crawfish. Catfish po-boys all around? Trin, chocolate milkshake or Diet Coke?"

"Chocolate milkshake. I can get Diet Coke anywhere. Mom makes hers with real ice cream and chocolate syrup."

"Then I'll have one, too," Jock said. He sensed this annual fetching of the crawfish from Mr. Poo-yie had become a family ritual that always included a stop at Mom's.

"Same for me," Mack ordered.

Joe yelled the order across the small space separating their table from the counter and the kitchen. A reply came from a black woman of generous proportions, her hair done up in a purple do-rag, her body covered by an apron splattered by the fat from the fryers. "I'm old, not deaf, Mr. Joe. Same order every year. How's Poo-yie doin' out in the paddies? He got more years on him than me."

"He seems same as always."

"Don't we all? No complaining about the arthritis or the backache." Mom turned to her fryers and sild fresh-cut fries into one and catfish fillets breaded in cornmeal into the other. While they cooked, she slit the French bread rolls and dressed them down with mayo, tomato, and lettuce before turning to a milkshake machine that must have been fifty years old. Still, it churned out the four drinks in no time at all.

The catfish po-boys came piping hot, two large fillets each to a sandwich. Mom set the platter of French fries in the center of the table and brought out the chocolate shakes two at a time.

"Not much help today?" Joe asked.

"I let the Catholics have off, and it's mostly Catholics around here. Business is going to be slow, but Mom's does not close on Good Friday." She took a seat in a battered leather chair by the cash register and flipped through a movie magazine.

"This is great," Jock acknowledged with mayo dripping down his chin, quickly swiped off with a paper towel. "Did Mr. Poo-yie say the crawfish were purged?"

"Yes, he sees they don't eat the day before, and that clears out their intestines," Joe answered.

"I don't see the difference when we strip that out of the crawfish before we eat them," Trin added, taking a big suck on his thick shake.

"The ladies like them better this way. Ever eat crawfish before?" Mack said with a little challenge in his voice.

"We have them in Australia. Balmain bugs we call them. Smaller than these, though. It's a harsh land, and the natives and first settlers ate most anything. We still do."

"Something you have in common with Cajuns. Don't forget to suck the heads. It's the best part of a crawfish," Mack said, a glint in his eye. Both his dad and brother shrugged, an inside joke Jock guessed.

They polished off the whole meal, three big men, and one slight with a voracious appetite that belied his size. Joe left a tip about the same size as the whole tab and wished Mom a Happy Easter on the way out the door. So full Jock wondered the roads didn't bring the entire meal back up, he dozed off, took some ribbing about it when they returned to the ranch, but was given a pass by Mama Nell who said he wasn't used to Louisiana time yet as she scurried between the house and the barbecue pavilion.

The place surged with activity as if someone had

kicked a termite mound. Small children, toddlers, and crawling babies raced around a circle of their mothers. The dogs fetched any balls thrown. More cars and trucks arrived behind theirs, with women carefully bearing covered desserts and their men handling any extra dishes. Most of the horde gravitated toward the pavilion. He was pleased to be here and wanted to be one of them.

He scanned the crowd for Lorena and found a tall, golden girl instead, the model Josee Riley, who immediately made her way to the group of men and lowered her head to kiss her shorter fiancé without a hint of embarrassment. Trin rocked up on his toes a little to return it with enthusiasm. When they came up for air, he introduced his intended to Jock.

Josee cocked that stunning blonde head. "Have we met before?"

She did dazzle in person, even when casually dressed and made up. He couldn't deny that. Trin was a lucky man, but no luckier than he if he wed Lorena.

"Briefly. I escorted Samantha Harris to a posh affair in Melbourne a couple of years ago. You have a good memory."

"You'd be hard to forget."

Again, Jock searched for Lorena. "Some women don't think so. Have you seen Lori?"

"In the barbecue pavilion, helping to set up the tables, I think."

"Thanks. See you later." Maybe he'd been rude, but cornered inside the pavilion, Lorena would hardly cause a scene, not with all her relatives swarming about the place.

He entered the domain of women and edged

through to his target. "Lori, could we…"

"No, we couldn't. Are you here just to take up space or be useful?" She turned her dark gaze on him.

"Useful, of course. I…"

She shoved a pile of newspapers at him. "Cover the tables double thick. I have to help Mom with the relish trays."

Off she went and left him standing there like a newsboy with the latest edition. He spread the newspaper as directed until Joe grabbed his arm. "Hey, help unload the crawfish, and I'll let you watch my culinary magic when I cook them. I have a crawfish well built into the indoor grill, but we're going to set up the propane burner outside to do two batches at a time. That big guy over there by the built-in boiler is my son-in-law, Junior Polk. He and Dean are heading up the second pot since they have the most experience."

Jock leaned across several shorter women to shake Junior's hand. "Pro Bowl cornerback for the Sinners as well."

One of the short women, Corazon, embraced Junior's thick waist. "Also, my son and *padre* to two children already."

"Good on ya."

"Come on. Timing is everything." Joe led him away.

He helped with the propane burner and hauled water for both deep pots. Bearing a tray of small, ripe strawberries with a pink whip in the center, Lori passed close once. She wouldn't have stopped at all if her mother, following behind with an immense relish tray of celery, cherry tomatoes, green pepper slices, and baby carrots arrayed around a yogurt dipping sauce, hadn't said, "Let Jock try our Louisiana berries. They are the best."

Smiling, he took a handful and agreed. The other men snatched a berry or two and grabbed some celery sticks and carrots to tide them over as if lunch at Mom's hadn't been enough. "Somehow, I imaged we'd have pork rinds and cracklings," he remarked.

T-Rex, as sullen as a teen boy could be, answered, "Not with Mom watching our diets and Mawmaw forbidding any meat at the Good Friday picnic because it's still Lent. We can't even add sausage to the crawfish." He let loose with what was really bothering him. "I can't believe y'all went to Poo-Yie's and Mom's without me."

Mack said, "No room in the back with Jock taking up all the space."

So he *had* intruded on a manly family ritual, but he'd been invited. Maybe they thought he'd turn them down and chase after Lorena instead. Still, the journey had been interesting in many ways. He felt right at home with the male camaraderie. His family had no special traditions except a bowl of cherries at Christmas.

"You'll have your turn again next year, son. We wanted to get to know Jock better." Joe chucked lemon halves, sliced yellow onions, and pods of garlic into the bubbling water. "Run inside and make sure Dean and Junior are ready with their potatoes. Give them my special seasoning sack, but tell them to be sure they don't add it until we boil the crawfish." He lowered the mesh bag containing the spices into the hands of T-Rex as if offering him gold.

"Dad, Junior is a chef when he isn't playing

football, and Dean barbecues all the time."

"Doesn't mean they know it all. Now, go."

T-Rex raced off as his father lowered an entire sack of small, red potatoes into the water. "That will take about twenty minutes, then the crawfish go into the pot until done, and the frozen corn for another fifteen. Gotta let the cooked mudbugs rest about forty-five minutes. Time for a cold one."

As if cued, Brinsley, the family butler, arrived with a tray of longnecks sweating from the cooler. He appeared exactly as in the magazine articles Jock had studied about the family, but the butler hadn't yet switched to his summer attire of Bermuda shorts and sandals with socks. He wore a white linen suit covered with a long, black apron to protect it.

"Brinsley, you read my mind."

"I should hope so, sir."

"Take the last two into Dean and Junior. Don't let anyone else swipe them."

"I shall guard them with my life."

The process of boiling crawfish was long, three beers long, Jock learned. Only two interruptions occurred. Joe's eldest granddaughter, introduced as Wynn, Dean and Stacy's daughter, tugged on her pawpaw's jeans and begged for mudbugs to race, a reprieve similar to pardoning a Thanksgiving turkey. Her brother, DJ, and Lizzie lined up behind her, and each selected a pair of the largest, gripping them behind the head and clear of the claws like old pros at this business.

"Mind you don't pinch the babies with those," Joe instructed as they ran off, shouting their thanks. "Sometimes it seems weird to be called pawpaw," he remarked.

"Sexiest pawpaw in the whole world." Nell comforted as she offered them first chance at a cheese and cracker tray. "Remember we have children and old folks here. Go easy on the salt and cayenne and especially Joe's Hot and Spicy."

"I'm sure Dean and Junior's batch will be milder, but I'll try," her husband answered. He upended the crawfish into the boiling water and added his sack of spices and several good douses of liquid seasonings from various bottles. "We have time now if you want to go watch the races, Jock. No betting allowed."

He grinned, more than happy to leave because Lorena sat in the circle of moms dandling a huge brown baby boy on her knees. Could be his son one day if only she'd listen to him. In the short time it took to cover the space, the kids had drawn a big circle in the dirt and dumped their candidates in the center. Like crawfish and politicians everywhere, they tried to escape by going backward, tail up, but pinchers forward. They had no compunction about crawling over their adversaries and taking a swipe at them along the way. Annie and Dre held their squirmy toddlers tight while May rested quietly in Jessie's lap. DJ won the first round, holding up his now named crawfish, Santy Claws, who retired to a sand bucket.

Jock moved his gaze off the second heat and looked up to find Lorena studying him. She smiled so sweetly, he wondered what went on in her mind.

"Oh, you haven't met another of my sisters. Jock, this is Xochi, Junior's wife and mother to these two, KC on my lap and Pilar," she said.

Jock leaned across the circle to shake hands with

yet another of Lori's siblings. He swore a small electric shock passed between them as they touched palms. He looked into brown eyes so warm and sympathetic he believed he could spill his greatest secrets to this person with the pretty tan face and long, black hair waving down her back. That smile and slight chuckle—like being offered hot cocoa.

"Pleased to meet you. Jock Brown, Aussie," he introduced himself.

"I know. We gossip about nothing else. Welcome to Lorena Ranch, and best of luck in trying out for the Sinners. I'm sure you will succeed."

Lorena did not appear pleased with this pronouncement. Her smile turned to a frown. He shifted his attention to the toddler clinging to her mother's yellow sundress. "Pilar, you want to race a crawfish?"

The child nodded but said, " 'Fraid."

"Okay, you little rippers, who has a crawfish for Pilar to race."

Wynn, being a girl and the most mature, offered one of hers. He took it behind the head and transferred it to the child that way. Pilar tossed it inside the circle, not as close to the center as it should have been. She won easily, though DJ cried, "No fair."

"I win." Pilar, who showed every sign of growing up as attractive as her mother and not as massive as her dad, celebrated by jumping up and down.

"You did. Now let's put him in the bucket with the other winners." He helped her do that. "Make sure he doesn't escape. Just push him back in with this stick if he tries to get out." Pilar plopped down beside the bucket, happy to do just that.

"What happens to the winners?" he whispered to

her mother.

"Oh, *la Libertad*, freedom to live on in the ditches of Lorena Ranch. I think Daddy Joe wants you."

Yes, he was being summoned to the boiling pot again. The frozen cobs of corn had descended into the hot water, and the potatoes were being warmed again. Joe scooped out the mudbugs with a huge slotted spoon, assigned them to a cooler to rest for forty-five minutes, and dumped the water. "Let's get moving on the second batch. Jock and Mack get water. T-Rex, make sure Junior and Dean know where we are in the process. Theirs should be coming out now. He clapped his hands and sent them scattering to bring off his play for perfect crawfish.

Seated at the newspaper-covered tables, the family ate in the late afternoon as the men dumped piles of crawfish, corn, and potatoes in front of them. For those who needed more, Junior had supplied a vat of his potato salad, and someone had contributed trays of sliced French bread, plus what remained of all the relish trays. Jock sat next to the grand dame of the family, Mawmaw Nadine, and not by accident. She'd summoned him from the crowd and beckoned to Lorena to sit at her right side opposite in a strange Last Supper tableau. He had to say her eyes and tongue remained sharp even if her legs had succumbed to a wheelchair.

"Lori, glad to see you come home at last." She squeezed Lorena's hand in an iron grip.

"Oh, I'm only taking a break from training until Maisie has her baby."

"Hmpf. Who'd you bring to the ranch here?" She signaled toward Jock with a sharp jerk of her wattled chin that set the skin flapping.

"This is Jock Brown, an Aussie Rules football player. He hopes to get on with the Sinners."

"Jacques? You French?"

"No, J-O-C-K, like an athlete."

"That what your mama wanted you to be?"

Ah, the interrogation began. "In Australia, it's another form of John like Jack is here. Mum said it meant God is gracious."

"You Cat'lic, then?"

He'd prepared his answer. "I was baptized Catholic, but really don't practice it since my mother died."

"You don't hold that against God, boy. We all got to die sometime. Me, I plan to go later, not sooner. On Sunday, you'll go to church wit' us. All the men do except Teddy. The Baptists got him at an early age, but Xochi balances that out."

He hadn't planned an answer to this and thought Lori, with a slight smile on her lips, enjoyed his predicament. "Since I'm Lorena's guest, I think I should go with her." He returned a much broader smile and waited for her to deny she'd invited him to the ranch.

Before Mawmaw could counter that, Edie spoke from a place at Jock's elbow where she'd squeezed in between him and T-Rex. "Have you eaten crawfish before. Let me show you how to do it. First, you rip off the head."

"Gotta suck the head. Get all the good stuff out," her twin brother said with a leer.

This again. Why not? He'd eaten worse things on a dare. The innards of the head came out easily in a fatty mass that didn't taste all that bad, but somehow, he liked that it had been purged. "Not bad."

T-Rex showed his disappointment with a scowl, while Lori might have given a nod of approval for his nerve. Edie disregarded the interruption. "Now, squeeze the back and crack it a little, spread it out and remove the little legs, pull out the meat, and strip the vein in the top."

"The legs are really where they carry their eggs, and that vein is an intestine," T-Rex added, determined to gross out an Aussie. Fat chance of that!

He popped the meat into his mouth and reached for another and another. The meal ended when only shells and corn cobs remained on the newspaper. Lori had offered to peel for Mawmaw as the mothers along the table did for their small children who accepted the tails like baby birds being fed. She'd been rebuffed with, "When I can't peel my own crawfish, you put me in a nursing home and not before." Jock grinned at her again.

"How about dessert? You try my bread pudding," the old lady offered. Mawmaw's famous bread pudding borne by Nell who led the way was followed by a procession of women: Josee carrying a fancy crystal dish of chocolate mousse, Xochi bearing a cake made into the shape of a lamb, Annie with two strawberry pies, and Stacy balancing a huge tray of store-bought cookies.

Mawmaw disapproved of all but her own dessert. "I make my bread pudding from stale buns that would go to waste, but all these sweets before Lent ends?" She shook her iron-gray head with disapproval. Outside the pavilion, Joe and Nell presided over the second set of tables where children already stuffed cookies into their mouths, and adults took a taste of everything offered—except bread pudding.

"I'm sure there will be lots more on Easter," Lori said. "No one has to eat dessert if they don't want, but I'll take a little bit of bread pudding."

Jock saw an opportunity. "I'll have just the bread pudding, too."

Mawmaw sat behind her creation piled high with meringue and dripping with rum sauce doling out scoops to people who lined up for it. She gave Jock a substantial portion and Lori a somewhat smaller piece. They'd won her approval.

****

After the long day ended when the children rested in their beds and the men helped Knox Polk clean the pavilion area and burn the garbage in a rather smelly bonfire, Lorena summoned the chosen women to her bedroom and shut the door. She hadn't invited her practical mom or Edie, clearly besotted with Jock already, and frankly, was rather glad her acerbic sister, Jude, worked Good Friday at the hospital to have Easter Sunday off. Jude rarely liked any man, and she wanted to be fair—maybe. The long-legged and limber lounged on her carpet: Stacy, Alix, and Josee. Annie sat on the edge of the bed, dangling her feet, and Jessie took a space by the bathroom door in her wheelchair. The desk chair of honor went to Xochi.

"Well, what did you find out, Xo? He's full of deceit, right? I'll bet his aura is black," Lorena pressed.

Her sister saw auras and worked as a *traiteur*, a traditional herbal healer. Some said she had a healing touch also. The first of her talents remained something of a family secret. Whether a person believed in

Xochi's powers or not, she rarely got it wrong.

"Sorry to disappoint you, Lori, but he comes across as definitely…"

"Don't tell me he's another white knight like Dean and Matt."

"So is Trin," Josee added, though her fiancé didn't look the part.

"Pink," Xo finished.

"Pink! I can't believe that huge bloke reads as pink." She kicked the edge of her bed, almost sending Annie to the floor.

"Yes, he's an optimist who takes joy in life. I sense past challenges have made him resilient as he's overcome them and learned he can do so again if the need arises. He blushes pinker when he's around you, Lori. Deep feelings there."

Although none but Xo could see this phenomenon, Lori found it hard to imagine a blushing pink Jock Brown. If his mates could, they'd laugh themselves senseless. "Do you know what he did to me? Took me to the most wonderful places, treated me like a princess, all to get an introduction to Dad, and a tryout for the Sinners team."

"How do you know this as he seems to be very taken with you?" Xo asked.

"Because two of his teammates announced it at my going away party back in Melbourne."

"But Jock never said this?"

"No, he was stuffing his face with sausage at the time. When he went at his pals, Augie threw them all out."

Josee, the most worldly of the bunch, asked, "Did you sleep with him? Is that what makes this so bad?"

Xochi stared at her, waiting to read her very essence. "Only once." She punctuated that with a pointed finger.

"How was he?" Alix, the other family female jock, asked matter-of-factly.

"Adequate," she snapped.

Xo blinked. "Now who's lying?"

"Okay, great, considerate, let me go first—twice." Good thing she'd left Edie out of the mix.

"We should all be *used* that way," Stacy drawled.

She'd depended on these women to see her point, and they weren't. "He followed me home without my consent, latched onto Dad right away with some story about not knowing how to get to New Orleans, a downright lie since I'd told him we didn't live near there."

Annie, kind Annie, spoke. "Sounds like a lie of desperation if you haven't given him a chance to straighten things out. I think we should vote on giving Jock a second chance." She put her own small hand into the air, and all the rest, large and small, bejeweled and plain followed.

"Good thing my room is not a democracy. All of you out of here." She pointed the way.

"We are only expressing our opinion. Go ahead and miss out on a good thing if you want," Stacy, always bossy, said as she left.

The last to go because of the traffic was Jessie. "Sleep on it, Lori. You might feel different in the morning."

Oh, if only her closest siblings hadn't been male. Sleeping on it would not change her mind one iota.

Chapter Eleven

Lorena attempted to sleep even later on Saturday, especially since she hadn't done much but toss and turn the night away after the betrayal by her sisters who were supposed to take her side. Exercise, she needed exercise more than bed rest. A good morning's ride would lighten her mood. She dressed in jeans, boots, an old tee, and went to breakfast. Unless the routine had changed, Corazon would set out chafing dishes of scrambled eggs and bacon, letting everyone make their own toast and beverage with the house so full of people all rising at different times. Near ten, probably not much left, but she'd survive.

How could it be possible that Jock still sat at the kitchen table thickly buttering his toast while Edie watched with rapt attention, and T-Rex scraped the last of the eggs from the chafing dish holding the Mexican version with cheese and peppers. She'd have to make do with the plainer offering, a single piece of slightly charred bacon, and the last of the coffee in the carafe. Lowering two slices of whole wheat bread into the toaster, she declined to greet any of them. They didn't appear to notice.

Jock opened a jar of blackish-brown goo and put a thin layer over the buttery toast. She recognized it immediately as Vegemite, an Australian staple that no American in their right mind ate. He sliced the bread in half and offered a piece to Edie and one to T-Rex.

"Go on and try it. Lots of vitamin B. My mum always said as long as I ate my Vegemite, I'd grow up big and strong."

"Too late for me," Edie quipped.

"It gives girls rosy cheeks."

Smiling, innocent Edie took a huge bite before Lorena could shout, "No!" She watched as her baby sister struggled to get it down.

"Now you, Rex. After all, I sucked a crawfish head."

"No big deal." Her brother crammed it into this mouth, perhaps working on the theory that the bread would stifle the taste. He drank half a glass of milk as a chaser. "Way worse than crawfish heads."

"Yet similarly fishy and salty," Edie said, leaving the rest on her plate. "What is this stuff made of?"

"Mostly leftover brewer's yeast extract with spices and flavoring to make it tasty."

"Big fail." T-Rex wiped his tongue with a paper towel.

"Good thing you don't like it. I only brought four jars along to tide me over."

Did Edie flutter her eyelashes as she said, "It certainly made you big and strong, Jock. You have any brothers back in Australia?'

"Yes, but they're puny, only six-three and six feet tall. One is nearly finished with his EMT courses, and the other is studying to be a doctor, Michael and Nicolas, Mick and Nick."

"If you and Lori get married, maybe I'll get a chance to meet them."

"Positively, but they're a bit old for you."

"Medical training takes a long time. I could be out of college by then."

Lori had enough. "I'm standing right here trying to eat what you people left for me. There is no possibility of a wedding."

Naturally, her mom walked in at that moment. "Stop teasing Lori. I want the two of you to get over to Mawmaw Nadine's and take her to Mass."

"Hey, it's not a Holy Day of Obligation," T-Rex protested. "Why can't she go with Corazon?"

"And I'm not Cat'lic, no," Edie said in a fairly good imitation of her grandmother.

"Don't disrespect Mawmaw. Corazon has already left, and Nadine wants to go. You can drive one way and T-Rex coming home. Her aide will need you to help with the wheelchair. Now off with you. Lori, you know the rule. Last one down cleans up the kitchen."

"I was hoping to go riding. It's been ages."

Jock rose. "I'll help."

"That's the good attitude. I have a few last-minute errands to run before tomorrow. See you later." Off her mother went having handily left them alone together.

For the next fifteen minutes, only the clatter of plates and cutlery being rinsed and put in the dishwasher interrupted the stark silence. Jock filled the sink with soapy water to clean the pans while she wiped down the table. He scrubbed and left her the easier task of drying.

"We make a good team, eh?" he had the gall to say.

"If I decide to go into the cleaning business, you'll be the first person I'll hire."

"I'm truly flattered."

No more banter with Jock. She wanted her ride.

Tossing the dish towel aside, she made for the kitchen door and the pathway to the barn. Jock grabbed a hat fit to keep off the rays of the outback from his face and neck and tailed her all the way into its horse fragrant interior. She hadn't had a personal mount since leaving for college and selected the eager red quarter horse mare who thrust her blazed nose over the stall door first. After leading the mare to the crossties, she went into the tack room, slid a bridle over one arm, lifted a blanket and western saddle off the rack, and went back to her chosen ride. Jock lolled nearby.

"Want me to help with that? Looks heavy."

"I've been saddling my own horses since I was a kid. You'd probably get it on backward, city boy."

He moved closer, keeping the end that kicks far off and the large head only a few paces nearer. The mare bent her neck to ogle him. "Does she bite?"

"She's not a dog, so no, though she could. Probably hoping for an apple or some sugar. Most of my dad's horses are descended from his first quarter horse stud, Lazy Boy. This is Lazy Linda. They all have lazy in their names, but none of them are. They were bred to race short distances and herd cattle. Intelligent, they like to work, and they make good pleasure horses, too." Damn, he'd made her talk to him.

"I'd give it a go if you have one big enough for me."

"Really, you want to learn to ride? Fine, lead out the horse on the end."

"This one with a little gray around the muzzle. I'm not sure about that glint in his eye."

"That's Rascal, Teddy's horse. If a handicapped guy can ride him, so can you."

"Stands to reason then." Jock opened the stall, and the horse walked right out. So far, so good. "Do I need to tie him?"

"Not Rascal. He's been specially trained, but you can carry your own saddle."

Humming happily to herself, Lori saddled Jock's horse, explained how to mount, and the basics of neck reining. She thoroughly enjoyed seeing the big guy so uncomfortable, the way he'd made her feel at her going away party after Augie put him out.

"How do you stop him if he runs off?"

"Pull back on the reins, but it won't be a problem. Rascal is a typical male. He'll follow my mare anywhere."

"I think I know that compulsion."

As she'd predicted, his horse fell into line right behind hers. They encountered Knox Polk as they exited the barn. The ranch manager's usually smooth mocha forehead wrinkled, and the lines around his mouth deepened. "From the way he's sitting that horse, I'd say this boy has never been riding. You sure about taking him out on Rascal?"

"Well, he won't fit on any of the ponies. I'm sure Rascal will be on his best behavior." Lori set her heels to Lazy Linda and urged her into a fast walk. Rascal jogged along behind.

"This isn't like an old western where the cowpokes put a greenhorn on a bucking bronco, is it?" Jock called out to her.

"Is he bucking? Then no."

A mile out, she moved Lazy Linda into a trot and heard Jock's nice, firm buttocks slap against the saddle. He probably held onto the horn for dear life. She notched it up to the smoother, but faster canter. Was that a gasp coming from behind? Once they reached an open field, she initiated a gallop to the other end, then pulled up to see if Jock still remained in the saddle. He did, but none too steadily.

"Looks like you could use a break," she hinted.

"No, no, I'm good. I can hang on as long as you." Sweat dripped from under his outback hat though the day hadn't gotten all that warm yet.

"Get down and stretch a little. You aren't used to this."

She had to admire that he slid off Rascal's side with a certain amount of athletic grace despite his running shoe catching in the stirrup for a second before he shook free. She really should have allowed him time to put on boots. Still, not a chance Rascal, being so well-trained for Teddy, would run off with him, but no telling what else the horse would do. Jock bent over and did some very impressive stretches that strained his jeans. His hammies were fine, and his quads even better. She enjoyed the view without dismounting—and waited as Jock flexed deeply again.

Rascal delivered a strong head butt to Jock's rear. As his rider went facedown, the horse neatly plucked the hat from his head and waved it around.

Jock vaulted to his feet and brushed at the dirt now smearing his Bondi Beach T-shirt. "What the bloody hell! I bought that hat in Alice Springs. It's barely used. Now it has horse slobber all over it."

"Stop being such a girl and take it from him." Lori egged him on. Of course, every time Jock reached for the hat, Rascal retreated a few steps and waved it around some more. Once he got hands on the brim, a tug of war ensued between man and beast. Perhaps, man won when Rascal let go and sent Jock to his behind. Maybe not, as the horse made another grab. Jock crawfished backward, still on the ground.

"Come on, Lori. Call him off."

"He's only playing with you, but if you insist." She formed her hand into the shape of a gun and said, "Bang."

A ton of horseflesh hit the ground, not very far from Jock. He stared at her finger as if he expected to see smoke rising from the tip. "What did you do to him?"

"Nothing." She made a hand gesture. Rascal arose, shaking himself off very much like a large dog. He bared his huge, yellow teeth in an equine version of a smile. "He's only acting out a little skit he performs with my dad for the kids when Camp Love Letter is in session."

"You should have warned me."

"I could have, but where would the fun be in that. Mount up. I'll take you home to soak your sore muscles."

"I'm not sore."

"You will be. I recommend a long, hot shower before the games begin after lunch."

"Games?"

"Yes, you'll enjoy them."

"As long as they don't involve horses."

****

Jock did shower, long and hot as she'd recommended. He washed the dust from his hair, and the horse stink from the rest of him. Knowing how easily an athlete stiffens up after being knocked around, he kept moving up and down the stairs and around pathways meandering among the live oak trees draped with Spanish moss as thick as a shower curtain. Lori let him know she'd wipe down and curry both horses since he didn't appear up to it—which he'd started to deny, but thought better of it. He suspected Rascal might initiate the game again, and small heaps of straw-studded manure sat outside each stall awaiting removal. With his recent luck, he'd end up face-first in one of them to Lorena's delight.

He didn't see her during his rambles but heard the babble of female voices coming from the vast trophy-filled den as he passed. He caught Lori in the midst of an apology to the other women as he lingered in the doorway.

"Sorry about last night. I let jet lag get the best of me. You are all entitled to your own opinion."

"What opinion?" Edie asked.

"Nothing, really."

He suspected nothing meant him and lurked in the hall a while longer. Someone poured wine judging by the glug of the bottle. Edie begged to be included, and her mother granted a half a glass.

"Anyhow, I brought gifts for all of you from Australia. Josee, I hope I'm not interfering with your wedding arrangements, but I got small opal necklaces for each of the bridesmaids and a larger one for mom to wear. Just pass them around and choose one you like. If you don't want to use them for the ceremony, that's fine, too."

"The gowns are blush. I think they will work out beautifully," Josee assured her. "By the way, we have to get you to New Orleans for your fitting. May isn't that far off."

"I'm glad I'm home for Trin's wedding and can be a part of it. I've missed so much in the years I've been gone. Oh, Corazon, these are for you. They're tea towels imprinted with native symbols for water and emus and women sitting in a circle exactly as we are now."

"So bright. I like them. I think I will sew them together and make a new apron."

"I have some carved bowls for each household. Take your pick. Boomerangs, real ones, for the guys. They can try them out after lunch."

Boomerangs! He'd have a chance to show off a bit. While no expert, he'd gotten the knack of throwing them when hanging out on the beach. Jock crept off, then thundered up the stairs again to grab his tin of Anzac biscuits, perfect to accompany wine.

Returning, he knocked politely on the door frame. The hen party seemed surprised to see him bearing his own gift. "Hope I'm not interrupting anything important. Thought you might enjoy some authentic Australian bikkies to go with that wine. These were developed during World War I to provide nourishment for the troops."

Edie widened her eyes. "Do they taste better than Vegemite?"

"Much better, not that there's anything wrong with Vegemite. There's a recipe on the tin, and you can use it to store any you make. Here, pass them around. Fine with wine."

Mama Nell rushed to pour a glass for him. He gave the offering a swirl, a sniff, and a sip. "That's a nice shiraz. We grow a lot of these grapes in Australia."

Lori pursed her mouth as if the wine weren't fruity and a trifle sweet. "Go ahead and boast that you own a winery."

"Half a winery," he corrected. "I still have a lot to learn from my partner."

The ever-inquisitive Edie asked, "Will you have to sell it if you move here to play for the NFL?"

"Wasn't planning to. I've built a house there. Lovely country, right, Lori? American football players have a much longer off-season than footy teams. Plenty of time to go back and forth and enjoy the best of both worlds—if I make the team, but I wouldn't have traveled this far if I didn't have confidence in myself."

"Confidence is only part of what you need to be a Sinner." Joe Billodeaux spoke as he entered the room.

The rest of the male contingent followed. T-Rex snagged a handful of the Anzac cookies with the insatiable appetite of a teen. Trin squeezed in next to his fiancée and seized a cookie, too. Mack waved the tin away and went to lounge by the huge, stone fireplace. Dean and Tom loomed behind their wives. What they'd been doing while Rascal terrorized him, he had no idea.

The ever-affable Joe asked, "Have a nice ride? Knox said Lori put you up on Rascal. Was he up to his old tricks?"

"I'd say so if that includes stealing my hat and head butting me into the dirt."

Mack snickered. "Be glad you only ended up in the dust. When we were kids, we saw him dump a famous movie star into a wheelbarrow full of manure. He's a great horse."

"Really?" So he'd been right to assume those little

heaps of dung might be a trap for the unsuspecting.

"Oh, he is." Jessie stood up for the animal. "I get up on him every once in a while. He just likes to play."

"Dogs play. Seems like horses push you around."

"Only if you let them," Lori said.

Rex reached for more cookies, and Corazon swatted his hand away. "We have make-your-own tacos for lunch in half an hour, shredded chicken or beef, all kinds of toppings, and corn chips. Plenty of desserts left from yesterday. Who helps me get it on the table?"

Jock stood up first. "I do love a good taco. Tell me what to do." He swore he heard Lori grinding her teeth at beating her to it. Most of the women got up and abandoned the den to the men.

"I'll call Teddy to herd the children this way. He's probably exhausted by now even with Dre helping him," Jessie remarked as she wheeled from the room.

With his long arms and great balance, Jock juggled lots of dishes to the dining room table with the aplomb of a trained waiter. If he sometimes collided with Lori, that couldn't be helped in the close quarters. While he'd rather be having a beer with the men in the den, he'd scored big points with the women, all but her. The more on his side, the better.

Chapter Twelve

Let the games begin, he thought. He hoped they involved contact with Lori. After lunch, he discovered what the men had done that morning—outlined fifty yards of a football field in lime over the bare parking area near the barn. All the cars now sat along the driveway. Just a friendly game of flag football coming up, Joe claimed, though the preparations seemed elaborate for that. He began to regret the four loaded tacos, handfuls of corn chips, a beer, and a serving of chocolate mousse that looked like someone had gouged a handful out of the center sometime during the night. Not that Junior Polk, who showed up with his family to devour his mom's tacos, had eaten anymore lightly. He had height on the big cornerback but not weight.

Evidently, the family warmed up a little first with a game the children demanded called Over the Barn. Tom and Alix, the married kickers for the Sinners, lined up some distance away, and each booted a football over the high arched roof of the stable. The kids raced to the other side with DJ and Wynn returning with the balls.

"Want to try? We have some good Aussie kickers in the NFL," Tom offered with a friendly smile on his freckled face.

"It doesn't matter if you miss. This just for fun," Alix said more seriously.

While he didn't see his role in American football as

a kicker, he'd done plenty of it for the Magpies. "I'll give it go, but my arse is a tad sore from that head-butting horse." Jock sized up the height and distance, dropped the first ball, and sent it hurtling toward the ridge of the barn—where it teetered for a moment before falling down the far side. Having judged fairly well the first time, he put a little more leg and loft into the second kick. It soared over with a good foot to spare.

Stacy held back her two children. "Let the younger ones have a chance."

Lizzie and Pilar retrieved the footballs this time with the pack of toddlers who had no idea what to do with it on their heels. They appeared happy simply to run.

"Let's try the boomerangs next," Lori said, handing them out to the men. "Here's a lefthanded one for Alix. Try them out."

Trin's ended up in the dirt. The athletes in the family sent theirs flying fairly easily but failed to get a good return. Jock borrowed Trin's and threw it into a wide curve. He jumped to catch the boomerang as it returned to him. "All in the wrist, mates."

The quarterbacks caught on fairly quickly, the others not as well. Jock stood by Edie, answering her incessant questions. "They really used those to kill animals?"

"More to break legs, then mob the animals with spears. When you live in a land with little hardwood, it's handy to have the weapon come back to you."

"Have you ever hunted with one?"

Before he had to confess to learning from a bunch of beach bums, T-Rex, who'd had several successful tries, claimed, "Mack said he doesn't hunt. Can you believe it?"

"I think it's wonderful you don't shoot innocent animals." Edie beamed at him.

"No need in Melbourne. Most people hunt on the cattle and sheep stations, rabbits and roos who compete for the grass."

"You eat kangaroos?" Her large, brown eyes appeared stricken.

"Sure, he does. Tastes like steak, he said. The tails are the best part." T-Rex continued to needle his tender-hearted sister.

Lori stepped in. "They are like the deer here, herd animals that must be culled from time to time. Rabbits are considered to be in the same class as rats as they do even more damage." She squeezed her little sister's shoulder. "You've heard it all from Dad, and you eat venison and rabbit."

"I know, but kangaroos carry babies in their pouches. You'd never kill one, Jock."

"Me, no. Like Rex says, I don't hunt. Here now, no whingeing." He put a comforting arm around Edie's shaking shoulders. She turned and burrowed right into the comfort of his chest. Helplessly, he patted her back. "There, there."

"Cut it out, Edie. I know you're tougher than that," T-Rex said. "Who killed a cottonmouth with a rock?"

Strangely tearless, Edie raised her head. "It was a venomous snake. I thought it might bite Brody."

"We have plenty of those in Australia. Good to know if we're in the outback together, you'll deal with the reptiles for me." That had her smiling again, but not Lorena.

"I think frisbee throwing is up next. Are you playing, Edie?"

"No, I think I'll sit with Mom and Annie and watch Jock." Edie removed herself from his shirt front and went to take a seat in the shade as the afternoon grew warmer.

"I'm in," said T-Rex.

"Good, you can be my partner." Lorena moved toward the pile of brightly colored plastic disks piled on a table. When they'd all paired off, he found himself standing alone until Lil the dog came to sit his feet. She stared at him, expectantly. He stood there fingering the edge of a disk, not expecting one hard-thrown to come sailing his way. It went high, and he jumped to catch it with his left hand. Lil whined.

"I threw that one for the dog, doofus. She likes to play." Lori, of course, making him look bad to the dog lovers, and they were all dog lovers as far as he could tell.

He crouched down on Lil's level and scratched her ears. He gave her a sniff of the red frisbee. "Sorry, girl. This one is for you." He pitched it high but not far out of consideration for her age. Lil got right under it, and with a small leap, caught the disk in her jaws. She brought it back and waited for another toss, which he did happily. His old man never let them have a dog. Just another mouth to feed as far as he was concerned. Jock thought maybe he'd get one after he knew where he stood with the Sinners.

"Does Brody want to play?" he called to Edie. She put a finger to her lips and pointed to blankets laid out on the ground where the toddlers and even the older children formed a napping puppy pile with Brody snuggled in among them.

"Okay, form a circle," Joe commanded. "Only one frisbee. If you drop it, you're out. I'll start." He sent his winging to Dean on the other side, who chose a short pass to Tom. Tom nearly bobbled it but recovered to send an easy one to his wife. Alix caught Trinity off guard, sending him to sit with the non-participating women and babies. The frisbee came Jock's way again and again. He fended off the onslaught and moved fast to take out Tom, T-Rex, Matt, and Junior.

Lori did some heckling. "Afraid to throw it to a girl?"

No, he was not. He removed Alix, Stacy, and Josee with quick high throws. He shot the next at her. She returned it with a vengeance. There might have been only two of them left in the game the way they concentrated on each other.

"Hey," Joe called. "Still here." Not anymore when Lori caught her dad unaware. Smiling at his daughter, he handed her the frisbee and watched her take careful aim at Jock. The disk headed for his throat, but he stepped aside and let it clip his shoulder instead. The frisbee fell to the ground.

"You win."

"You let me win. You could have caught that."

"Maybe I'm tired of playing games." He allowed that to sink in before turning his back on her. If he'd won, she'd most likely be angry that he had.

"Now that we're all warmed up let's play football. I'll take Jock for my team," Joe said.

Dean, quarterback for the other team, selected Junior. Lori refused to join Jock and volunteered to play with her brother. In the end, only the women under the trees remained to watch. Sitting with an iPad on his lap, Teddy had joined them.

"Xochi, Edie? You want to join in?" Joe encouraged.

Xochi shook her head. "Nursing mother here. Won't be a pretty sight if I start leaking or KC wakes up and wants his dinner."

"No, thanks," Edie said. "Last year Rex didn't just capture my flag, he threw me over his shoulder and ran across his goal line with me. That had to be cheating."

"Teddy is the ref. It won't happen again."

"Still, no. How about Dre? She's tall and not nursing. Dean's team needs another person."

Color swept the pale cheeks of the nineteen-year-old mother of a toddler. "Go on," Annie said. "Have fun. Plenty of us short people here to watch the babies."

"Edie, hand out the flags. Let's get this game on the road," Joe said with some impatience.

She went from person to person handing out red or blue kerchiefs from a basket. When she got to Jock, she sank one deep in his hip pocket. "Do you know how to play? It's no tackle, so when someone takes your flag, you're down."

"I get the idea." She'd certainly planted that flag very firmly. If only she'd been Lori.

"Edie," Mama Nell called. "Sit down and let them get underway."

Joe called his red team into a huddle. "Jock, go long. The rest of you keep blue team from getting close to him. He clapped his hands. They hunkered down. Joe stepped back behind his line and threw a spiral close to fifty yards and high. Jock, who'd run like the devil was biting his bum to get into position, rose, and caught it midair before Junior reached him. He had only to step across the goal line to score. After that, Junior guarded him all the way, and even so, he'd managed to make another touchdown for his team.

The ball went back and forth between the teams. Dean's team had more women with his wife, Lorena, and Dre, which should have been a disadvantage, but all were in great shape. The same could be said of Joe's reds with Josee and Alix contending. They stayed one touchdown ahead. Teddy called time. "One more possession each. Dean gets the ball."

Joe huddled with his people. "They need this score real bad, or we win. Be on the lookout for tricks."

Dean handed the ball off to—someone. It seemed most of his players ran forward hunched over, guarding something precious. Then Lorena broke from the pack and streaked toward the goal line.

"Get her, Jock," Joe shouted.

Dre attempted to protect the blue runner mostly by standing in the way. T-Rex forgot they played flag and knocked her over, but she grabbed his shoulders as she fell and pulled him down on top of her. She groped for his flag and waved it in triumph as Jock, following orders, vaulted over the pile they made in the center of the field.

He thundered down on Lori, but oh, she was fleet. They raced to the ten-yard line when he got close enough to pluck the flag from her pocket and end the play. Instead, he went in low, scooped her off the ground, slung her over his shoulder, and reversed toward his own goal. She still hung onto the football but used her feet effectively, kicking him in the belly. Didn't hurt much, but her shrieking, "Cheater" in his ear, nearly deafened him. Still, he didn't put her down until they'd crossed the line. He tried to wipe the cheeky grin off his face and almost succeeded. She spiked the ball in his face. He deflected it easily with his footy reflexes.

That's when he noticed the silence. Those on the field stayed in place while the spectators gaped at them.

"What? Isn't that called an interception?" he said. "Didn't Edie say you used it last year?"

"You know perfectly well that is not an interception. You've been studying the NFL rule book. Liar," Lori spat at him.

"An intervention, then?"

"Not that either. You are impossible to deal with."

"Are you going to take your football and go home?" he asked, the grin returning.

"I am home. You are not. Go back to Australia." Lori stormed off.

Teddy cleared his throat. "Yeah, that play was interesting but still illegal. I'm giving the points to the blue team and calling the game a draw. We've got two dozen pizzas that should be delivered fairly soon, and I'm not eating mine cold."

T-Rex offered a hand up to Dre. "You're more of a fighter than I thought." She smiled. "Hope I didn't hurt your insides with you being a mother and all."

She frowned. "My insides are fine, thank you." She dropped his hand and joined the exodus of women herding children toward the pavilion for washing up and eating dinner. Another woman with her knickers in a twist, Jock decided, glad he wasn't the only one in trouble.

The men gathered around Teddy and his iPad.

Jock, unsure where to go, stood on the edge of their group.

"Here's the height of his kicks. I got that when I sat on the gallery. I clocked his first fifty-yard run. Impressive. More impressive what he did with Lorena on his back while being kicked in the gut. She's no lightweight and fairly fierce when angry. He also captured more flags than the rest of you. I filmed that left-handed catch of the frisbee, too. His hands are big enough to do that with a football."

They discussed *him*. "Ah, right here, mates."

Joe looked up from the screen. "We don't usually give prizes today, but you just won a private workout with the Sinners.

Chapter Thirteen

A light knock on his door awoke Jock along with Edie's sweet, girlish voice saying, "Time to get up. If we don't leave early, we'll have to stand in the back of the church for the Easter service."

Right. Easter. He took a quick shower and shaved close. Luckily, he'd brought along his custom-made suit and tailored shirt in the garment bag, thinking he'd need it for an interview with the Sinners hierarchy. Never suspected he'd be going to church. He straightened his tie, the one the salesman said had enough green to bring a pop of color to his eyes. He didn't see it. Anyhow, not wanting to be late, he went to join the noisy chaos downstairs.

Platters of croissants, cinnamon buns, and Danish filled the dining room table along with fruit plates and pitchers of juice and milk. Two urns of coffee guaranteed no one would go without caffeine. Children swathed in large napkins to keep the stains off their finery dominated the large kitchen table.

He fetched his jar of Vegemite from the refrigerator and held it up. "Anyone want some? Willing to share. Okay, no takers." He swore Lori's eyes widened when she glanced at him. Good or bad?

"Word has gotten around," she said as she wiped DJ's face clean of cinnamon bun icing.

God, she looked finer than a spring day in her

floral dress. She'd worn her hair loose and pinned back from her face with a red camellia on one side. How he wanted to remove that blossom and kiss the side of her neck. For a moment, she was all he could see—that and a vision of future Easter celebrations with her as his wife and the children theirs—until Edie touched his elbow.

"I'll try it again. I imagine Vegemite is an acquired taste like caviar. You look spectacular in a suit, by the way. Every woman in church will want an introduction."

He put a spoonful of Vegemite on the corner of the plate she held out. "Now, we wouldn't want that. I'll stand in the back, perhaps." His eyes still focused on Lori.

"You stand out wherever you are, Jock. I'm sure you know that," Lori said.

"If you stand beside me, no one will see I'm there because you look so wonderful," he answered.

Next to him, Edie sighed so hard he felt her breath on the hand that held the Vegemite.

"I wish someone would say that to me. I can tell Lori didn't appreciate the compliment."

"You're very pretty today as well, Edie." Pretty, but very young in a white and lacy dress that made her seem like a girl ready for her first communion. All she needed to complete the picture was a short veil on her curly, black hair. Not the compliment she wanted, of course. His gaze scanned over the little ones and their mothers. "I'm in a room full of lovely ladies."

He hoped that would do. Again, Jock held up the Vegemite. "Must get my vitamins today." He adjourned to the dining room to fill his plate with rolls and fruit and managed to get all that down and a cup of coffee before he heard Mama Nell directing everyone to various vehicles.

She stood by the door handing out spring flowers from a grocery store bouquet as the children filed past. "You are going to ride with Pawpaw in the van. Don't bend your flowers. Edie and Dre go along to keep order. See you at the church."

"Do I need a flower for admission?" he asked.

"Not unless you plan to go to the nursery and help decorate a cross for the procession. We don't have much in bloom except a few late camellias and azaleas, hence the supermarket bunch. I'm not much of a gardener. That talent belongs to Xochi, but her family will be at Ste. Jeanne's with Mawmaw Nadine, Dean, Rex, Trin, Mack, Matt, and his boys. Teddy is driving his van to our church. You'll be with us women in Stacy's SUV, I'm afraid."

"No worries. I'm honored to escort all of you."

"Don't let him drive. Aussies use the left side of the road. He'll put us all in a ditch."

He started to say, "Would not," until he realized Lori had made the comment. "I guess you'll have to teach me how to drive over here."

"Fat chance."

She pushed past him trailing a light perfume that made him wish they'd stayed home and made love while the others were out. Sacrilegious thought. Sorry, God. But if she sat near him, he knew where his mind would wander.

He stood by the open door of the SUV handing each woman inside until only he remained. Stacy beckoned him to take the seat beside her for the sake of the legroom, and off they went past burgeoning cane fields like the ones he'd seen in Cairns and glorious mounds of pink and purple azaleas somewhat past their prime. They passed the plain frame historic Catholic church in town with its large but overflowing parking lot and departed from Main Street, USA, to a rather small but elegant red brick Episcopal church half-covered in vines and with no parking to speak of.

The white van stood waiting. Lorena and the moms debarked without his help and went to claim various children clutching wilting daisies and stiff stalks of purple statice.

"If you'd like to go ahead, I'll park your Ute. I promise I won't wreck it," he offered Stacy.

"I assume that's an SUV. Thank you so much. DJ can be a handful. Just follow Joe. He's great at finding spaces." She tossed the keys and grabbed her son's arm before he made a getaway into the street.

Feeling a bit strange to be in a driver's seat on the wrong side, he pulled out carefully behind Joe and trailed him to a nearby bank lot, usually empty on Sunday but already filling with the cars of Easter Christians. When they both got down, Joe pointed the way back to St. Luke's Episcopal. "I have to get to Ste. Jeanne's before my mother starts thinking I'm turning almost Cat'lic. Enjoy the service."

Easy to follow the flow of well-dressed people walking swiftly in order not to miss the processional at the protestant sanctuary. He joined them but stood in the rear, trying to locate the mob of Billodeauxs amid the crowded pews. There—he spotted Lori's long, black hair or thought he did. A lot of dark hair in the congregation along with some very bleached blondes and a few who appeared totally natural like Stacy, Alix, and Josee. Ah, there she sat with them, a nice contrast. Stacy saw him and waved him to their row. Lori ignored him.

"Smush over everyone and let Jock take a seat."

He slid into the space allowed, far too narrow for his frame. The side of the pew dug into his ribs, and his legs scrunched up against a kneeling bench. A man behind him politely tapped his shoulder. "Would you mind slouching a little? My wife can't see the altar."

Stacy whispered, "Put the kneeling bench down. You can use it as a footrest."

Good advice. Still, he hoped the service wouldn't be long. The lily-scented air hung heavy as priestly vestments from all the potted flowers bedecking every corner and windowsill of the church. He caught a whiff of incense just as the organist in the loft hit a loud chord that had everyone rising to their feet. He struggled upward and because of his height was among the first to see the priest enter swinging his censor behind the altar boy carrying the cross. Another carried a large Bible. Behind her, a second cross made of flowers contributed by the children was held up by two of the bigger ones. The rest tagged along after. Some kids peeled off to squeeze in beside their parents. Older ones went to the front to settle among the lilies like so many bright spring buds.

The sermon did run short, but the musical interludes and communion ran long as nearly everyone rose to get their wine and wafer, often while holding wiggling children between their knees as they awaited the blessing. Teddy and his wife in their wheelchairs, a child in each lap, sat in the front and had the eucharist delivered to them. Vaguely remembering his mum saying Catholics should not take communion in another church, he elected to stay in the pew but stood to let everyone else pass. Mostly he feared making a fool of himself. Without Stacy prompting him, he would have bungled the sit, stand, and kneel routine. Some of the common Easter hymns he knew. Others he tried to belt out with confidence using the hymnal, though knew his voice wasn't good, just loud. He guessed Lori might have let him mess up as part of her revenge, an act of vengeance he didn't deserve.

Afterward, another long line formed to shake hands with the priest, a short, bearded man, fortyish, who certainly knew to keep a sermon brief on a day like Easter. Nell introduced him to Fr. John as a friend of Lorena's from Australia.

"Anglican, then?" The inevitable question.

"Not much of anything."

"I'd say you are a great deal of something. Please come worship with us again. Any baptized Christian is welcome to take the eucharist with us. Now, you'd better move along before the hospitality committee captures you. They're headed our way." Nice guy, sense of humor, too. Good on him if he presided over his marriage to Lori one day.

Nell waved to the ladies determined to reach them, but she'd evaded more determined paparazzi. "Have to get the grandchildren home for the egg hunt. We'll talk next Sunday." She uncorked the bottleneck the Billodeauxs created and hustled them toward the white van for their getaway. Joe waited behind the wheel.

"You escaped early."

"Went out the side door right after communion

since I had a good excuse. Xochi, Mawmaw, and the rest of the guys will be behind us. We'll beat them home."

Ah, the Billodeaux competitive spirit showing up again. Jock boarded next to Stacy, and they raced back to the ranch. The gate opened like magic before them, giving access to the long oak alley. Mama Nell orchestrated the whole situation, as usual, directing some of the women to spread the Easter eggs hidden in the pavilion around the corral and others, including Lori, to keep the children inside and occupied until that was accomplished, and Xo and her children had arrived. He saw his opening.

"Ah, I could tell them a story about the Easter bilby in the den if that would help."

"Really, that would be wonderful." Mama Nell blessed his idea.

"Let me get something upstairs. Just a mo'."

He took the stairs two at a time and retrieved his shopping bag full of chocolate bilbies and one slender book. By the time he returned, the Billodeaux grandchildren, including Xochi's Pilar, sat more or less in a crescent, crisscross-applesauce, as they were taught in nursery school or at the library. He recalled story times well, a free activity his mum could take three rumbustious boys to and get some rest for herself for a short period of time. He'd been the one to read to his brothers, also, as his hard-working mum rarely had the time. Nothing to it. Yet he was strangely nervous. He sat on the floor with the little kids, his own legs crossed, and drew out a picture book.

"This is the story of the Easter bilby," he began, instantly interrupted by DJ.

"You talk funny."

His older sister elbowed him. "That's rude, Mom said. You weren't supposed to say anything."

"Quite all right. I speak differently because I come from a land far away on the other side of the world called Australia. If you visited me there, people would think you talk funny, but we have lots of American visitors so they wouldn't mention it. We also have many strange and interesting animals found nowhere else. I know you are familiar with kangaroos and koalas, but…"

Lizzie shot up and began to jump up and down, holding her hands like a roo. Annie's little boys began to wiggle and unfold. Jessie pushed her daughter down, and in a schoolteacher's voice said, "If you don't stay in your places, there will be no story time."

Whew. Saved from disaster. Jock held up the book. "*Easter Bilby's Secret* by Kaye Kessing and Alison Garnett. There's the Easter Bilby on the cover. He's very tiny but has big ears and a long nose. His large eyes let him see in the dark. The old Easter Bunny has retired and trusts the bilby to deliver eggs all over Australia—but how with Cat and Fox waiting to eat him?"

Now he had them. The smallest creatures built a thorny hut that Cat and Fox could not penetrate, and inside that hut, the wombats dug tunnels all over Australia so that children had brightly colored eggs on Easter morning. Sure, he had to pause now and then to explain words and point out the various creatures, but on the whole, he thought it went well. He glanced toward Lori, who stood by the fireplace with her arms folded, resembling her brother Mack but so much prettier. She gave him no feedback.

Sitting on the floor with the kiddies, Edie did. "That was wonderful, Jock. You're really good with children."

"Thanks. Now, I have treats all the way from Australia—chocolate bilbies for everyone. Let's see, nine grandchildren, one for each, and three left over."

Lori finally spoke. "Save one for Beck. That's Dean's oldest son. He's in Germany with his mother this year."

"Righty-O. Would you fancy one for yourself."

"No, thank you." Her rejection threw a chill over the room, cold as a bucket of ice. The kids didn't notice, but the women surely did.

"I'd love one," Edie said.

"There you go. Cute as it is, promise to eat it before it goes bad. Remember, the ears are the best part. I'll save the last for Corazon. I'd bet she's getting a bonzer dinner on the table right now."

Stacy appeared in the doorway with an armful of small baskets, all identical. "Egg hunt time. Let's leave the chocolate until after dinner. You'll get them back," she added as a few small faces screwed up to cry. She handed each child a basket as she confiscated the bilbies and asked her daughter, Wynn, to lead the way to the corral. The older children stampeded for the kitchen door, the toddlers bobbled along behind, and the babies rode their mother's hips.

"Sorry, didn't mean to cause a kerfuffle with the chocolate," he apologized.

"A second more and they would have been coated head to foot. You don't know small children."

Lori approached. "He should. He raised his two

brothers."

He couldn't tell if she'd given him a compliment or a criticism.

"They were older when I took over their care. At the age of these children, I'd have been in the lead getting to the egg hunt—if we'd had an egg hunt."

"Come along and watch. It's a riot. DJ will try to fit too many in the basket and spill them all. This is the first egg hunt for Annie's toddlers. They have no idea what to do. As for the babies, they'll gnaw on the plastic egg with no clue something is inside." Stacy pointed the way.

He left the bilby bag in the kitchen with Corazon, who removed a stuffed pork roast from the oven with care. He gave her a peck on the cheek and slipped a bilby into her apron pocket. "Here you go, dear, for all your hard work."

At the corral, Pawpaw Joe opened the gate and let loose the hunters. Any manure had been raked, and no attempt to hide the eggs had been made. DJ overfilled his basket immediately. Annie's toddlers picked up an egg each, then sat down, pried it open, and began to gorge on jelly beans. The babies did indeed teethe on the eggs they were handed. What a great family moment. He couldn't hold back a smile. Jock took out his phone to record the scene and tried to get Lori into the picture, but she turned away.

Another Billodeaux had shown up, Jude, Annie's twin. He'd almost mistaken one for the other until he noticed the stern eyes and an almost perpetual frown as she watched the egg hunt. Short of stature like her sister, she hiked herself up on the fence to be at his level.

"You're the Aussie who followed Lorena home. Saw you briefly at the airport. You're hard to miss. I managed to skip church by driving in this morning but got here in time for the meal, the leftovers, and this, plus the egg pocking. I often win. Look at those rug rats run."

"So you're the doctor up from New Orleans for the day."

"Not a doctor yet. Just a humble med student. I was a surgical nurse." The way she said it, he gathered surgical nurses probably knew more than med students, and it grated on her.

Nothing humble about Jude. He formed two impressions: She liked to win and had no great fondness for children. He doubted he'd gain acceptance from this family member no matter what and decided not to try. "I'm enjoying all the family activities."

"Enjoy while you can. Lori wants nothing to do with you."

"I've noticed, but I don't give up easily."

"It's your time to waste. I'd book your ticket back to Australia early." She slid off the fence. "I've got to get back to the house before one of them recognizes me, and I'm covered in sticky handprints. See you at the egg pocking."

The event ended shortly after his conversation with Jude. Stacy issued another order that no candy was to be eaten until after dinner. They trooped inside to wash and line up for the buffet, another groaning board anchored by a large ham at one end, and the pork roast at the other. In between, the sides: both rice and cornbread dressing, candied sweet potatoes, the green beans made with a can of mushroom soup and crispy onions on top that he'd attempted to cook once for his brothers, and on and on. Edie stayed next to him, naming each dish, and warning some would be spicy. She sat beside him as he ate.

"The kids might think you talk funny, but I love listening to you. I even like the way you hold your fork upside down."

"Most of the world eats the way I do except those who use chopsticks. See, it's more efficient. Stab that meat with the fork. Saw it off with the knife. No need to put the knife down each time."

"I can see that." She tried the method herself. "It does work. I might eat this way all the time from now on."

"If you want everyone at the Episcopal Day School to stare at you, go ahead," Lori said.

He hadn't noticed her proximity for once. Her constant hostility might be making a dent in his adoration after all. Maybe she'd become the woman he always wanted that did not want him, and he'd have to give up on her. His optimism kicked into gear. Nope. He simply needed more time.

"I'd say that's Edie's choice. Continental dining habits could be a conversation starter in the cafeteria. There are two sides to every story."

"Not every story."

"Yes, every story if you look a bit deeper."

This back and forth could have gone on all day, but Joe announced the egg *paque* contest, yet another Billodeaux test of skill. Nell summoned Lizzie to pass out a boiled egg to each person who wanted to play from her basket. Everyone decided to participate except the babies and toddlers. Lizzie went back to the kitchen for a second basket. Jock recognized hers among the dozen. He asked if he might have the green one with the bunny drawn on it, identifiable only by its big ears.

"That's a special egg. A winner egg—I give it to you."

As it turned out, it was a winner egg. The object appeared to be to pock another person's egg and put them out of the game. He sheltered Lizzie's egg in his big hand, letting only the pointed nose stick out. With his speed and force, he moved down the line making conquest after conquest, and blew by Jude, at least earning her respect, until he came to Lori. Should he let her win? Bloody hell, no. She hadn't appreciated that in frisbee or his funny stunt in flag football, simply scowled at him the whole time. She wielded one of May's scribbled eggs, but though her hands were fairly large, her fingers were long and slender and unable to give her weapon the protection it needed. They circled each other, choking up on the fighting end of their eggs, feinting, then drawing back. At last, he struck, making a dent in her egg all the way down to the yolk.

"Didn't let you win this time. Happy?"

Lori surrendered her damaged egg to the bowl of losers destined to be deviled for the evening meal. "I lost fair and square. But losing to you will never make me happy." She moved away, rubbing her hand. Maybe he'd bruised it a trifle.

Lizzie replaced her, holding up an intact egg, one of her lesser creations. "I beat Wynn, Pilar, and DJ. DJ smooshed Wynn's egg so hard, egg guts went everywhere. Wanna play?"

He felt as if every Billodeaux waited in judgment. Yes or no? "Sure."

Lizzie held out her hand. "I want my egg back because it's a winner egg."

"Okay." It took him several minutes of maneuvering to reach a point where Lizzie could smack into his mostly unguarded new egg and do a little victory dance.

"The winner egg, the winner egg!" Lizzie showed her dad, her mom, May, and everyone else in the room.

Jock went to stand by Teddy. "That girl is really something else."

"She certainly is. Thanks for letting her win. Usually, I'd say that isn't a good thing, but you made it seem like a real fight, and she's so proud of that egg. I caught it all on my phone."

"Evidently, the winner egg was only on loan to me. It couldn't be beat. I hope you won't send that video to the Sinners. They'll think I lack the will to win. Say, Teddy, you and Lorena were close, correct?"

"Like a fourth triplet. She roomed next to me and never complained about using a handicap bathroom, even though she had to stoop way over to use the mirror. She protected Trin and me from anyone who hassled us. Lorena has a loving heart and a fierce spirit."

"I'm only seeing the fierce spirit."

"Maybe you should stop getting in her face for a while. Give her time to miss you."

"She says she won't."

"She could be lying to protect that loving heart. Give her space, then try again, less aggressively. I did have to keep trying with Jessie."

"Thanks, mate. I'll take your advice."

Chapter Fourteen

Lorena stayed in bed the next morning as long as she decently could without being sick. She heard the departures, not as many as last night when the New Orleans contingent of Jude and Dean's and Annie's families departed, hauling tired children and large bags of leftovers and candy. T-Rex headed to school with a roar of the truck he'd gotten for this eighteenth birthday. Her mom went to the clinic, judging by the tinny sound of her small car. Her dad strode out to the barn, punctuated by the hard slam of the kitchen door. A second small car turned over and moved away, probably Corazon going for groceries depleted over the weekend. She suspected Jock laid in wait for her at breakfast. No sense putting their meeting off until later.

She threw on nothing special and didn't bother with makeup, only taking time to braid her hair to deprive him of the pleasure of seeing it loose. Last one down, she'd have to make do with whatever was left to eat and clean up, another thing she could blame on Jock. But she found only Edie lackadaisically pulling apart a croissant leftover from yesterday.

"What, no Vegemite today?" She took a couple of Danish from a platter and nuked them back to freshness. As she poured lukewarm milk from the pitcher into her coffee, she asked, "No school?"

"How soon you forget. Ste. Jeanne's had spring

154

break last week. The Day School is off this week. I don't know what I'll do with myself now that Jock is gone. I had plans to show him around—the Tabasco plant, Vermilionville, the Shadows—but you drove him away by being so mean."

The first bite of Danish stuck in her throat. "You mean he left, went back to Australia?"

"No, to New Orleans with Dean and Stacy. If you'd bothered to say goodbye to anyone last night instead of hiding out in your room, you'd know that. He's staying with them until Dad arranges the workout for him. That might be a couple of weeks since all the coaches are scattered for the offseason. I'll never see him again, thanks to you. He's the greatest guy I ever met. What did he do to you, anyhow?"

"He used me, Edie."

Her baby sister suddenly perked up. "Sexually?"

"What would you know about that?" It shocked her that cheerful little Edie possessed any knowledge of sex. Of course, their mom would have given her the talk well before now about respecting yourself, safe sex, and not giving yourself to just anyone.

"I'm eighteen, Lori, a senior in high school. I know about sex."

"Are you active? Jock didn't take advantage of you, did he?"

"No. He treated me like a pesky little sister, which I guess I am. The way Dad and Rex guard me, I won't have sex until I get to college. Maybe I won't have a date for the prom or what the Day School calls the Spring Graduation Dance to emphasize education."

"It is better to wait, Edie."

"Like you did. Dean and Tom were in college by

the time you grew old enough to date. Trin and Mack were supposed to keep an eye on you, but Trin always had his face glued to a computer screen, and Mack didn't care. He wasn't going to miss out on his fun to stop yours. Tell me you didn't do it with that baseball player who won all those stuffed animals for you."

She took her time, finishing her Danish and thinking what to say. "I won't lie to you. I did. We found ways and places, but it wasn't all that good. Teenage boys don't have much skill, and college guys aren't a lot better. Wait for someone really special."

"Like Jock. He's really special. I can tell by the way he put up with me. I'll bet he made love to you and was really, really good. Don't lie."

"We did once but didn't know each other well enough to call it making love. He was considerate."

And so much more. Her mind wandered back to his beautiful house, the king-sized bed, his strong body arching over her, those arms and legs thick with muscle keeping his weight off her. That second time in the bathroom satisfying her again and tenderly washing her body. He'd been so perfect, the best lover she'd had in her lifetime—but he'd only desired one thing, which made the betrayal even worse. She'd been so close to falling in love with him.

"He wanted an introduction to Dad and a tryout with the Sinners. He used me to get that or would have if his teammates hadn't ratted on him. All that bull about not knowing where New Orleans was situated from the ranch, just another lie to get what he wanted."

"I guess he did lie about that, but Lori, he couldn't take his eyes off you the whole time he stayed here. Why didn't he ignore you once he met dad? He kept trying to get your attention no matter how rotten you treated him. I think most guys would have given up on you."

"Oh, Jock says he does what he has to do to get what he wants."

"Obviously, that's you. Jeez, I'm still in high school, and I can figure it out. I do hope a man wants me that badly one day."

"Men always want a woman that badly until he's had her a few times and gotten bored with her." Mack lounged in the doorway. Trinity stood there, too, almost tucked under his taller brother's arm.

Though he made a good point for Edie, somehow the comment riled Lorena, as if there were no such thing as love. "You mean men like you."

"I won't deny it." Mack moved into the kitchen and emptied the coffee carafe to the last drop. "You get to clean up. We ate earlier."

"Why aren't you on your way back to Dallas? You usually beat it out of here as soon as you can after a family gathering. Trin, did your beautiful fiancée go back to New Orleans without you?"

"She drove here by herself and wanted to return to working on the Josee's World game. Mack and I stayed because we needed to have a talk with you without all the chaos."

"And Mom and Dad butting in on it," Mack added. "You, too, Edie. Get lost."

"You'll have to carry me out and tie me up. I think this conversation could be very educational." Prepared to fight for her right to listen in on whatever the brothers had to say, she clutched the edge of the table to prevent removal.

"Leave her," said Trin. "We aren't going to get raunchy."

"Good thing you told me in advance. We don't like this guy for you."

Curious, she asked, "Why not?"

"I spent time doing research on him. His story is easy to find: grew up in a rough neighborhood, mother died when he was fourteen, father a drunk. He raised his two younger brothers and gave up the chance of a university education to play Australian Rules Football and get them out of the slums."

"Aww," said Edie. "That is so great."

Of course, it was. Lorena had thought so when she first heard his story. She needed a reason to hate him. "Find any dirt?"

"Puts away a fair amount of beer. I noticed it here, however, no more than most athletes if you exclude Mack. Doesn't touch hard liquor, but owns part of a vineyard."

"Hey," Mack objected. "I can hold it, and so can he."

"Yeah, but he doesn't look for a fight when he has one too many. Only scrapes I could find were during games when he defended his teammates. As for women, he's tapped to escort some pretty famous babes by his agent I gather, has some casual sex, but not much, no one special in his life."

"Tell me something I don't know about Jock or Mack." Lori shook her head, very disappointed.

Trinity poured a glass of orange juice and gulped it down as if he needed the extra energy to continue.

"What, does he have a secret wife, two wives, a dozen illegitimate children, a drug habit?"

"No, not that I could find. It's just that he's so Aussie."

"What exactly does that mean?" She'd lived in Australia for two years while they had not.

"You know, so friendly, up for anything you throw at him. We figure in a while he'll want to go back to Oz and take you with him—permanently. We wouldn't see you much."

"You mean if he doesn't get on with the Sinners?"

Mack smirked. "Oh, he'll get an offer because Dad and Dean are backing him. They're really impressed with his skills. If they had that much faith in me, maybe I'd be catching balls for the Sinners and not the Cowboys."

"It's not your ability they doubt, Mack. It's what you do off the field that concerns them and Mom, always a chip on your shoulder and a beautiful woman on your arm who you'll dump for the next to come your way. It's a wonder *you* don't have a love child," Lori informed him.

"I follow Dad's advice about always wearing my rubber raincoat, that's why."

"A rubber raincoat?"

Trin explained. "Condoms, Sis. You girls got Mom's talk. We got Dad's, but none of this concerns Jock and you becoming a permanent resident of Australia."

Lori huffed. "First of all, if Jock makes the team, he'll be here half the year. I might not if I go back into training with Maisie. Second, I won't be seeing him anymore. He only used me to get introduced to Dad. Third, while I appreciate your Cajun need to keep family close, what I do is none of your business. Are we done?"

"Hmm, we thought you might be playing hard to get. He's so totally into you even the guys noticed," Trinity said.

"See, the guys saw it, too. Why can't you, Lori?" Edie had kept her mouth shut until now to escape ejection from the room.

"Because he's a liar."

Mack shrugged. "I hate to give him credit for anything, but he doesn't lie any more than most guys. If he didn't want to lay my sister, I might like him."

"Language, Mack!" Trin's head jerked toward Edie. His cheeks turned red.

"I know what that means. Another reminder that I am not a child," Edie said.

"Well, Dallas, where a man can say what he wants, calls." He picked up a leather overnight bag he'd left in the hall and came forward to give each sister a peck on the cheek after slamming his brother on the back in a manly goodbye, out the door and into the Jag that surged down the lane in a blast of power taking Mack back to Texas.

Trin, who'd nearly been toppled by the blow to his back, grumbled, "When will he grow up?"

"Mom says when he finds the right woman like Dad did. I think Jock believes he's found the right woman—and she doesn't want him. I wish he'd wait for me to get through college, and I'd marry him. Come on, Lori. I'll be a good sport and help you clean the kitchen." Edie began clearing the table.

"I guess I have spare time now that I'm my own boss. I'll pitch in, too. It will be like old times, the kind we don't want to lose if you go to live in Australia."

Trin carried milk and juice containers to the fridge.

Lorena had a lot to ponder as she rinsed the dishes before putting them in the washer. Would she abandon her large family for her career or for a man she loved, a man like Jock, but not him?

Chapter Fifteen

When Lori awoke the next day, the big house seemed empty without the overwhelming presence of Jock Brown. His outsized feet no longer thudded down to breakfast, giving her ample warning of his imminent arrival to torment her with his charm. She could have slipped out the kitchen door to avoid him, but no, she'd stayed to watch him share his Vegemite and enjoy the reactions of his victims. Today, the kitchen sat quiet and clean with only a covered dish and a half pot of coffee waiting to greet her.

Of course, it was a weekday, not a holiday anymore. Her mom would be at the free clinic seeing to the mental health of the poor. Dad—probably exercising one of the horses since he no longer had a houseful of kids to ride them. She could help with that as soon as she had breakfast. As for Edie, she, too, had gotten a vehicle for her shared birthday with T-Rex, not a truck but a Honda Insight, a hybrid that purred compared to her brother's roar. She'd be off early to socialize with friends. With Jock gone, no reason for her to hang around her older sister.

Had she really slept that late? Even Corazon had abandoned the kitchen, off on an errand, or visiting Xochi and her grandchildren. She'd left Lorena a plate of food to nuke in the microwave. A peek under the cover revealed congealed scrambled eggs, sausages, and a dollop of grits with a half-melted butter pat in its center. Toast was up to her, but thank God, a good two cups of coffee remained. She heated her food, gulped down coffee, and turned off the machine. Then to the barn to see if she could make herself useful.

Her dad had Lazy Loser in the crossties for a vigorous brushing after a ride. Unfortunately, his name had proved to be true, unlike his sire, Lazy Boy, who once raced on the quarter horse circuit and won. While other offspring of Lazy Boy were snapped up when offered for sale, Loser remained at the ranch to be gelded and turned into a placid saddle horse—the one she should have put Jock on since Loser loathed moving much beyond a gentle trot and frequently stopped to munch grass along the way. Jock had strong arms to pull the big head of the horse up when it lapsed. Strong arms to hold a woman gently but tight. Lori shook her head to clear the thought as if she'd gotten water in her ear. That reminded her of the cold pool plunge with Jock.

"Dad, want help exercising the horses?"

"I could use it. How about we take Rascal and Lazy Linda out for a ride together? The old boy still likes to get out of his stall, and the mare is getting a little pudgy with all of you gone."

"I'll get them saddled." She led out Linda, the horse she'd ridden with Jock. Also, belying her name, the mare was a perfect lady, responsive to commands and not a malingerer when it came to faster speeds. She'd been a broodmare a few times, and all her foals went for high prices. Broodmare, maybe that's what Jock wanted of her—to give birth to his gigantic children. She's seen the way he watched the little ones at the egg hunt with a sort of loopy grin on his face that said, "I'd like to have some of those one day." Well, not with her, though she thought her hips were big enough to accommodate his child, unlike little Annie who'd needed a C-section to birth Matt's large baby. Jock in her head again. She shook it harder this time, more like a bug in her ear than water.

She and her dad rode in companionable silence on a perfect spring day low on humidity and high on acres of blue sky above. Even the bayou running alongside the bridle path seemed less muddy and attempted a little sparkle on its surface. When they came to a place where the dirt and grass were a trifle disturbed, she remarked, "That's where Jock had his little tussle with Rascal over his outback hat." She wished she'd kept her mouth shut because she'd opened the barn door of opinion.

Her father said, "A little mean-spirited, no, not warning him about Rascal's tricks?" He threw a little Cajun accent in to soften her up, she was sure.

"Jock is big enough to handle it."

"Right, he is. I tell you, me, you two are like school kids where the boy keeps showing off to get attention, and the girl won't give an inch—though she'd like to." Her dad pulled up, took off his battered barn Stetson and ran his fingers through his still thick iron-gray hair.

"Maybe she wouldn't like to at all. Maybe she didn't want to be used to get invited to the ranch and meet you."

"I have to say he showed ingenuity there, even came with—what do women call that?—hostess gifts. Helped out where he could and didn't complain no matter how we challenged him in the games. I think he's worth a second look. The Sinners are giving him a tryout next week after Buck rounds up the other coaches. Want to come along and see what he can do on a real football field?"

"Not in a million…" She stroked the braid that had tumbled over a shoulder to give herself time to think. "Yes, I would like to see him fail."

Her dad gave her that smile that drove women wild once upon a time but had always been the way her father smiled at his children. "I wouldn't set my heart on that, sugar. The boy has talent to spare if he can adjust to American football. The coaches won't go easy on him."

"Good!"

"You know your mother gave me a second chance."

"So I've heard a million times."

"Just keep that in mind. I think we've given the horses enough exercise. Let's get them back to the stable, give them a good brushing, then shower and grab lunch."

"I'll help, but I think I'd rather go for a quick swim to get the horse off of me."

"You know that water is still *tres* cold, *cher*."

"Exactly what I want." After all, men took cold showers to get rid of their lust. Why not an icy plunge for her?

As soon as the horses were stowed, she set off for the pool and donned one of the bikinis she'd left there before she'd gone to Australia. Without a second's hesitation, she dove into the deep end, resurfaced, and did some fast laps that should have driven all thoughts of Jock away. Instead, she recalled how great he looked in a Speedo, how easily he'd lifted her in the air and gone under with her, and worst of all, the heat of his body so close to hers, the only warm spot in the pool.

Since the cure failed to work, she went to the pool house shower and turned on the hot water. The only hope for her appeared to be Jock's imminent return to his native land once he bungled his tryout.

Chapter Sixteen

The week before Jock made his bid for a place on the Sinner's team passed as slowly as a snail inching its way up the stem of a tall stalk of sugarcane. A drizzly rain set in for three days, making neither riding nor swimming palatable. Working out alone in the exercise room quickly grew old. In desperation, Lori phoned her former volleyball coach at the Episcopal Day School and offered to do a seminar for the team if they'd meet at the gym on Saturday with the net set up. She was well aware that some of the girls might be playing soccer and possibly could not attend, but oh, how she wanted the all-out exercise.

Coach Pat Swope greeted her in the high school gym, where Lorena had played her early games. All six starters perched on the foldout bleachers and the six subs behind them as if they'd lined up by rank. Her introduction went as expected—the pride and joy of the EDS volleyball team who had gone on to glory at LSU and now partnered the Amazing Maisie Morton of Australia in beach volleyball and intended to go to the Summer Olympics. Coach Pat, a sturdy woman with a short cap of hair as gray as the whistle around her neck and who never seemed to change, rattled off Lorena's impressive statistics as if she'd kept a scrapbook.

"Any questions for Lori before we hit the court?"

One of the two blonde girls, who sat close together,

whispering to each other while Coach talked, put up her hand. They were both taller than the rest of the team. "Why aren't you playing for the United States, Miss Lorena? My dad says it's a shame."

Not again. "You might not be old enough to know that Maisie Morton and her former partner took the gold in the last two Olympics. It's an honor to be chosen by her—and I feel I am proudly representing America as well." The youth of the girls and the fact that they called her Miss Lorena made her feel as old as Maisie. "Look her up when you get home, and you'll see why she's called amazing."

Her friend whipped out a phone.

"Not now. I'd put that away for the time being. Feel free to call me Lori. What's your name?"

"Petra Lamperez."

Ah, daughter of a prominent lawyer in town. EDS had its share of snobs and mean girls. She suspected Petra was one or the other or both by that cocky ponytail styled to the side and the nerve of her to ask such a question. "And your friend?"

"Lissa Matlock. We're the Outside Hitters."

Tuition at EDS ran high so that one probably belonged to the Matlock Motors Man, owner of the biggest auto dealership in town and prone to doing his own corny commercials, something his daughter had to live down, maybe by being good at volleyball.

"I played Middle Hitter here at EDS."

"No surprise there," Lissa answered.

True, the Middle Hitters were usually the tallest on the team, and she had been for all of her high school years, but in college, six feet wasn't that odd. She'd experienced some teasing. "How's the weather up there?" But one hard glance from her Billodeaux brown eyes put an end to that. She didn't come from a football family for nothing and had her own game face. As she recalled, she'd used it once on Angus McCall, Jock's mate, very effectively. Right now, she cast it on Lissa. "Let's get started with a little exhibition. First team, take your positions. Your serve."

The server put a soft ball just over the net. Lori set it up for herself and smashed it back between the two lines for an easy kill. Next time they tried a more subtle play, server to setter to outside hitter who sent it obliquely across the court. With no one in her way, she arrived in time to return it to Lissa, hard and short enough for her to miss. The ball crashed up against the girl's body. The crunch of broken glass followed.

"Hey, you broke my screen!"

"Never bring your cell phone onto the court."

In that moment of commentary, they tried to get a quick serve to the very back of the court. She intercepted the ball and returned it just inside the boundary, another kill. At twelve to zero, she asked the subs to take over and nailed all but one of the rest of the eleven points needed to win. Her single hesitation to end the game came when she looked over the net about to cram the ball into the face of a short girl, blue eyes wide with terror, mouth full of braces opened in a silent scream as she tried to shield herself with her hands rather than return the ball. Then she realized every shot she'd taken was aimed in anger at Jock Brown because she still wanted him, lust not love, she assured herself. She pulled her shot, sent it over softly, and let the child return it without really trying to deflect it over the net. Next time, she did end it.

"My apologies. I got carried away. We have only one other person on the court with us in beach volleyball and plenty of room to get where we need to be. Y'all are more constrained." She accepted a towel and a bottle of water from Coach Pat.

"One thing I hope you learned. Don't let your attention drop. Look for holes and weaknesses in the other team."

"Is that why you bobbled that single point?" Petra asked, her perky ponytail looking a little stringy after her exertions. Not that she wasn't still sassy, which could be an asset to the team if used for the benefit of the group.

"Yes," she said simply as if kindness and mercy had nothing to do with it. You couldn't go easy in volleyball. "Get some water and a little rest, then line up, and I'll work with each of you on your weak areas."

She kept her word and sent the team away with valuable lessons learned, even offering to pay for the damage to Lissa's phone to which she got a shrug.

"My daddy will get me another one. No biggie."

Coach Pat sauntered over. Low-voiced, she said, "Thanks for putting Petra and Lissa in their places. They're my best players, but not the best teammates." She shook her head. "I'll never have another one like you. You be sure to win the Olympics, so I can brag about it for the rest of my life."

"I'll do my best."

"Now that you're of age, how about a cold beer in a dark bar?"

"It would be my pleasure once I shower." She didn't take long.

Still, a strange feeling, having a drink with her

mentor. The last time she and Coach Pat really talked, she hadn't been legal drinking age. They discussed volleyball, of course, then about living in Australia, and finally got to the big Aussie she'd brought home, not that she'd suggested the subject.

"Does everyone in town know about Jock Brown?" She slammed down her bottle and beckoned for another.

Coach Pat raised her silver eyebrows. "This is Chapelle, Lori. Most of the EDS faculty goes to St. Luke's. Hard to miss a man that big even in the Easter Sunday crowd. It didn't take long for the hospitality ladies to pump Fr. John dry of all he knew. Friend of yours, Australian, not religious. They passed the word over carrot cake and coffee. Our minister has him sized up for conversion—via marriage, I think."

"That won't happen. He's in New Orleans now and will be heading back to Australia fairly soon." No disguising the edge to her words, as if she'd just thrown sharp blade toward her old coach who held up her arms in defense.

"Hey, hey, you know my girls can come to me and talk about anything on their minds: school troubles, family troubles, boy troubles. It wasn't like you to be so aggressive. You used to help your teammates improve. What's eating you?"

How inappropriate if she'd answered Jock Brown. "Petra and Lissa got on my nerves, that's all."

"So you took it out on the whole team? Really? And that one lapse?"

"My mind wandered and then returned to its senses."

"There's more."

"Jock Brown used me to get an introduction to my father. He pretended to accidentally land in Lafayette when he knew damned well where New Orleans was from here. He wants to play for the Sinners, and now thanks to Dad, he's getting a tryout next week."

Coach cocked her head. "He didn't have to use you for that. Your father shakes any hand offered, signs autographs by the dozens, and is always on the lookout for new talent."

"But Jock didn't know that. Instead, he took me punting on the river, and to see the fairy penguins and a platypus, plus a date at his private winery—like a hero in a romance novel."

"Did you enjoy the attention? Seems he went to a lot of trouble when he could have just asked for the intro."

"I enjoyed it too much and didn't keep up my guard."

Coach Pat touched her hand in a maternal gesture. "This is funny advice coming from me, but letting your guard down isn't always bad. The girl you let score on you, out of kindness I suspect, is my least confident player. For the rest of her life, she can say she got the drop on the famous Lorena Billodeaux. It will do wonders for her. Maybe Jock Brown will do wonders for you."

"Stop. Everyone is on his side, Dad, Mom, now you. I was looking forward to a nice vacation since Maisie practices year-round. She's pregnant again. That's why I'm home now. I'm so bored. I'm going crazy. Hence, my rather ugly exhibition, taking out my excess energy on high school kids." She peeled off the bills to pay for their beers as if to announce their discussion had ended.

"I heard about Maisie's condition. The whole world of volleyball is wondering if she can recover in time. When's the baby due?"

"December."

"Good, I might have a remedy for you. Tulane is looking for an assistant volleyball coach. Even though it wouldn't be permanent, I think they'd be glad to have you for a semester. You'd be staying in New Orleans, though, maybe too close to that man you despise. I'll text you the information if you think you can handle being in the same city as him." Was Pat Swope challenging her, knowing she always rose to one?

Teacher and former student stood. No shaken hands here. Out on the sidewalk, they hugged, and Lori realized she could have rested her head on Coach Pat's if she so desired. Still, her mentor, now a friend. Getting into the too-small car she'd borrowed from her mother, she set out for the ranch, running through her options of places to stay in New Orleans. Any of the family would gladly put her up, but she settled on Jude, the one woman Jock Brown hadn't enchanted.

Chapter Seventeen

Lorena sat on the second row of bleachers next to her mom. She wore that same yellow dress she'd stripped off at Jock's home by the winery and paired it with oversized sunglasses and a large straw hat pulled low, causing her mother to remark that she resembled Jackie O. hiding out from paparazzi.

"Who?" she asked.

"Jackie Onassis, Mrs. Kennedy."

"Really?" She stared at the locker room door, waiting for Jock to appear for his workout. In front of her, on the first row, sat the coaches her dad and Marty Buck had lured from their offseason activities. They waited with all the patience of a pack of hounds wanting to be fed. The men checked watches, got up, and helped themselves to water, though as Louisiana days went, this one could be described as mild, no more than eighty degrees and with tolerable humidity. Crusty old Coach Buck wore a Sinner's cap to cover his increasing bald spot, but most of the rest went bareheaded. Maybe she had overdone her disguise to prevent Jock from looking into her eyes or guessing her thoughts.

Tom and Alix sat with the coaches to judge the candidate's kicking ability on the field, though as far as Lori could tell, they'd already bonded with Jock while lofting balls over the barn. As usual, the couple's thighs touched, and their hands clasped together. Her dad and Dean completed the contingent of judges. Those two had made up their minds already. Hadn't Dean brought Jock to the training center every day to teach him the ins and outs of American football?

She'd come to the city with her parents but turned down an invitation for a cookout at Dean's house even though he'd be making his famous brick oven pizza. She wanted to rest in Jude's relatively quiet, kid-free environment and prepare for her interview at Tulane, she claimed. Mostly, she didn't want to see how good Jock would be with Dean's children, and heck, also their dog. Everyone appeared to love him except Jude and her triplet brothers. Of course, she'd come for the interview, but more to watch Jock Brown fail and be sent back to Australia with his damned dingo tail between his legs.

The locker room door cracked open. Jock trotted out and—oh, no, he'd worn the snug black shorts and sleeveless, vertical-striped black and white jersey of his old team. She heard a few snickers from the front row as Jock moved toward them and stopped before Coach Buck. The coach eyed him up and down and drawled, "Son, this ain't a tryout for referees."

Coach got a quick comeback. "I am aware of that. I proudly wear the guernsey of my Aussie rules team, the Magpies founded in 1892." His remark made the Sinners, an expansion team that Joe Billodeaux at quarterback took to greatness, sound like newcomers.

But someone upfront asked, "Isn't a guernsey a cow?"

Sure, she wanted to see him humiliated but not for using an Australian term. She spoke up for him. "He means his jersey. Guernsey is what the Aussies call them."

Ignoring her, Coach Buck, who expected his rare jokes to be appreciated, not put down, continued. "In our leagues, we have fierce birds: eagles and seahawks and falcons."

Tom came to the rescue. "Also, cardinals and ravens." That earned a few chuckles and gave Jock the time to form another answer.

"Magpies protect their territory, their nests, and mates quite fiercely."

"I'm no birdwatcher, so don't know about that. I do know football, our kind of football. What position did you play down under?"

"Ruckman." Anticipating the next question, Jock added, "When the umpire bounces the ball to start the game, I rise up and try to tip it to one of my teammates rather like basketball."

"That's all you do?" Coach Buck reset his cap as if ready to go home.

"No, I kick goals and play forward for a break. Bashing into another man as many as fifty times a game does wear out a fellow."

"That often? We just use a coin toss once in the beginning. So how do you rank as a ruckman?"

"Highest paid in the league, one point two million."

"In Australian dollars," Lori said. This time several heads turned her way.

Tom called up the calculator on his phone and announced, "That comes to $816,812.72 American."

About what an average NFL player might earn at the beginning of his career, Lori knew. The sum made

Jock seem undervalued. Wasn't that what she wanted?

"Look, I know being a Sinner means hard yakka, and I'm up for that, but I want a fair suck of the sav."

This time all the heads in the first row turned toward her. "Yakka is hard work, and he only wants a fair chance."

Jock flashed her that cheeky grin of his. "Righty-O, fair dinkum."

How had she become his official translator? "He really means it. By the way, he is perfectly capable of speaking plain English." Jock smiled again, this time a little impish as if he were playing with her—and probably was.

"Fine, if you have potential, I think we could come up with that amount of money. Have you warmed up before coming out? No injuries on my watch."

"I did my stretches and rode the bike in the locker room. What do you want me to do?"

The special teams' coach, with his big belly and short legs, elbowed Buck. "I'd like to see him kick. Plenty of Aussie kickers in the league and big as he is, he might do for the return team, too."

"A drop punt, a torpedo, or maybe a banana kick?" Jock laid out his repertoire.

Not familiar with most of the terms, the coach went with the drop punt. "Go out to the thirty-yard line and see how far you can send it."

Tom offered Jock a ball and a murmured good luck. He went to his position, took a couple of steps, dropped the ball, and sent it into the end zone. He did the same at twenty yards, but when asked to place the ball into the coffin corner to the left just before the goal line, he shanked it badly out of bounds. The special team coach remarked, "Looks like he'd make a strong punter with more practice in case mine goes lame."

Lorena, just behind the team's kickers, heard Tom whisper to Alix. "Don't worry. He has great leg but no finesse. You're a better punter. Besides, our contracts run for another year, and if you go, I go." He squeezed his wife's hand.

"Okay. Dean, you claim he has good hands. Send him downfield to see how fast he can cover the yardage and catch your passes."

While her brother gave Jock his instructions, Lorena could only think of those good hands on her breasts, kneading them with lightly callused fingers. Lust, not love, she reminded herself.

Dean sent Jock racing to the end of the field. On the bench, the coaches started their stopwatch apps on their phones. Coach Buck, who used technology but hated it, clicked an actual watch and turned it off as Jock moved to receive one of Dean's perfect spiral passes. He caught it with ease and several after that. At a nod from Buck, the next soared in high, way too high for most receivers to catch. Jock leaped up and seized it from the air, a solid catch. Dean's next came in very low. Jock dove to prevent it from touching the ground, eating turf along the way. He rose up, his jersey streaked with green, and waggled the ball in the air. Damn, Lorena thought, he was so good, even great.

The coaches conferred. "For a big guy, he's fast, really fast." "He can catch anything with those huge hands." Joe Billodeaux nodded, sage that he now was, and said, "Another Gronk."

Coach Buck held up a hand. "But how will he handle the ball when he has competition? Can he hang on to it? Where are those boys? Should have been here by now."

As if cued for a timely entry, Junior Polk and Matt Keaton rumbled from the locker room in their exercise clothes. "Sorry, coach. The kids are having an ice cream party at Matt's house and wanted us to stay. Hard to say no to a quick cone on a warm day," Junior explained. Pink dribbles down the front of his shirt verified his excuse.

"I had to scrape mine off my legs and promise we'd be back later," Matt said.

"Whatever, get out there and try to strip the ball from the Aussie. Both of you play defense this time around."

The four men set themselves up two against two, though neither tried to prevent Dean from throwing the ball. Comfortable as one of the best cornerbacks in football, Junior dashed after Jock. Matt, a prime running back, caught up with them easily by the time the ball started its downward arc. Neither moved to intercept, but Junior went after Jock as soon as he caught the ball. He tried to punch it out and got a sharp elbow in his ribs for his trouble. Matt, attacking from the other side, received a strong, stiff arm.

Jock surged over the goal line and spiked the ball. "A bit of fun, eh?"

"Should have worn pads," Junior said, rubbing his side.

On the next try, Junior went for an interception instead, getting in the way, raising his arms high and about to leap when Jock did the same, using his opponent's substantial rump to push off for the catch. "Butt pads, too. I'll have cleat marks on my behind tonight."

"Sorry, mate. That's a common move in Aussie rules. Not sure if it's allowed in yours. Want to have some more fun? Matt, you're on offense with me. Pretend you're blocking behind me as I run with the ball, but Junior is about to take me down coming in from the other side. Get ready to receive the ball."

They played out the scenario as described, and when Junior reached out to make the tackle, Jock punched the ball he cradled back a few feet hard into Matt's arms. Matt took off for the goal passing both men who were now on the grass. Coach Buck whistled them over to the bench.

"Explain exactly what that was."

"In Aussie rules, we call that a handpass, like a lateral except the ball is punched out instead of thrown." Jock picked up another football, ready to go again like a dog with endless energy for frisbee. He glanced up at Lorena as if seeking her praise. Good boy, she felt like saying, but didn't.

"Not sure if that's legal here, but I'll be damned certain to find out if it is. I do like me a trick play now and then. And Junior, no tackling today."

"Yes, sir. I got carried away."

"Good job, all of you. Why don't you hit the showers while we discuss whether we have a place for Jock on our team?"

Junior let loose with a huge laugh. "I'll be happy if he's playing for our team and not against it."

Glaring at him, Coach Buck snapped, "Junior, Matt, you can get back to your ice cream party. No need to stick around while we debate the matter."

"You're all invited," Matt said, extending the offer

to his in-laws.

Jock spoke up. "Ice cream would hit the spot about now. Are you coming, Lori?"

He'd shown his eagerness too soon and given her a quick out. "No, I'm going for a job interview this afternoon at Tulane and can't afford to get messy. Nice work today." She threw the dog a bone, a rather dry one. In fact, he'd been fantastic, spectacular, magnificent. He'd surely get an offer.

"So you'll be staying in New Orleans? You and Maisie are done?"

"No, it's only for a semester as an assistant volleyball coach to pass the time until she decides if she's going to another Olympics. Don't start any rumors."

"Not me."

Coach Buck, ready to get on with it, snarled, "I told you to get a shower. Come back when you're cleaned up."

"Righty-O." Jock trotted for the locker room with a smile on his face that said he knew he'd performed well. The door closed behind him.

Buck stood and turned toward the bleachers. "This was a private workout. None of you are to mention a word of it to anyone else. Especially, you, ladies. I allowed you to be here as a favor to Joe. Now, let's get started. Who wants him?" That began the uproar.

Dean dove in as if he covered a loose ball. "I need him for my tight end."

"Return team," the special teams coach shouted.

The lanky coach for the offense backed up Dean, and the rock-solid defense coach called, "Cornerback, paired with Junior we couldn't be beat."

Joe repeated, "Another Gronk, I tell you me."

Buck held up his hands. "All right, we want him. Couldn't agree with you more. We can work out the details later."

Lorena and her mom climbed from the bleachers and prepared to depart. "Could you drop me off at Tulane before you go to dote on your grandchildren?" They formed their own little cluster away from the men.

"Certainly. Jock really was impressive today."

"He'll get a contract. He deserves a big one, but I think Coach Buck will try to get him to sign as low as possible."

"I wouldn't put it past the old goat."

In what had to be one of the world's fastest showers, Jock reappeared. Water droplets still caught in his sandy hair as if he'd just emerged from the waves at Bondi Beach, and he'd made a hasty change into khakis and a black tee promoting the Magpies. His eyes glittered green as the sunlit vines at his winery. He possessed that confident air of a man who knew he'd done his best to impress. He looked her way again. Only his swift return betrayed how badly he wanted to be on the team. He should have played it cooler, Lori thought.

Coach Buck waited a long minute before nodding. "We think we can use you somewhere with the Sinners. You might have to start out on the practice team, and that doesn't pay what you've been getting. If you practice well, might be we could move you to a backup position since you don't know the game that well yet. Who knows, you might have a future with us."

Lori could not prevent herself from whipping off her sunglasses and pushing back her floppy hat to shake her head in a vigorous no. Her tight braid slashed back and forth. Whether Jock saw her action or not was uncertain, but his relaxed posture stiffened.

"I didn't come here to be on the practice squad or serve as a backup. Yes, I have much to learn, but I'll make first team in one position or another or go back to footy."

"If you are that determined, I'll have a contract drawn up for you to consider."

Bless him, her father saved the day. He withdrew a card from a pocket and handed it to Jock. "This agent represents Dean, Tom, and Alix and also handles all my post-career deals for advertising and such. Tell him Joe sent you and don't sign anything until he reads every word."

Coach Buck puckered his wrinkled lips as if reconsidering. "Maybe we can match what you made with the Magpies."

"Not good enough," Joe answered for his former houseguest. "Do better. Jock, you ready for that ice cream?"

"I could gnaw my arm off."

Her dad put a hand on Jock's shoulders, even though he had to reach up a little, and steered him toward the parking area. Dean, Tom, and Alix trailed behind.

Lori resettled her hat and sunglasses. "I don't want to ride with Jock," she told her mom.

"No worries. Isn't that what the Aussies say? He's going with Dean." Mama Nell squeezed her around the waist. "He seemed to want to please you as well as the coaches. And I have to say you tried to help him. This might work, after all."

What had she done? Encouraged Jock to stay when she wanted him gone, gone, gone.

Chapter Eighteen

No matter what the time of day, the interior of Mariah's Place always seemed to be set at dusk. Lorena entered with her new boss, Tulane's premier volleyball coach, who'd happily taken her on short-term, and after much chitchat suggested they go get bar food and a beer at the night club to seal their deal. Only six p.m., the lounge had yet to awaken fully, nor had the legendary and outrageous owner, Mariah Coy, who claimed the Sinners football players as her own and all of Joe Billodeaux's many kids as her surrogate grandchildren.

Lori breathed a sigh of relief at seeing Mariah's exclusive table with its reserved chair for her long-deceased lover, Billy, still vacant. No one could create a scene like Howdy McCoy's birth mother, who had rediscovered her famous Sinners' kicker son late in life. Heck, he'd bought her the club where she held court in low-cut sequin dresses that glittered in the gloom, a Dolly Parton-sized white wig, and comparable boobs. Somehow, Lori wasn't in the mood to be crushed to Mariah's vast cushy bosom and interrogated about her future plans and any men in her life.

She and the coach took seats at one of the four tops spaced around the small checkered dance floor and ordered a tray of sliders and the cold draft beer always on tap. Plenty of time to eat and escape before the bouncers, most of them members of the Sinners practice team, made the rounds of tourists who'd brought children into the bar in hopes of seeing famous football players and cadging autographs. They'd point out the cards on each table decreeing that families with offspring under eighteen were requested to leave before the entertainment began at eight. Parents with good sense simply left. Others were escorted from the premises as discreetly as possible, usually with a dad or a teen braying that they hadn't seen a single Sinner. As if team members were paid to be there when they had better things to do before training began again.

Not that Mariah's had more trouble than most French Quarter bars, less probably, but the owner wanted her "boys" to relax without undue adulation from the customers. Lori planned to be long gone before the drinking and the dancing began.

The beer appeared at once, and the food not too long after, every small hamburger juicy and dripping with melted cheese and various toppings. As two tall, athletic women, modestly dressed, who played in a lesser-known sport, they attracted little attention. Maybe mother and daughter, perhaps lesbians, by any guy trolling for company might assume. Continuing their conversation about volleyball and Masie and Australia, they ate at a leisurely pace, had a second beer, and barely took note when a band began to set up. The next customers to enter weren't framed by sunlight. The group caused a stir, four hearty men with thick Aussie accents calling for drinks, and catching Lori's notice even though none of them resembled or sounded like Jock. Still, she had the urge to flee.

"It's getting late. My sister will wonder where I am."

"Sorry to keep you. This has all been fascinating. Can I give you a lift home?" her new boss asked.

"No, I can walk from here. Looking forward to working with you."

"Likewise." They split the tab and shook hands as if they'd just ended a match.

She'd almost made it to the door when the spotlight shone on Mariah's table where the proprietor appeared in all her gaudy splendor as if she'd simply materialized from a gossip magazine. Despite her age and inappropriately high heels, Mariah homed in on her and crossed the floor with the speed of a greyhound at the dog track. The spotlight followed her progress. Mashed against the woman's deep, gasping marshmallow chest, she became a celebrity, too.

"Lorena, honey, heard you were home. I hoped you'd come to see me." She spun her captive to face the room. "Lorena Billodeaux, folks, Joe Dean's little girl, and a famous volleyball player in her own right."

The table overflowing with Aussies clapped and hooted. "Amazing Maisie's partner. Come sit with us. Buy you a drink."

"Sorry, she came to see *me*." Mariah aimed a long, red-lacquered nail at their group. "Behave now. Don't make me put you out on the curb." Then, relenting, she sent them a pitcher of beer before leading Lorena to her table and seating her next to Billy's vacant chair.

"Aussies, they drink a lot, love to party, and usually cause trouble, but still, I like them. I heard you brought one home with you." Mariah rested her chin on the cage of her manicured fingers and prepared to soak in the details.

Figured that word had reached her all the way from

the ranch. All it took was one of the family to stop by for a drink. Might as well reveal the story which Mariah probably knew already and escape as soon as she could. As the time for the entertainment approached, the door to the club opened more and more frequently, making her nervous that the next might admit Jock.

"Just a guy who followed me home to meet my dad and try out for the Sinners. He's nothing special to me."

"Oh, I heard he's very special as a football player and can't take his eyes off you."

How had the news traveled so fast from the practice field to Mariah's ears in a few hours? "No one is supposed to know about his tryout." Coach Buck would assume she'd been the leak.

"They won't hear it from me." Mariah locked her enhanced vermilion lips with a twist of two fingers. "Will the wedding be here in the Big Easy or at the ranch? You know I'm good for the champagne. I should meet this young man first, though, and let you know how I feel about him. I've had tons more experience with men and can smell a stinker from miles away."

"There is no wedding, and I already know he stinks. I…"

She had her back turned from the door and her eyes on Mariah, but she knew exactly when he entered. The table of Aussies erupted. "Jock, Jocko Brown, right here in New Orleans. Pull up a chair and have one on us."

"In a bit. I have to pay my respects to the famous Mariah first."

Lorena kept her back turned, which didn't prevent Jock from striding over and grasping the back of Billy's chair. If he sat, he'd lose big points with his hostess, but a friendly hand guided him to the other unoccupied seat. Of course, her brother, Dean, showing his protégé around New Orleans. He pressed Jock into place, grabbed a spare bentwood chair, and took the space next to Mariah.

"Let me introduce you to the newest Sinner, our Aussie Swiss Army knife, Jock Brown. After the day he had, I thought it was time I brought him around to meet you."

Jock reached his hand across the table, lifted Mariah's ornate fingers to his lips, and lightly brushed a kiss across them. "*Enchanté*, Miss Coy. You are as fabulous as I've heard."

Mariah sniffed the air as if scenting for bullshit, then broke into a smile displaying her perfect dentures. She accepted the compliment as her due. "I do believe you, big boy," she said in her raspy, smoke-damaged voice that went low and flirtatious.

How did he do it, always knew what to say and how to act whenever he met a person? Must be a gift along with his athleticism. Lori stood. "I was just leaving for Jude's place. I'll let you get acquainted."

Jock immediately turned his attention to her. "How did your interview go? Will you be staying in New Orleans until January?" he asked as if he truly cared.

A little belatedly, Dean chimed in. "Did you get the job?"

"I did, thanks for asking. Now, I'll be going."

Jock rose. "Let me walk you to the apartment. These streets aren't safe."

She laughed. Taller than most men and with a fluid athletic stride that proclaimed she could and would knee any skeezy guy in the nuts, she was rarely challenged on the streets of the city and simply ignored catcalls and lewd suggestions. "I'll be fine. I don't need your help."

"Come on, Lori, hang with us a little while, and I'll drive you over to Jude's," Dean suggested.

Mariah snapped her fingers to catch the attention of her bald bartender, who had been a fixture there forever. "A bottle of bubbly for two celebrations. Enjoy my children. I have to prepare for my opening act." Dean helped her from the chair and escorted the elderly singer backstage, pretending she didn't need help with the couple of stairs. Ah, that was it. Her brother had tipped Jock about how to treat Mariah. Too bad they were alone now. His Aussie fans began to call for attention again.

"I'm leaving. Why don't you go sign autographs or something?" She set out for the exit only to find her way blocked by an entering couple: the man with the very lean build of a strict vegan, a professorial beard, and John Lennon wire-rimmed glasses, plus a young woman who clung to him like an adoring undergrad likely to be sleeping with her mentor. Though rather plain, she'd made an effort with light makeup, sparkly clips holding back lank brown hair, and a classic little black dress adorned with a crystal necklace. Her companion took the easy route, black turtleneck, and slacks.

"I can't imagine why you wanted to come to this tourist trap," he said.

"Because everyone does. Look, look! There's Dean Billodeaux, the quarterback for the Sinners and about the most handsome football player alive. I don't know who the gigantic guy is, but I bet he plays football, too."

Lori glanced behind her. Dean had reemerged from escort duty, leaving Mariah backstage, huffing the oxygen that let her sing exactly one song.

"You know I don't follow sports, and I can't believe you allow yourself to be distracted by them when the world is in disarray."

His words drew her attention before she could say, "Excuse me," and push by them lest Jock caught up with her. Oh, her lucky evening, Stuart Fogler, her ex-boyfriend with another young woman who swallowed his crap whole. Lori had to give her credit. Upon spying Dean, she'd dropped her clutch on Stuart's arm, snatched a napkin from a nearby table, and headed for her brother with single-minded purpose showing in the blue eyes enlarged by her own dark-rimmed glasses. Scholarly, but a fan and not a groupie. Good, Dean hated when a woman wanted her breast signed. He might have fathered a child out of wedlock with the scheming Ilsa but took his football dead seriously. Removing an always handy pen from a pocket, he prepared to honor the request coming his way.

"Really, Alicia, I thought you had more intelligence than to throw yourself at football players." Stuart shook his head in a reproving manner. Lori noted he'd tamed his long hair into a man bun worn low.

"For heaven sakes, Stu, she only wants an autograph."

"Oh, Lorena, I didn't see you towering over us. Still, hanging around playing your childish game? I completed a two-year stint in Ethiopia, returned and received my master's in African studies, and am now working toward my doctorate. Alicia is in the sophomore class I'm teaching. Until now, I thought she had a true dedication to bettering the world."

The hell he hadn't seen her. Right now, she wished she had a volleyball to cram down his belittling throat, but she held her temper. "I'm glad you're achieving your goals, Stu. I've been in Australia training for the next Olympics."

"What will that get you?"

Jock's voice boomed out behind her. "Probably a gold medal, she's that good."

"Your new man? I always knew, in the end, you'd go for brawn over brains."

Before she could frame her reply, Jock answered. "Yeah, a shame I left my medical studies to play footy, but I might get back to them someday. You think sports have no purpose? They bring us together. They divert us from our troubles. The Olympics unites the world in goodwill. Anyone who would sneer at what Lorena has to offer doesn't know a bonzer woman when he has one. Are you aware you're blocking the door, mate? Let me help you out with that."

In a tour de force exhibit of passive-aggressive behavior, Jock moved alongside Lorena and placed his hands in Fogler's armpits. He raised him as easily as he did a hundred-pound weight and set the scrawny man aside. "There you go. Out of everyone's way. Shall we leave, Lori, or did you want to speak to this tosser some more?"

Her "Let's go" was drowned out by Stuart's outraged voice shouting, "He assaulted me. You all saw it."

Maybe they did, but no one rose to help except the table full of Aussies who lined up behind Jock like a rugby team ready for a scrum. "This wanker giving you trouble, Jocko?"

"Nothing I can't handle, mates. He mocked Lorena."

"Not our Lori. We can't allow that."

One second more and blood would have hit the tiles, but with impeccable timing, the lights dimmed, a drum rolled, and the emcee announced the incredible Mariah Coy. She swooped onto the stage showing remarkable legs for her age from the slit in her skirt. "We have some great entertainment tonight, and I'll be singing for you in a minute, but first, thank you for clearing the doorway, Mr. Brown. Others wanted to get in, and he blocked a fire exit. Sir, you will have to leave. As for anyone Australian, a free drink at the bar, and that also goes for volleyball fans."

"How did she know what was going on out here?" Jock asked under the sound of feet thundering toward free liquor.

Lorena pointed to the side of her head. "She wears AirBuds under that wig. I think they double as a hearing aid. Mariah is never out of touch. The bartender or one of the bouncers probably cued her. I'm sure that's how she knew I was here since I didn't ask anyone to call her. She lives over the club."

As she spoke, the bouncers, wearing as much black as Stuart but more impressively, closed in and herded the man toward the door. His protest, "But you saw he put his hands on me," did no good.

"You were blocking an exit," said one.

"I didn't see nuttin'," replied the other.

"Alicia, Alicia, we have to go." Stu's slender wrists waved her way like flags on a windy day.

Alicia emerged from behind Dean, where he had tucked her when it seemed like a fight might break out. "Thanks for the autograph. This is the most exciting evening I've ever had."

"Oh, you'll have more—but I'd choose another date," Lorena advised.

"I hope you do win a gold medal," Alicia whispered as her prof seized her arm and pulled her into the night. The bouncers stood by for a few minutes to make sure the troublemaker stayed out.

Lorena waited, too, not wanting to run into Stuart again. Jock stayed by her side. "Champagne or an escort home?" he asked, leaving the choice up to her.

"Home. You don't need to come along."

"I do with an angry ex lurking nearby. I've heard about Josee's experience with hers."

"Stuart? I could have lifted him aside myself if I'd thought of it. He's a lightweight despite his heavy thoughts. He despises how my father made his fortune, but our family foundation has helped more people than he ever will spouting off in a classroom."

"I'd like to do that someday—have a charitable foundation and not spend my money on cars and wineries."

"Not to mention putting your brothers through college. If the Sinners pay you what you're worth, you'll have that chance."

His countrymen again beckoned for him to join them. Jock shouted over the din, "Back in a mo'."

"Should take you longer than that, mate," one of them guffawed.

He offered the guy a strong middle finger and gently guided her into the darkness with a hand on the small of her back. "Which way to your sister's unit?" he asked, clearly not going anywhere else.

Refusing to admit she enjoyed that slight touch or his verbal defense of her, she pointed the way and swung off at a fast clip, not that she could outrun him. Though the spring night was balmy, she worked up a sweat. People enjoying the French Quarter ambiance gave way before her. He kept pace, of course, not even breathing heavily. Stuart would have been winded by the time they reached the side street where she turned and moved into the alcove where a door led to Jude's apartment over the Korean electronics store on Canal Street. They hadn't shared a word since leaving Mariah's.

She began working the many locks and safeguards her dad had installed. "We're here. You can go back to your admirers now," she said, trying very hard to make sure he knew she was not among them.

"Not going to invite me in for a bottle of water after that sprint?" Oh, his grin, shining in the moonlight.

"No, Jude might be sleeping. Med school is tough even if she did get to skip a lot of the classes because of her training as a surgical nurse. She's on the fast track to an internship, and I don't want to be a bother."

"Righty-O then." He grasped her shoulders as gently as he had touched her back, leaned over, and bestowed the lightest of kisses. "Good to be near you again, Lori."

She wanted to push him away, sputter how much she hated him, but she didn't. Instead, wordless, she slipped inside and set the alarm, guarding her heart against falling in love with him again.

Chapter Nineteen

Dean kept him on a tight schedule. They left early
to work out at the training center, both with weights and
treadmills inside and out on the field with him wearing
full gear, all the pads, and a helmet. Dean wore sweats
or whatever, claiming his protégé needed to get used to
wearing the uniform and head protection while he did
not. Not all teams had air-conditioned domes. Jock
Brown could expect to play in both snow and high
humidity elsewhere. He'd better accept being
encumbered by more than shorts and a jersey. Once the
quarterback began throwing him those perfect spirals
over and over, he generally forgot about the
impediments and immersed himself in being the best
receiver.

Before noon, they stopped for a water break.
Another hour and they'd quit for lunch as the day
warmed like hot milk simmering in a pan to make café
au lait. Afterward, out came the rule book with Dean
testing him on his knowledge of NFL rules, so many
rules. He informed Dean that footy had about twenty
basic rules, though each had subsections: no kicking an
opponent, tripping or maiming, no hitting an umpire, no
tolerance of racist remarks, sometimes forgotten by his
teammates, or throwing the ball as it was deemed too
dangerous except for the handpasses. Holding a foe
who didn't possess the ball, about the same as the

American rule, but a carrier could be slammed hard to the ground in a tackle as long as the hit came between the shoulders and the knees.

He removed his helmet, glugged water from a cooler set out for them, and admitted, "I love your long passes. Can't see how they can be dangerous when we wear all this protective gear."

"Wait until someone like Junior hits you as you come down from catching one before you speak."

He might as well come out with it. "I kissed Lorena last night. I love her, too."

Dean eyed him over the rim of his paper cup. "You're running well, and I don't see any bruises, so I guess she wasn't offended."

"She didn't say a word. Simply ducked inside that fortress your dad set up for his daughters and closed the door."

"Yeah, our father probably knows what happened. Did you notice the camera hidden under the fire escape? No? If she didn't struggle, he wouldn't say a word for now. Hurt her and watch out."

"It was barely a kiss, just a brush of the lips. Teddy said I might be coming on too strong. I need to give her time to get over her bit of mad."

Dean took a seat on the bleachers and poured another cup of water. "Ask me anything about football but not about women or love."

Jock poured some of his drink into his hands, scrubbed his sweating face, and raked water through his hair. "I'm finding it hard to wait."

"Just don't do what I did, get angry and frustrated, and take up with another woman because she lied to you. Above all, don't get that other woman pregnant.

That's my advice."

"You see, she thinks I'm the liar. I mean, I'd forgive her, right? She believes I only took an interest in meeting your dad and getting a tryout. Bloody oath, not true."

"Lori should know no one needs an introduction to our dad. He always has a hand out and takes new talent under his wings. You impressed him at Easter, impressed all of us, and here we are, getting you ready to fight for a starting position on the Sinners team. You might have jumped the gun a little, but there are always open tryouts in the spring. She could have told you that and sent you on your way."

"I tried to court her first. Gave it my all, but we didn't have much time. I wanted to tell her my intentions about the Sinners and her, but she wouldn't hear me out. How did you get back with Stacy after your plans went shithouse?"

"Look, among the Billodeaux men, there are two ways to go—say you are wrong and grovel or make a grand gesture. Matt tried for the grand gesture, big honking ring, down on one knee in front of the whole family, which would have gone great if my father hadn't punched him, hit Annie instead, and sent her to the hospital. Me, I groveled."

Hard to believe a man who stood so fearlessly in the pocket waiting for his receivers to get downfield would grovel. "You? Shocker. Don't think I can do that, mate. My mum groveled to protect us from our pop when he was sloshed. Never did her any good. No groveling for me."

"I can only say ask for Leslie at Schifferman's if you want the big, honking ring. He'll be of more help than me. Now strap on that helmet, and let's return to football."

"A grand gesture has to be more than a ring, don't you think?" With reluctance, he fastened the strap and prepared to get back to work, feeling way too encumbered.

"Well, Trin and Junior saved their lovers' lives, but I don't see it happening again. That pretentious prick at Mariah's was Lori's ex, and she could kill him without your help."

"Figured as much. So who can I ask for help on reaching Lori?"

"Ordinarily, I'd say Trinity or Teddy are the sensitive ones, but Trin is out since he's too close and protective of Lorena."

"Teddy did say to give her space and be less aggressive."

"Then that's what you should do. Jesus, I'll be glad when all my sisters are married, and I won't have to deal with this anymore." Dean led the way to the twenty-yard line and let him practice kicks for a while. Easy enough to allow one part of his brain to work on the problem of Lorena while the other guided his feet. When he'd expended the pile of balls, he asked Dean, "Who would be the best person to see about grand gestures?"

"Inside the family, Tom. Outside, probably X-avier Hopkins. He usually comes to voluntary training sessions. I'll introduce you, then I've done my part, right?"

"Righty-O. I wouldn't want to get Tom or you in any trouble with Lori."

As they hit the showers, he made a mental list of

details he had to take care of that didn't include staying with Dean indefinitely. He could hardly invite the man's sister up to his room, now could he, or take her out in a borrowed car. Maybe have Luca ship his custom-made tuxedo. Grand gestures called for grand clothes, and other than the one good suit, he hadn't brought any with him. Needless to say, he couldn't buy off the rack with his size.

He begged off the afternoon rules practice. He'd been over some of them so many times Dean's kids, who were always around, could answer the easier ones. Their dog might be able to bark them by now. No seeing the playbook or learning those moves until he'd signed his contract.

Taking on getting a vehicle first, he did a tad of research on American cars large enough to hold him in comfort, but not a full-sized Ute. No sense in having one of those to drive in the congested streets of New Orleans, though many did, including Dean. Sinners seemed to favor Escalades. For now, he'd rent a mid-sized Lincoln Aviator, good enough for Matthew McConaughey, good enough for him, in black to show team solidarity. Sleeker than the Cadillac, and did he really need screens in the rear seats to entertain passengers? Parking assist appeared more useful in this crowded city. Amazing, simply amazing, how fast a man was able to lease a high-priced vehicle for three months when Dean put in a word to the salesman. He had options to buy or upgrade at the end of that time. Swell for all of them since Dean no longer had to cart him around like a show horse in a trailer.

As for getting a more permanent place to stay, he'd had kind offers aplenty. Staying with Dean for a while made the most sense, but Matt had offered to put him up, too. Much as he enjoyed children, three toddlers underfoot and a spare, barely legal sister-in-law seemed a bit much. Tom and Alix suggested he room with them in their large brownstone condo, and Junior offered his empty apartment below them, vacant unless he came in for training sessions before the season began. He backed off both of those when he learned they possessed windows directly across broad Canal Street with its crowds and clanging trolleys from Jude and Lorena's place. Alix told him, a person might be able to see directly into their bedrooms if their shades weren't always drawn. He could just imagine what Lori would think of that—spying or stalking, she'd name it.

He didn't drag Dean along, especially since he'd driven the Lincoln straight from the lot. Instead, he contacted a real estate agent about flats in the old quarter itself, dropping the magic word Sinners as his future employer. The agent, Cal, a big fan, would get him the best deal.

Outrageous prices for places with cracked plaster walls and the grime of years built in, small rooms with high ceilings made him feel gigantic. Most had a tiny, ornate balcony or a leafy courtyard to make up for their interiors. After several refusals, the determined agent, sweating in his yellow jacket, said, "I sense you want something historic, yet modern," as he removed a jaunty hat with a feather in the band to mop more moisture from the bald head beneath it with a matching pocket square.

"Um, yeah," he'd replied, having no idea what the fellow meant.

Next, Cal offered a second-floor unit created out of

an old brewery building with high open beams, hardwood floors, and wide doors. Tall, double-sealed windows with shutters just for looks let in light and kept out noise. Outside, worn bricks and French Quarter ambiance, inside entirely new. Only two blocks from the Mardi Gras parade route, the agent added, and not very far from the famous Mariah's Place, where the Sinners hung out as if he imagined Jock to be a party animal.

It was the second fact, not the first that grabbed him. That, and the scale of the place which suited his size. Another winner, private garage space on the ground level. Sold! Or rather rented for a pretty penny for twelve months. Close enough to Lorena, yet in the other direction from Mariah's, a central place where they just might run into each other by accident.

The agent, flush from the afternoon heat and his commission, gave him the names of several reliable places to rent furniture sure to please. Mention that Calvin Benson sent him and get a discount, and certainly a kickback for ole Cal. He wrote on the back of his business card and poked it in Jock's direction. "This place can get you an Alaskan king bed made in Canada."

"A what?"

"Biggest bed on the market, nine by nine feet. You'll never feel cramped. You could have a three-woman orgy in a bed like that."

Why did everyone assume professional athletes were into orgies? A few maybe, not him. The scowl on his face redirected Cal's comment.

"Make that have your wife, your kids, and your Great Dane piled in there. Don't forget to say I sent you." Good advice. The man knew how to hustle.

At the furniture store, the Alaskan king platform bed was indeed impressive. It could only be bought, not rented, as they were custom made. It did come with a set of enormous sheets, two oversized pillows, and a spread, silky and silver, that needed only to be tucked in to look decent. He envisioned Lori's black hair spread across it, the feel of it against her body.

The furniture salesman cleared his throat. Not a good idea to envision anything of the sort while shopping. He stepped behind the waist-high dresser in the showroom set and pretended to check the quality of the backing until his johnson settled down. He took the matte black dresser and night tables that accessorized the bed, and a floor lamp with a stand as thin as a licorice whip and a shade that matched the bedspread.

Adding in a vast sectional sofa of dark brown leather with a recliner built into one end and its matching coffee table, he figured to be nearly done with furniture shopping except for a big-screen telly and a place to sit down for meals right off the open kitchen. Four substantial wooden chairs spaced around a pedestal table with the same dark stain seemed like plenty for now, all but the bed leased to own, depending on how the next year went. He had no illusions that if he were badly injured or didn't perform as expected, he'd be cut loose after taking this bold step and on his way back to Australia without Lorena Billodeaux by his side. All or nothing.

With delivery pending the next afternoon, he spent time soaking in the atmosphere of his new town, watching kids tap dancing on the sidewalk for coins, and placing a few dollars in their bucket, breathing in the scent of salami and oregano wafting from Central Grocery, home of the giant muffuletta sandwich. He inhaled too much-powdered sugar off his order of hot beignets which made him cough, quickly washed down with chicory-laced coffee. At the French Market, he bought the largest and freshest of the bouquets available. "Smell that freesia," the florist said. Whatever it was did have a great scent. A box of pralines, a pound of dark chocolate fudge, and a small bag of organic dog treats rounded out his purchases. Feeling vaguely homesick for his native Queen Victoria Market, he made his way to the Jax Brewery parking lot. He maneuvered his newly leased car through the traffic and back to Dean's house.

Letting himself in the rear gate by the key he'd been entrusted with, he failed to go undetected. The children rushed him, and the white, poufy dog, Brody's brother, immediately sniffed out the treats as quickly as Winn and DJ did the candy. He handed Winn the pralines and DJ the fudge with the caution not to open either until after dinner. Stacy came right behind to settle them down. He presented the svelte blonde, blue-eyed Stacy, the epitome of a footballer's wife, with the blossoms and dog treats. Possibly, she didn't eat sweets, but her children would.

"For Mati," he explained about the little, brown sack. At the mention of his name, the small white dog sat up in the begging position. "And for your kind hospitality. I should be out of your way by tomorrow afternoon."

"You were no trouble at all and are welcome to visit anytime. Of course, we'll probably see you at Josee and Trin's wedding in May, right?"

"I'm not sure I'm invited." Why did he feel like staring at his shoes like a boy seeking a date for a formal dance?

"The whole team is invited. I'm in the wedding party—and so is Lorena."

"Well, not exactly a team member yet and not so sure Lorena wants me there. I wouldn't want to cause a kerfuffle."

"It's up to Josee who gets invited. We both voted for you." Stacy raised the bouquet to her perfect nose and coyly inhaled its scent.

"I didn't know I was standing for office."

"We voted on giving you a second chance with Lori."

"Women do that?"

"You'd be surprised what women do to help their sisters. Unfortunately, Lori vetoed our vote. I'd say the wedding would be a good place to try to impress her again. She must be mellowing toward you by now. I mean, you are perfect for her. We all think so."

"Not her closest brothers and one of them is the groom. Not her roommate, Jude, either."

Stacy waved a long-fingered, graceful hand dismissing the naysayers. "You won't know if you don't try. The wedding is formal. Do you have a tux?"

"I've sent for it, strangely enough."

"Xochi would say there are no coincidences, but good. I'll let Josee know she needs another lobster dinner. Nothing like a wedding to restart a romance."

Despite orders, DJ had opened the fudge and gouged out a portion that went directly into his mouth. Wynn immediately told on her brother. "Mooom, Mr. Jock said not until after dinner."

"Mr. Jock is right. Hand it over." Stacy confiscated the pralines, too. "Here, give Mati one treat each. Dinner is nearly ready." With the cock of an eyebrow, she added, "But you and Lori might want to consider not having children."

Shock must have registered on his face since she continued on, "Joking. They are the lights of my life even when covered in fudge."

She made everything sound so easy when nothing about Lorena was. Perhaps, Lori didn't want the family he'd been assuming they'd have. Never had a moment to discuss that subject thoroughly when she'd asked if he wanted children while lying naked on his bed. Bloody hell, yes, he wanted children, hers. For him, she was the perfect footballer's wife, strong and athletic, dark in her beauty, mother of his offspring. Would she give him that second chance?

Chapter Twenty

He had no time to worry about future sons and daughters the way Dean kept working him and the other players who wandered in for voluntary practice. They met at six a.m. and kept it up until noon most days. Lunch with Dean, Matt, Tom, or the likable X-avier Hopkins with whom he began to plan a grand gesture.

He'd stocked his fridge with the necessities: milk, butter, eggs, bread, cold cuts, and beer, but mostly he took dinner somewhere in the Quarter. Why cook when the best food in the world could be had a block in any direction? He discovered he had the appetite to eat the whole wheel of a muffuletta, generally enough for four, and gigantic fresh seafood platters. Good thing he worked off those calories nearly every day in the week or he wouldn't fit into the custom tux which had arrived lovingly packed in tissue by Luca. Evenings, he had a nightcap at Mariah's untroubled by people who didn't know he was famous in another country. Lorena never showed, busy, he guessed, with her new job or wanting to avoid him.

"Stay cool," X-avier advised, echoing Teddy. "Let her miss you." He doubted that to be true.

May, the start of summer by another name, came on fast with still higher temperatures and more drenching humidity. Yes, it would worsen, his friends assured him, but an Aussie could take it considering summers at the bottom of the world when most sports weren't played due to the heat. But that heat was dry, he reminded himself as he changed out of soaked clothes and took a very necessary shower. At least, Dean had finally allowed him to practice in shorts.

"Hey, X, what about lunch at my place?" he asked as the lean running back primped his afro in front of a mirror. "I don't have any Devon or polony on hand, but we can swing by Central Grocery for muffulettas. Josee's wedding is coming up fast, and we need to work on plans for winning Lorena. Might be that will soften her up."

"Even if you did, I don't think I'd eat anything called polony. Sounds like Spam. I swore when I became rich, I'd never eat Spam again. And what the heck is Devon?"

"They're Australian sausages. Hard to get here evidently. So muffulettas it is." He waited impatiently for X to finish his do. His own short, sandy hair required little more than a toweling and a quick run through with a comb. "I do have some Fourex in the fridge."

"That better be beer. What do you think? Should I go cornrows for Trin's wedding?" X-avier regarded his sharp features set in a mocha complexion he liked to say was more chocolate than café au lait.

"I have no opinion on that whatsoever, but you could probably bring it off. I'll drive the Aviator and spare your Camaro any scratches in tight quarters. You run in and get the sandwiches while I circle the block."

It said a lot about the efficiency of Central Grocery or the density of French Quarter traffic that he'd had to go around only once. X handed off the two butcher paper-wrapped purchases as handily as he would have a football and vaulted into the vehicle while the queue of cars paused for a red light. At the condo, Jock used his fob to open the garage door and park inside before the Italian bread grew soggy from the olive salad heaped on top of the mound of thin-sliced cheese and cold meats. An inner staircase led up to his place.

X nodded his approval of the space. "Parking and so new you can still smell the paint."

Sometimes he thought it too new. With only himself living there and little furniture, the high ceilings echoed, and the vast open area seemed to cry out for children and dogs to fill it. He'd do his best on that.

"Great windows, but you need drapes to keep the paparazzi from filming you in a bath towel," X further commented as he roved around, taking in the details like a potential buyer.

"Right now, I'm not on their radar. I thought Lori would like it here, the location, and the newness. She can get drapes if she wants and more furniture."

"You seem about to burst with confidence about bringing her here. I don't see why you need me to help." X looked straight back to the open door of the master bedroom and ejected a soft whistle. "If she doesn't like the bed, I'll take it off your hands."

"Only thing I bought outright. I'll give you a card. Say Cal sent you. If the deal doesn't work out, I'm taking it back to Oz."

"Along with Lorena?"

"That remains to be seen. Right now, she's sore that I barged in on her family. She thinks I used her to get the tryout. Not true, but she's in a bit of a snit about it."

"Tom did mention that. He'll help because he likes you, and you aren't likely to take his or Alix's job." X eyed his physique. "I'd say they have you pegged for a tight end. That's what I played in college, but the Sinners wanted me for a speedy running back. I dropped a few pounds to play that position and ain't sorry I did. Not eating like this, though."

He told X to make himself at home and popped open two beers. They spread out the wrappings like placemats on the dining table and dug into the feast. With one-quarter of the nine-inch loaf eaten, he put out a jar of dill pickles and a bag of Zapp's Spicy Cajun Crawtators to round out the meal.

"Can't get enough of these crisps," he remarked.

"Kettle cooked potato chips from right here in Louisiana, a crawfish boil in a bag," X responded as he dug into the sack and dumped a large handful next to his meal. "Okay, we got protein, carbs, a beverage, and a vegetable." He waved a dripping pickle spear in the air. "Now how do you want to impress Lorena enough to marry you—classic romance down on one knee, an announcement at a sporting event, something with music under her window with a boombox, or what? Tell X what you got in mind."

"I'm not sure. Classic seems trite. Boombox has been done, and I can't really sing, but some big arena isn't special enough for Lori."

"And really embarrassing if she says no in front of thousands."

"There is that. Back in Melbourne, I told my mate I'd walk five-thousand miles across the outback in summer for her. Maybe we can work with that. You know that song 'I'm Gonna Be' about walking five-hundred miles to fall down at her door but change the lyrics to five-thousand miles. Here, I printed out the song and thought maybe you could sing it for me, then I'd propose." Suddenly, the remaining half of the muffuletta lost its appeal. He'd face the meanest bastard on any team without a qualm, but proposing to Lori sent a trickle of cold sweat down his back. He'd left the printout on the kitchen counter, got up, and handed it to X-avier.

"Yeah, I know the song by The Proclaimers, a Scottish group." X studied the sheets. "This part about falling down drunk next to her isn't very romantic."

"But there's an Aussie feel about the song, and it says exactly what I want to say to Lorena. Not the drunk part. We'd leave that out, and the havering. I thought that meant vomiting, but it turns out it's only talking foolishly. Otherwise, I do want to wake up next to her every day, give her all I have, and grow old with her. Will you sing it for me? This has to work."

X took another swig of beer and shook his head. "My voice is too light for this."

"We'll think of something else." His optimism failed. Wrapping the remaining half of the sandwich in its paper, he stowed it in the fridge. No need to go out to dinner tonight, but a couple of drinks at Mariah's might help.

X took no notice as he continued to study the song. "Matt Keaton has a nice rich baritone that would work. But you need more than one man singing for a true Grand Gesture. What you need is a troop of marching men. The whole team in heavy boots pounding out the beat. Even the most frog-throated can do the da-da-das. We leave out the more elaborate stuff. I did something similar for Teddy's wedding, and have songs planned for Trin's, but this will be spectacular."

"You certain Trin won't mind if you do this for me. I'm not his favorite bloke. Fact, some of the team members aren't very keen on me either."

"Those are the ones afraid that you'll take their jobs. The threat of a talented new guy being signed makes us all work harder. As for Trin, after all I did for him, no way he's going to diss me. That's why I'm the best man. If you make Lori happy, Trinity will come around eventually." After another study of the song, X looked up and stated, "You have to sing the chorus."

He chugged the last of his beer. "Ah, yeah—no. Don't think I can, mate."

"When actors can't sing, they just chant the words. You can do that nice and loud, right?"

"For Lori, I could. I will."

Having finished his lunch, X wadded his sandwich paper into a ball and lofted it into the kitchen sink. "I'll take these sheets with me. It's going to be work and lots of rehearsal. I think I can get most of the guys who do voluntary practice to stay the afternoons and help out, especially if Dean and Tom are on board."

"You think Dean will do it? He seems kind of straightlaced."

"Tom tells me he once dressed up like a cheerleader to help him with Alix. The man can do unexpected things on and off the field when it comes to teammates, and the others will follow along. Tom is always good for any gag."

"It's not a gag. I'm dead serious."

"Sure, you are. I hope to be so nuts over a woman someday that I don't even ask for a prenup." With a grin, X gathered the pages and awaited his ride back to his red Camaro.

They were on the road in more ways than one.

Chapter Twenty-One

Jock walked along the gilded gallery of the Roosevelt Hotel ornamented by potted palms in huge jardinières to the reception room where Sinatra once crooned, and Louis Armstrong wailed on his trumpet. Not overwhelmed by the huge troupe of bridesmaids and men in formal wear, he reentered the famous Blue Room after a quick trip to the loo. As a celebrity in his native land, he'd been to plenty of high-class affairs. Hence, the custom tuxedo he wore. He eyed the crowd, still thick after the meal, that had started around three-hundred and dwindled only a little since.

The reception of Josee and Trin was the extravaganza he'd expected. A live band played on the dais. Towering flower arrangements dominated by white roses tipped in pink decorated the tables. The remains of the lobster and steak dinner with fancy chocolate mousse served in crystal cups for dessert were being cleared. Tiny golden boxes of truffles to take home remained. A bottle of decent champagne left in a cooler sat stationed at every table to be replenished as needed, compliments of Mariah Coy. Posh, very posh, indeed.

As promised, all the Sinners were welcome. Now he had only to sign the contract hammered out so laboriously by Joe Billodeaux's recommended agent to become one permanently—at least for the next year.

Yet he hesitated. Holding out for more money, the agent asked? Nope. Offered two million for one year of his services plus the incredible twelve million as a signing bonus, how could he complain about such a bonzer deal? If he didn't live up to the footy films he'd supplied that showed his athleticism and determination to win even if the watchers had no idea what the game was all about, he deserved to be sent home. However, as he understood, that twelve million was his to keep. He wanted to tell Lori, but she might already know. The word had come through just the day before this event.

Of course, he hadn't been invited to the actual wedding ceremony as he wasn't family or close friend. Yet he told himself, yet. Fifty select people had gathered lakeside at the bride's home for the nuptials, the other two-hundred-fifty invited to the reception only. Not that the party lacked anything a guest could want.

He'd had no chance to get near Lori as a photographer herded her from one spot to another with the rest of the large wedding party. Merely getting them all lined up for any shot seemed to take hours: around the gigantic but tasteful wedding cake shrouded in white lace icing, arrayed in front of the flower-bedecked head table, bouquets still in hand, watching the first dance of the bride and groom, and so on. He wondered if Lori wanted such a wedding. He'd be happy with a barbecue at the ranch, but bride's choice.

He had gained a dance with the gorgeous bride, catching Trinity's scowl out of the corner of his eye, but Josee had been gracious. He'd admired her engagement ring, an Australian opal, one of the milky variety, but huge. An heirloom stone, she'd called it.

Each bridesmaid wore a similar but small pendant of the same courtesy of Lorena. Recalling watching her clean out the jewelry counter at the airport made him smile, but he doubted if Lori remembered that flight as fondly. He must get her alone while glamourous romance filled the air.

X had warned him against making any move before his Grand Gesture. To let her believe he'd given up enhanced his chances of delighted surprise, X's words, not his, but X as best man couldn't keep an eye on his actions. Most of the folks he knew here were in the wedding party. Very sensibly, he'd been placed at a table with other bachelor Sinners who hadn't brought a plus one. All of them seemed intent on rooting one of Josee's model friends, but in the meantime, they needed to amuse themselves. He drew on his special party skills and summoned a waiter for a tray of clean champagne glasses and another bottle of Mariah's finest.

Building a pyramid of crystal, making sure each glass had enough of an opening to receive some bubbly, he carefully poured the wine into the uppermost flute. As it overflowed, the champagne cascaded down the sides into each glass and ended filling in the last in the bottom with not a drop wasted on the tablecloth. He'd learned from the best, his partner in vintages, Luca, and knew exactly the number of glasses needed and the volume of fluid. His audience applauded. He began at the top and dismantled his creation, placing the glasses into waiting hands. He seized the last one for himself, not that he hadn't consumed plenty already. His hands remained steady, but his feet felt like dancing.

Had Lori noticed the trick? No, she danced with

one of Trinity's gaggle of dags, all decked out in ill-fitting tuxedos like ungainly penguins. He swore the bloke breathed in the space between her breasts and danced with his eyes closed, letting her lead. Enough of this bulldust! He'd wait no longer, Grand Gesture or none.

He strode across the floor and tapped the dweeb's shoulder. Looming over the nerd like a killer whale homing in on its favorite prey, he said, "Excuse me. May I cut in?"

"No cuts," Lorena answered.

The poor little geek looked from one intimidating figure to the other. He swallowed hard. "Happy to step aside. Save another one for me, Lori."

"Not if you don't stand up to this—this tosser."

She could have come up with a worse Aussie term or added bloody to it. She must be in a good mood, as mellowed by champagne as himself. He gave the guy more incentive to retreat with a feral orca grin

"I think I'll ask Edie. She's more my size." The dag disappeared quickly as if someone had hit his delete key.

"That was both mean and rude. It probably took him an hour to work up the courage to ask me."

"If he'd stood up to me, I'd have stepped aside. Besides, he was sniffing your cleavage." Taking in a quick whiff, he said, "You do smell terrific."

"Some expensive French perfume Josee gave each of her bridesmaids."

"Worth whatever she paid for it. You think I didn't need to buck up my courage to come over here?"

"Not with your overwhelming self-confidence."

They were beginning to block other dancers, their

combative stance the start of a scene. He didn't want to do that to Josee and mar her wedding. "Just the end of this dance. We don't want to upset the nuptials. I have something great to tell you."

"Fine," she huffed and allowed him to hold her at arm's length as they began to move together.

"My contract is settled. As soon as I sign it, I'm a Sinner for a year at a mere two million."

"That is mere for what you can do. Don't sign."

He took advantage of her outrage on his behalf to draw her closer, near enough to whisper in her ear. "With a twelve million dollar signing bonus."

Her smile emerged brilliantly and genuinely happy for him. "That's more like it."

Lori raised her arms to hug his shoulders. He linked his around her waist and drew her against his chest. Her head rested there as if they were in bed together. His hand stroked her hair down to the braided bun at her nape. How he wished to untangle it and strip the gown of palest pink off her shoulder to pool on the floor. Right here, right now.

He turned them toward an exit and caught sight of Trinity coming down off the second tier of the ballroom with his face full of determination. Fortunately, well-wishers impeded the groom on his way, and his former boss insisted he sit with him and his wife for a moment. Then X-avier mounted the dais and captured a mic. He presented a husky black woman, her hair in cornrows that matched his, as Caressa. She wore hot pink with attitude. The two intended to perform a series of duets, starting with "Unforgettable" in honor of the bride and groom. "Would the guests please clear the dance floor and let the happy couple come forth to dance?" X requested. He'd be busy for a while.

The moment couldn't be more perfect. Jock danced out the door into the gallery shining with gilt. He'd heard X sing at the rehearsals and joined to Caressa's voice, pure magic. No one would notice their absence or leave before they returned.

Lori's head jerked up. "Why are we out here? The dance is over."

"It's just beginning." He dug out the key card he'd gotten earlier in the evening when the emcee announced that rooms had been set aside compliments of the bride and groom for those who had come far or felt they were in no condition to drive home. He'd cadged one early, hoping she'd soften toward him—and she had. Perhaps. Because now Lorena pulled away from his embrace.

"You think because they're paying you fourteen million dollars, you can have me, too?"

"Not a bit. If I can't have you, I don't want their offer."

"You'd better take that room. You must be drunk. And if you say drunk on you, I'll slap your face." She quivered with outrage—or some other emotion.

"I was going to say not too drunk to perform. Why can't you believe I want you more than a big contract?" This wasn't going well. He had to act before she left him hard and alone. Twirling Lori behind an ornate pillar shrouded by a palm on one side, he laid his lips on hers, not too hard in case she bit him, but firmly, asking for her response. She answered him with equal pressure, equal desire. Her lips moved against his.

"What did you say?"

"I said one more time won't matter, only once more."

"Righty-O, we'll start with that." He pushed back a palm frond to lead her away but ducked when he saw Mack coming down the corridor with one of the model bridesmaids, the leggy redhead, not the brunette. He'd danced with them both, but neither compared to Lorena. "Wait. Mack is passing with a woman."

She glanced out the small space he'd made. "Catriona. I noticed you danced with the models but never came near me, and I thought you'd finally gotten over us. I heard them later discussing which of them you'd bed tonight. They were considerably more interested when Mack told them you were the next big thing in football."

Ah, so X had been right. By staying away, she'd had time to miss him. Jealous, perhaps? "Sorry to disappoint them, but I only want you. Coast is clear. Let's go."

They sped to an elevator and rode it to a beautiful but modest room featuring a two-poster queen-sized bed, understated furnishings, and black and white photos of the city on the walls. He wished he'd reserved a luxury suite. "Want to go to my new place? It's got a better bed," he asked.

"No time for that. I have to be back to see the bride and groom off on their honeymoon." She tore at his bow tie, opened his jacket.

He understood this wasn't going to be slow and gentle sex but rather tearing off the clothes sex. Her gown, a long, silky column, slid down her hips with ease. Under it, amazingly few undergarments, a suggestion of a bra, a wisp of a panty, until she stood only in her pink high heels and the opal necklace. Her hands loosened the cummerbund. He moved her back to lie on the bed while he struggled with the rest of the formal dress impediments. She toed off shoes that added four inches to her height and parted her legs.

He couldn't get out of his shirt with its studs fast enough and simply shed the slacks, the shoes, the socks, the black briefs, and joined her. She ran her hands under the shirt, stroking his muscles, taut with desire—as was what jutted out from under the shirttail. Her nails, kept short, still scored his back.

He'd palmed the condom he'd brought along in hope as his pants slid down and applied it now before going any farther. No telling what came next, but he had to slow down, give her pleasure first. Not easy when she'd begun to stroke his balls. Removing her hands, he held them over her head and applied himself to laving her nipples, making a trail down her center to where he swore he could feel her throb, so wet and ready he might have stopped right there.

Instead, he used his tongue to bring her to orgasm, careful not to do the same himself. While she still gasped from the pleasure, he turned her over and slid beneath her body. With his hands on her hips, he mounted her on his erection. She didn't move, still having aftershocks that he experienced as small squeezes against his penis. He could wait as she lay on his chest.

He busied his hands, removing the pins that held her hair so tightly coiled like the tiger snake he'd once compared it to. Then he unraveled her braid, his fingers parting each strand until they covered their bodies in black waves. Lori rose and moved slow, fast, faster. He hung on until he felt her come, and let go with the greatest relief at last. She continued to rock gently against him, her eyes closed and unreadable. Finally, she sank onto his chest again and rested, slept. He let her stay as long as she wanted to be there, the first of many times together, he hoped.

He felt the movement of her lashes against his nipple. Her eyes flickered open. She barely raised her head, and damn the clock on the nightstand. Lori swung from the bed. "I'll be late. We have to form an aisle and do the confetti poppers in fifteen minutes."

She raked her clothes from the floor and raced to the bathroom, slammed the door. He heard the sound of running water as she washed and a loud curse followed by, "My hair, what did you do to my hair? Everyone will know what we've been up to." She flung the door open and started for the exit, turning to face him before entering the hall.

"Tell them that heavy bun gave you a headache," he suggested, unable to hold in his grin. She looked amazing in her fury, so flushed beneath that fading tan, her dark eyes full of fire like the black opals of Australia.

One of her long fingers pointed his way. "Good idea. Just remember, this was a once and done. It will not happen again. I had too much champagne, that's why."

"Another good excuse, but I don't believe it."

"Believe."

"Oh, I will." He'd believe in having Lorena in his bed for the rest of his life. Unlike Cinderella, she scooped up both her shoes and raced toward the elevator.

He took his time reassembling his formal garb but didn't bother with the tie, letting it dangle Sinatra style loose around his neck. At the elevator, he ran into Mack similarly disheveled. For the first time, Lori's brother smiled at him.

"Catriona was smokin' hot. How about Katinka?"

How he wanted to say not as hot as your sister, but no sense getting pounded on in the hall. Let Mack believe they shared the same low morals. "I had a bonzer time," he answered.

They rode downward in companionable silence. In the ballroom, the confetti had settled, little puffs of it rising as the last of the guests assembled their small boxes of cake with the wedding date on it golden lettering and other take-home items. He searched for Lorena, but exactly like Cinderella, she had disappeared.

Chapter Twenty-Two

"Oh, man!" X-avier moaned. "You did exactly what I told you not to do. Made contact too soon." He tried to rake his hands through his afro and found the wedding cornrows in place instead.

Up until now, he'd been a welcome Sunday guest, sharing greasy bags of beignets and café au lait at Jock's table. Nearly noon. Everyone slept late after the lavish and long reception. Lorena hadn't answered his two phone calls, he told X. Probably had it turned off to get some rest. He demolished another doughnut and let the powdered sugar fall where it may.

"She slept with me, X. She wanted me as much as I wanted her. I have the scratch marks to prove it."

"Repeat to me what she said before you went up to the room." X knocked most of the sugar off his beignet and took a single bite.

"Something like, 'One more time won't matter,' and after that, it was 'a once and done'."

"Don't that tell you it's over. She satisfied her itch, and she's done."

"Lori didn't mean it." His stubborn optimism kicked in hard. "What makes you such an authority on women anyhow?"

"Raised by a single mother, a granny, and four aunts who sat around the kitchen table drinking coffee and talking about men as if I weren't in the room from

224

the time I could understand. Lots of valuable lessons learned. I don't know if the Grand Gesture will work now."

"I'll bet my arse it will. Is the team ready to go because I'd like to bring it off this coming Saturday before she forgets last Saturday."

"Not as polished as I'd like, but we have five more days to practice. If you were as good as you claim, she'll never forget it."

Jock thought he detected doubt in X's voice, but he barged on making plans. "I'll reserve the team bus to get everyone out to the ranch by mid-afternoon. After she accepts my proposal, we all go to dinner at Junior's place, open bar, my shout."

"How do you plan to get Lorena to the ranch? She lives here now."

"Teddy is creative. I'll give him a ring. Which reminds me, I have a private appointment to look at engagement rings this afternoon at Schifferman's."

"Dean always says you can't go wrong with Leslie, but maybe you should wait until she accepts and let her pick her own."

He shook his head at that. "No, I offer her the ring at the end of the song,"

"You could use an empty box and just not open it."

"I know exactly what I want to give her. They might have to special order, so it needs to be attended to now."

"Your funeral."

He checked his watch and considered the powdered sugar snow on his black Sinners T-shirt. "Get out of here with your negative vibes. I need to change before I see Leslie. But, X, really, I couldn't do the Grand

Gesture without your help. You're a real cobber."

"That better be a good thing."

"A best mate."

"I try. You sign that lush contract yet?"

"No, I'll get around to it."

"Fourteen million dollars, and he'll get around to it. Best of luck with Lori, my friend, best of luck. Don't call her again."

****

After changing into black slacks and a dress shirt open at the collar, he proceeded to the elegant black glass embellished with a gold S doors of Schifferman's. He entered precisely at one p.m. From what he'd heard of the legendary Leslie, the man would appreciate his punctuality. Idiotic to be intimidated by a jewelry salesman, but he admitted he was. Behind the counter, way to the rear, the small man waited, meticulously dressed, silver hair groomed to perfection, mustache exquisitely trimmed. The super clerk did not smile as Jock made his way past case after case of watches, necklaces with colored gems, and place settings for the brides-to-be. He stopped by a display of Australian opals, but none would do for Lorena. Moving on, he arrived in front of the god of engagement rings.

"Mr. Leslie, I presume. G'day."

The clerk tilted his head. "Simply Leslie."

Sounded like a bloody perfume for men. He put out a hand, and it swallowed Leslie's cold fingers for a brief shake. "Jock Brown, soon to be a Sinner."

In New Orleans, that could mean many things, but Leslie understood immediately. "Referred by the Billodeauxs, no doubt."

"Righty-O. Were you able to find what I wanted? I

didn't see anything close in that case of opals."

"I have scoured the vaults of all our stores and believe I have what you want." With a flourish of the wrist, Leslie drew a black velvet ring box from under the counter. "I hope this will do. A superb black opal mounted in platinum with two accent diamonds on either side and a sprinkling of smaller stones nestled in the custom design of the setting."

"An heirloom gem?" he asked, having picked up the term from Josee.

"Absolutely, though opals are far more fragile than diamonds." Leslie handed him the ring to inspect. "The setting is a bit heavy, and I am not familiar with Miss Billodeaux. If you like, we can choose another for the stone."

"No, she has strong hands and can handle this." He turned the ring this way and that, bringing out the fire beneath the black surface. The smaller diamonds caught in the twists and folds of the setting reminded him of the stars over the outback in summer and the song he'd sing to Lori. The clerk talked about carats and clarity, but he barely heard. This was the ring, dark and full of colorful depths like her.

"I'll take it." He drew out his badly abused credit card. The car and furniture rental, that great big bed, the substantial deposit on his living space pushed it toward its rather high limit. He held his breath while Leslie checked his credit and exhaled when it was accepted.

"I must say that you and Mr. Trinity know what you want." The clerk wrapped and deposited the ring in a tiny black and gold bag.

"Maybe the only thing we have in common. I'm an Aussie, you see. Only an Australian opal for me."

"As I divined. My best wishes to you and Miss Billodeaux."

"Thanks. Have a cracker day." Jock turned on his heels and marched out, murmuring the altered chorus of "I'm Gonna Be" as Leslie faded into the background.

Chapter Twenty-Three

Lorena wondered why her mother needed her help with a mutual birthday party in mid-May for Matt and Annie's two toddler boys, Daniel and Gabriel, at the ranch. Of course, she would have driven the three hours for the party scheduled on Sunday, not being held at Matt's Garden District house with the big lawn because her mom said she didn't want her dad trailering ponies to the festivities as he'd done the previous year. Considering that Jessie lived on the property and Xochi not far away, not to mention Corazon, who had baked something that smelled delicious before her arrival and stashed it away for the party, Mom really did not need her help.

But here she sat filling red and black balloons from a helium tank, an odd choice for little ones, but not these children who at their early age already mouthed, "Go Sinners" with gusto. She had questioned the need to do this when the party place in Lafayette could have supplied the balloon bouquets, and been snapped at by her mother. "They charge too much. Mawmaw would say, throwing away money on stuff we can do ourselves." As if the Billodeauxs were penniless. Regardless, a cake bought from Pommier's bakery in Chapelle waited in a box so sealed with tape and string that no one would be tempted to dab a finger in the frosting.

Her dad, T-Rex, and Teddy lounged by a party urn of coffee on the kitchen counter and discussed which ponies to saddle for the event, helping themselves at will, while Jesse and Edie worked the balloons into bunches. Stacy and Annie, also early arrivals, stayed upstairs, keeping the children occupied and out of the way or balloon mayhem might have ensued. They said their husbands would be along later after they settled some Sinners business.

Jude had declined the invitation based on having to study. Of course, Trin and Josee were still on their honeymoon at the usual undisclosed location. Mack never drove from Dallas for anything as paltry as a kiddie party. Otherwise, the whole clan was in attendance except Tom and Alix, who planned on coming tomorrow, they'd said, instead of riding with her and Stacy and the kids.

She heard a rumbling noise and glanced out the kitchen window. A perfect, sunny afternoon filled with the mockingbird's crazy mating song presented itself. Still, it might be thunder in the distance as Louisiana weather could reverse itself in a matter of minutes. Xochi, who had gone upstairs to change KC's diaper, dashed into the kitchen despite the burden of the large baby on her hip. "You've got to come upstairs and see this."

"Just a minute." She tied off a black balloon and handed it over to be added to the bunch. "What's up?"

"You have to see for yourself." Xo reversed and headed for the stairs with KC laughing at the wild ride.

Edie needed no invitation. She followed with her phone in hand, ready to photograph anything newsworthy as usual. Reluctantly, Lori arose and came along, hoping the excitement wasn't an impending tornado or simply the arrival of yet another pony for the grandkids. Her parents brought up the rear with Teddy, Jesse, and Corazon going outside to watch whatever.

She'd been feeling low since waking last Sunday as if she'd done something wrong when she hadn't, being a fully grown woman who knew what she wanted—most times. Jock had called twice while she slept off the wedding, and Jude let both go to voice mail. He wanted to see her again. Saturday night meant so much to him. Most guys wouldn't bother to call after a one-night stand because that's all it was, let alone say such sweet things, but she would not be lured into answering. Work and physical activity kept her thoughts occupied all week, and this party had the potential to lift her mood. She'd be fine and free of Jock Brown, the man who had humiliated her at the going away party, just when she thought she'd have to hurry back to Australia before he forgot about her, fooling herself that he cared.

She went to her old lavender and lace bedroom, where she stayed the night and moved out to the gallery. Xo and Edie stood in front of Teddy's room. At the other end of the long balcony, her mom and dad with Stacy, Annie, and the children clumped together. All gazed toward the source of the rumbling noise as it rounded the curve in the drive and entered the straightaway to the house. At least half of the Sinners team in their red jerseys, black slacks, and very heavy boots marched along, Dean, Tom, Alix, and Junior among them.

Jock led in a freshly pressed tuxedo, oh, and he looked so great in one, part of the problem on Saturday evening. The sunlight blessed his hair with a surfer's corona, and even from this distance, his eyes shone the green of summer leaves. X-avier Hopkins and Matt flanked him. With military precision, the group wheeled and faced her. X turned and directed the marching to a softer step while Jock moved forward. She should have run inside and locked the door immediately, but she stood there transfixed as he began to chant, sort of.

I would march five-thousand miles
And I'd march five-thousand more
In the outback, in the outback
In the summer, in the summer
To collapse before your door.

Da da da da, da da da da, the group shouted. X motioned for the marching to cease, and Matt Keaton began to sing. Annie had told her of his amazing voice, one that lulled all the babies in the NICU where they'd met during her infrequent phone calls to Australia. In a strong baritone, he sang a verse about being lonely and dreaming of her, going out and always coming home with her, of being the man who'd grow old with her. All the while he motioned to Jock, making it clear for whom he sang. She absolutely would not be brought to tears. A couple of hard blinks took care of that.

Da da da da, da da da da. More marching. Jock reprised what he'd said before and ended by falling on his knees. X gestured for all other sound to cease. Jock held out a black velvet box, Schifferman's for sure, and flipped the lid with one big thumb. The sunlight caught in the diamonds and lit the fire of the central black opal from within, a magnificent ring, a ring for a better person than she.

"Lorena Billodeaux, will you have me for your husband?"

The mockingbird ceased its mating call, and Lil, the ranch dog, stopped barking at the intrusion. In this void of silence, she could only say one thing, and the score would be even between them. "No."

Gasps and cries followed as she turned and slammed the French door, locking it and leaning hard against the panes as if he'd try to scale the balcony and drag her away. Maybe she wished that he would. That didn't happen. The doors in Teddy's room still stood open, and she heard Jock's voice as strong as when he'd proposed.

"We gave it a good go, mates, the best mates a man could have, but you heard the lady. The bus is waiting to take you to Junior's restaurant. Food and drink, my shout. Order whatever you like. I'll be along shortly."

She didn't see where he went because Xo and Edie stood in the adjoining doorway that connected the rooms through the bath. Tears rolled down Edie's childish round cheeks. Xochi stared directly at her, those usually warm brown eyes penetrating as if dissecting her soul. Probably only her aura. She'd never pressed Xochi to "read" her, but her sister did it now.

"This is awful, Lorena. I saw a man's aura change from pink to gray in seconds."

"What does that mean?"

"Profound sadness. I've seen it once or twice before a death."

"Jock is tough. He'll get over it. Now he knows how it feels to be embarrassed in front of all your friends."

"Was what happened in Australia really as bad as

this?"

She tried to be honest. "Maybe not, but he won't be bothering me anymore."

"I don't expect he will, but you did care for him, and little parts of you have died, too."

"Oh, for heaven's sake, what garbage." This had all been a setup, the whole family in on it except the missing few. She had some people to tell off and proceeded directly to the kitchen where she knew they'd be gathered.

Just before entering, she heard Corazon say, "Is okay. We use this for the party tomorrow. The babies will not care."

All eyes turned her way as she came through the door. She paused, taking in the entire scene: the table bedecked with the two balloon bouquets, a silver tray of Corazon's Mexican wedding cookies between them, and a cake with whatever had been inscribed in red icing now smeared and swirled into the white topping, unreadable. Their faces said "death in the family," but there had been none, not really.

"What did you expect me to do? Marry a man I don't love or even like to please all of you?"

Her father spoke first, as dreary as if one of his own sons had died. "At least when your mother turned me down the first time, she did it in private. To do that to a man in front of his team…"

"You could have accepted, then told him no later and spared him that awful embarrassment after all his efforts. I thought you were a kinder person," her mother said.

Her dad had taken to Jock like a kindred soul, but her mother's judgment hurt more. "You know he used y'all to get on the Sinners team and me only for an introduction to Dad."

She couldn't believe that T-Rex, not out of high school yet dared to chip in with his opinion. "Aw, you know no one needs an introduction to Dad, and from what I hear about that workout, he'd have made the team no matter when he performed for the coaches."

"But he didn't know this. He used me. I hate him."

Xo arrived, a little out of breath from hauling KC around. "She's lying. She does have feelings for him."

"I'd have married him in a minute; he was so nice to me. From what she said when the women were together, he's really good in…" Edie tried to add.

"Hush!" their mother said. "The deed is done and not well."

"You all conspired to get me here for a fake birthday party, and you talk about bad deeds."

"There will be a party for the boys tomorrow. The adults can drink the champagne chilling in the refrigerator. We hoped to have a little family congratulation party after the proposal before joining everyone at Junior's restaurant. It's over and done now. Lori has the right to her make her own decision," her mom said, smoothing the troubled waters as she so often did.

"I'm going to my room. I don't know if I'll be here tomorrow or not."

"Don't take it out on my boys. They need to get to know their auntie," sweet Annie beseeched.

"We'll see." She marched out of the kitchen to the heavy beat of her own drummer, more of a death knell than a celebration, and passed Stacy trying to get downstairs with her two children locked to her legs and demanding to see the ponies.

"Big mistake, Lori."

"Know-it-all. You've always been one."

"Sheesh, let the wicked witch pass."

"Where's a witch?" DJ asked, peering down the stairs.

"Maybe in the barn where the ponies are," his sister suggested.

"See what you've started." Lorena lashed her long braid back and forth as she shook her head and ran up the rest of the steps.

With everyone safely downstairs now, she locked all the entrances to her bedroom and flung herself on the mattress for a good, long cry. She should have been jubilant, but merely felt empty, bereft, now that it was truly over. She'd barely let a tear drop when Brody crawled from under the lavender dust ruffle and jumped up beside her. He trembled as he licked the wetness from her cheeks.

"Sorry, sorry. I forgot you were afraid of thunder. The bad men scared you, didn't they?" He barked as if agreeing, but then jumped down and whined at the hall door.

"Really, you need to go now?" She opened the door. "Go find Edie to take you outside."

Brody didn't budge but whined plaintively. Some things were more urgent than tears. She went down the stairs again, and turned toward the grand front door with its beveled windows, a way out rarely used by the family who still talked in the kitchen. Turning the deadbolt ever so softly, she cracked the door to allow Brody his freedom. The pouf of a dog raced out, pushing it wider.

Jock Brown sat on the bench in front of the graves of the previous ranch dogs, his back to her. Diamond Lil had her black head on his knee. Though hunched over as if punched in the gut, he stroked her floppy ears. Leaping up on the bench, Brody joined them, kissing his cheek with an enthusiastic tongue. Did everyone feel sorry for Jock?

Did she? Was this awful feeling in her stomach regret, not anger? Perhaps, she should apologize for making a fool of him, though he never had to her. Come on, Lori, she chided herself. Be the bigger person, not the wicked witch. Still, crossing the deep porch and going down those three steps took all the resolve she had left. As she moved toward the bench, Brody betrayed her with a sharp yap that brought Jock's head up from its hunched position.

"Off, Brody." She took the dog's place as he finally went to do his business. Leaving a safe space between them, she made herself say the words. "I'm sorry. What I did was cruel—but no more so than making a fool of me in front of my friends."

"Not my doing. Angus blurted out what I wanted to tell you and didn't get the time—that I did want to meet the great Joe Billodeaux and have a go at the Sinners, but that wasn't all. Didn't you hear me say you were more important to me than that?"

"I did, but believed you lied."

"No, I wanted to court you like a princess and ran out of time. Then you were on your way home and without giving me a chance to speak. I thought you didn't mean the things you said to me about quitting and going back to Australia. I suppose because even the worse situations have always turned out well for me in the end. Cockeyed optimist." He gave her one of his irresistible grins. Only this one did not reach full-blown and skewed to one side.

"I believe you now. A girl who loves tiny penguins and platypuses wouldn't hurt any creature she cared for. I can't marry you, Lori, but I can give you what you want. I called the agent and told him I wouldn't sign the contract. I'm going back to Australia, my team, my mates, my brothers. I was willing to leave them all behind for you."

"That's insane! You'd give up fourteen million dollars, American, and the chance to play for the best team in the league because I rejected you?"

"Not about the money. I proved I could get into the NFL. Without you, that's enough. No worries. The Pies will have me back. Their new ruckman can't jump as high as a roo and takes a hit like a baby koala. I'll most likely get more money, Australian money."

He stood, rising far above her. "A lot I need to do—get over to the restaurant and let the lads have a go at razzing me for being such a drongo first. Then I have to turn in the Aviator and try to wriggle out of my lease, get rid of my furniture. X will take the bed. I don't want it anymore. I'll see about getting a ticket home." He surveyed the live oaks, the mansion, the two dogs who listened to his every word with their heads cocked. "Bonzer here, though." He started to walk away.

"Wait! Do you need a ride?" She could do that for him, but it seemed like delivering a bull to slaughter. "And you aren't a drongo." He'd used the Aussie word for idiot.

"Big-time drongo. No, the Aviator is around the bend. I thought we'd be going there together." She couldn't discern any hope in his voice, though she'd called to him.

Jock dug in his pocket. "Almost forgot this." Not coming closer, he tossed her the ring box.

She caught it easily and took a closer look at its contents. "God, it is beautiful. Leslie?" she asked.

"I told him what I wanted, and he tracked it down for me. I usually know exactly what I want. I've learned now that doesn't always work out, does it? It's yours. Keep it. You can wear it on your right hand. No other woman should own it. Hooroo."

He turned and left before she could protest the gift, its cost, its meaning, his stride so wide he knew she couldn't catch up. Not that she tried, but stood there nearly paralyzed with something precious in her hands.

Chapter Twenty-Four

Her mother never lied. Sunday did bring a birthday party for the boys. No need to invite more guests with eight of the grandchildren there, and Dre and her son, Drew, showing up early, and surprisingly, Jude later. No one brought up yesterday or made a single ugly comment to her, but she spied Edie showing Dre something on her phone and heard the exclamation, "Oh, wow!" and a glance her way. Sometimes, she forgot that while Dre had a son, she was only a year older than Edie. She passed near their huddle and overheard, "I wish I could have seen that ring up close." "Me, too."

Why shrink from what she'd done? "It's on my dresser. He gave it to me before he left. Yes, it is spectacular."

"Watch Drew for me, Annie." Dre ran off with Edie to satisfy their curiosity. The other women might have liked to do the same, but showed adult restraint.

"Always," Annie replied. "I watch Drew while she takes her college classes. He's like one of my own. So nice of Jock to give you the ring. Most men would want it for a refund."

"Jock Brown isn't most men," Lori acknowledged.

Stacy joined their group. "I tried to tell you that. If you'd seen how hard he worked with Dean and how good he is with kids and dogs. Are you going to call me a know-it-all again?"

"If you refrain from calling me a witch and scaring your children, no."

"They'd probably be thrilled if you were—though they were a little afraid of Dre in her Goth stage."

Jude intruded. "I've come to your rescue. Leave her alone. She made the right decision. Not every woman wants a husband and kids and shouldn't be badgered into it.

But she did, not that she'd ever tell career-devoted Jude. Saved by the call to the little table under the live oaks where two-year-old Daniel and one-year-old Gabe sat on either end of the big sheet cake modified by thick wax candles showing their ages. Because Drew felt left out, though he'd had his party back in January, her mom seated him in the middle like a little yellow chick between two dark ducklings. The others sang the birthday song and urged the boys to blow out their single candles. "Cake?" said Daniel, the most verbal of the three.

"Dig in," their Pawpaw Joe urged, camera at the ready.

Gabe went face first into the red velvet under the frosting. The older and more sophisticated Daniel simply gouged out a piece with his hand while Drew scooped just the icing into his mouth. Pictures were taken and shown around, but she suspected Edie had captured the ring on hers as she heard exclamations that appeared to have nothing to do with the cuteness of cake-covered children.

The moms cut pieces from the far side of the sheet for the rest of the kids, and after cleaning up messy faces, turned the party over to the men who had the ponies saddled for riding. Wynn, the first-born granddaughter, raced to the barn to claim the elegant white horse she'd gotten on her first birthday. Except for DJ who always wanted the pinto, the others had no idea of preferences yet. Junior hefted his big son onto a hip and took Pilar's little hand to give his wife a break. Lorena claimed his seat next to Xochi in the shade where the women settled with coffee and Mexican wedding cakes.

"I need to know. How bad was it at the restaurant? Did Junior say?"

"I asked. Actually, the team came through for Jock. Many condolences and slaps on the back and guarantees that when he played for the Sinners, he'd have his pick of the babes."

"He didn't tell them, then. He really didn't give up his contract for me."

"The only ones who know that right now are Dean and Junior. He told them after the others had gone and asked that they not divulge it until he left for Australia. I doubt they'll be as sympathetic when they find out. Dad got a call when you went to your room and didn't look too happy, but he said nothing. I suspect his agent contacted him. You know our father. He's hoping Jock will change his mind."

"Xo, I think I've made a terrible mistake. First thing tomorrow, I'm going to find Jock and tell him I believe in him—and us. Oh God, I don't know where he lives, and I erased his number from my phone. Stacy!"

"What?" She poured chilled champagne into the plastic flutes held out by the rest of the women, Brinsley having the day off.

"I need Jock's address and phone number."

"Because I know it all?"

"Yes, because you do. Is that my congratulatory champagne?"

"Someone should enjoy it. Want a piece of the cake that read Best Wishes to the Happy Couple?"

"I don't think I could eat right now. Some champagne, please. Did you know only wine from that region of France should be called champagne? Everything else is sparkling wine. Jock owns half a vineyard. He taught me that."

Stacy poured for her, then perused the label. "Sparkling wine it is. I think I did know." She placed the half-empty bottle on a small table and found her phone. "Here, write it down on a napkin. Better yet put it in your phone. Don't lose it between here and New Orleans."

"I won't, but I don't have a car. When are you and Dean leaving?"

"Not until tomorrow when the children are over their sugar high. It takes forever for us to get going with all the kid stuff. Sorry. If I were you, I'd be on my way, well, hours ago. Maybe Mom will lend hers."

"She has patients tomorrow."

A set of car keys dangled in front of her face held by an unexpected source. Dre said, "That engagement ring is prettier than Josee's, and I saw what Jock did to get you to marry him on Edie's phone. You'd better go to New Orleans ASAP and tell him you changed your mind. It's the silver Lexus with the car seat in the back parked in the shade by the front entrance."

"You're right, Dre. If I can return the favor sometime…"

"I need it back for a ten o'clock class, but I doubt anything so romantic will ever happen to me. You know, a young woman with a kid."

"Don't sell yourself short. It's early years for you. Oh, I got each of the boys giant Lego sets. There's one for Drew, too, so there won't be any jealousy."

"Nice of you when you hardly know him. But run, run, don't lose Jock!"

"Xo, Stacy, tell everyone I'm off to New Orleans. I'll call." She raced across the lawn on her long legs and startled Corazon arranging a pile of gifts in the dining room. "Going after him," she shouted.

"*Buena suerte,* Lorena!"

She dashed up the stairs and down the long hall to dump her clothes and toiletries into the duffel she'd used for the weekend trip. To think, she'd received her proposal dressed in ripped jeans, athletic shoes, and a stretchy red tee that flattered her coloring, but really nothing special. What else? Anything else? The ring, oh, the ring. She opened the box, again astounded by its beauty. Right hand or left. Left, of course. Anything else? She threw open her closet doors and sought out the plush platypus, taking it along for good luck.

Slinging her shoulder bag over one arm, she raced down the staircase with its dangling chandelier and out the front door so rarely used, past the bench where she'd found Jock hunched, and over to a silver Lexus parked in the shade of the live oaks. Fancy car for an unwed teen mother, but she supposed Matt had bought it for Dre. Who cared right now? Put it in gear and go out the gate, the same one that Knox Polk in on the plot had opened for the team bus yesterday.

Over the rutted road to the slightly better main drag

of Chapelle, then off to the interstate at the first cutoff. Left or right on the highway? Three hours if she went through Baton Rouge with the I-10 always torn up and the sluggish traffic of the city, or two and a half through the small towns and across a long causeway into New Orleans. Her ring suddenly flickered with color. Left, the back way, it seemed to beckon.

Even gorgeous rings can be wrong. Once off the highway, the two-lane clogged with Sunday fishermen in their SUVs towing boats and four-wheelers, slowing to turn off for gas or a meal at Spahr's or IHOP or watermelon at a fruit stand. Not to mention that each village had at least two stoplights, enough to set up a tidy speed trap for extra municipal income, and she had to watch her speedometer. Lori ground her teeth in frustration.

At last, she broke free onto the causeway, never heavy traffic there, and emerged from its cypress swamp not far from the Louis Armstrong Airport. Into the city and off the ramp to the Vieux Carre. She knew the locale and how to get there. Fortunately, the tourists were thinning as they went to roost in various restaurants for dinner—which she could use herself having been fueled with only half a glass of champagne and a couple of cookies. Food could wait until they made up on that great bed he'd mentioned. Then they could dine wherever they chose to celebrate.

Jock's street, narrow like all in the old quarter, was further constricted by a small moving van taking up half the space. She squeezed the Lexus behind it and rushed to the wrought iron gate with two buttons to push for entry. Jock stayed in Unit B, not very far away now—if he'd allow her in at all after yesterday. She laid on the buzzer until someone answered, not an Aussie voice, but a black one she recognized from Trin's wedding, only not as friendly. "He's not here. Moved on out today."

"Please, please, it's Lorena. I have to see him."

"If you planning to return his balls, he's on his way back to Down Under where no one knows what happened yesterday. Best Grand Gesture I ever designed, and you destroyed it and him with one word."

"This is X, right.?"

"Sho' is. Get out the way because my new bed is coming down the steps—last thing to go. The furniture rental picked up their stuff a couple of hours ago. I'm going to leave the keys and the letter for the landlord saying sorry and to keep the security deposit and the last month's rent. Drove him to the auto dealer myself to turn in the car since all the guys who know about this stayed for the birthday party. Shit, Dean said we had a chance to take the Super Bowl again with Jock on the Sinners team. He made up for all the dudes who left for big money after we won last year."

"I'm sorry. I truly am. Where is he now?"

"We went straight on over to the airport. You know how early they want you there for those international flights. He said to come visit him at his winery, and I just might do that."

"Stop talking, and tell me when his flight leaves. Qantas, right?"

"Righty-O, as the Jock man would say. No idea when it takes off. He says they leave late in the day, feed you, then turn down the lights so you'll sleep some of those eighteen hours. That's the only problem I got with going to visit."

Two burly men who appeared to be using their day off from working the docks struggled down an outside staircase with the largest mattress Lorena had ever seen. They paused to rest for a moment at the bottom before pushing it toward the gate where she stood. The guy nearest to her elbowed the gate open with his hairy arm. She could have gone directly up but didn't think anyone in New Orleans would be so careless about leaving it open for a thief or a homeless person to bed down for the night in their courtyard.

"X, I'm changing my answer to a yes. Now, if you know more about the flight, tell me so I can stop him."

"I absolutely don't. Jesus H. Christ, he'll want his bed. Tell the movers to bring it back on up here." Certainly, he could hear their curses over the intercom. "I'll pay them double."

"You heard the man. Twice the pay."

"If he wasn't a Sinner, I'd drop this fucker on top of him and leave him to die," the one on the upper end said. But they began to slide the mattress backward as it swayed over them like an avalanche about to happen.

"I can't talk anymore. I have to catch his flight."

She checked her watch, six o'clock, bolted for the Lexus, and threaded her way to the ramp off Canal Street. Naturally, the traffic had thickened with people returning from a New Orleans weekend, but she stayed in the slow lane not willing to miss the offramp to the airport. For the first time, she wasn't grateful for the loan of a car because she'd have to cruise the multistory parking garage to find a space, no abandoning it in the drop off lane, or it would be towed.

Thank God or Cupid, she found a place on the third level just wide enough for the Lexus between two massive SUVs and crossed over the bridge into the terminal. Qantas—way down there. She sprinted the length of the terminal, dodging luggage toters and strollers and got into a very short line with the last flight for Sydney listed to take off at 8:00 p.m. No getting into the security area without a ticket, and that's where he'd be. Six-thirty, but still the gauntlet of the search line to endure. She began to ask for the cheapest ticket to gain entrance but realized in time that Jock wouldn't be crammed into a tourist class seat on the lower level of the plane, and she wouldn't be allowed on the upper level without paying more. She still hadn't paid off her flight home but no time to be cheap.

"Enhanced tourist class, please, on tonight's flight," she said, offering up her credit card and ID. "No luggage."

"All righty, no luggage." The clerk checking her in eyed her flashy engagement ring and probably wrote her off as a wealthy eccentric dressed down in an outfit much like she'd worn yesterday—no sense in dressing up for small children covered in frosting bound to give you sticky hugs. "I'll need to see a passport. This is a nonstop international flight. But they are boarding as we speak. It's a large plane. You should make it."

Her passport, where was it? She'd used it last going through customs in Dallas. Digging deep into her shoulder bag, she sought out the hidden zipper pocket where she usually kept it and found the reassuring outline of a small booklet. "Here it is! Please hurry."

Rather leisurely, she thought, as he checked the expiration date and matched her desperate face to the photo. The computer spit out a boarding pass. The clerk pointed the way to the concourse, which she reached on an escalator taking two steps at a time to the top. Running shoes might not be glamorous, but she made record time catching a plane until she came up against the security line and scoped out the shortest one. Dumping the purse into a container and sending it on its way, she waggled her boarding pass and passport and danced through the metal detector—which went off.

"Would you please step aside, ma'am?" A chubby black woman in uniform held up a wand. "Any joint replacements, metal objects, or jewelry on you."

"No, no." Then she remembered. "Only this," and held out her hand.

The ring merited a low whistle. "Someone loves you big time, sister. Take it off and put it in the bin, now go through the detector again."

She passed with no trouble and grabbed her purse from its container, preparing to run again. The TSA employee called her back. Now what? Damn terrorists everywhere for making flying so complicated.

The woman held out the bin. "I'd hate for this to end up in lost and found."

"Thank you so much." She slipped the ring on her finger and made the sprint to the gate with a long line for tourist class and a short one for those who'd shelled out more money. Once the boarding pass was checked again, she skirted the slow movers and beat them to the entry to the upper deck of the aircraft. Barely acknowledging the cheery welcome of the crew, she entered the first-class area where most of the rich and famous were already ensconced in their private pods. Some glanced up at the sweaty, heavy breathing person who had intruded on their space. Others turned their pods away from gawkers going toward the back. Jock had to be in one of those. She spun one around, then another, drawing shocked protests. A steward headed her way.

"You can't do this, miss. Cease and desist before I call security."

"I apologize. I was supposed to meet my fiancé up here—big Aussie guy, sandy hair, green eyes, great grin."

Jock always made an impression. "Next compartment, but I beg you no more disturbances."

"None, none at all, I promise." She broke through the curtains delineating business class—and there he sat being plied with orange juice and champagne that was probably sparkling wine by a stewardess only too pleased to serve him both. The flight attendant said something that made him smile, but not all the way up to his eyes. He nodded and failed to continue the conversation. The woman and her tray moved on to the next flyers.

He didn't notice her approach. How could he not when her heart pounded loud enough for all the occupants of the cabin to hear. Instead, he downed his juice and flipped through the airline magazine as if she hadn't destroyed all his dreams yesterday with that one word. She stopped abruptly by his seat, making two other late boarders squeeze by her in an aisle wider than most on their way to sit with the enhanced tourists.

"Jock, please, please look at me before they make me take a seat in the next cabin and buckle up."

"Lori?"

"Yes, yes."

"Yes, what?"

"Yes, I want you for my husband." She expected

him to jump up and proclaim his love to the world. That didn't happen.

"Did the Sinners pressure you to do this?"

"If my family couldn't convince me to marry you, the team certainly won't."

He set his champagne aside and placed the magazine in the seat pocket. "Then, why?"

Why? "Because the Sinners and my family love you. Because you are great with kids and dogs. Ah, because you're taller than I am. I don't know what else I can say, but we have to get off this plane before it taxis."

"What, not rich and handsome, too?"

"Yes, both." She waved her hand to show that mattered the least. His gaze followed the ring on her finger. The one said to have a connection that went straight to the heart.

"Not good enough, Lori."

"Huh, I…because you love platypuses." She unzipped her bag and drew out her wildlife park souvenir. "We both love you." She pressed the sleek little animal against her chest, protecting her heart in case he wanted revenge and nothing more from her.

Now, he unbuckled and stood, stooping over a little even in this more spacious compartment. Moving into the aisle, Jock retrieved his garment bag, seeming to take forever. "I might be needing my tux for a wedding."

"Yes, yes." It appeared to be the only word left in her vocabulary. She took his hand. He took her lips against his. The flight attendant told them to sit down, buckle up, and prepare for takeoff.

"Oh, sorry, we have to get off. Dire family

emergency. Just hold the plane for a mo'." Jock's cheeky grin betrayed him.

While the attendant's raised eyebrows indicated doubt, she remained polite. "Hurry. They'll be closing the door any minute."

Good thing both of them were long-legged and in great shape. They arrived at the closed exit just as the crew prepared to seal it. "Dire emergency," Jock repeated. Their rushed explanation had the crew reversing the process. The skyway had already begun to recede, not a long jump, but a chancy one. Hand in hand, they took the leap together and landed safely on the other side.

Chapter Twenty-Five

The phone buzzed in Jock's pocket, still on airplane mode, as Lori steered the Lexus down the parking garage ramp.

"Yes, she found me. We're on the way back to…I'm not sure where."

She heard X's whoop loud and clear. "Super Bowl, here we come!

"You did that? Great. My place then. You're a bonzer mate, X. See you shortly. No? Thanks for that, too."

"What?" she had to ask.

"X thought we'd be coming back and left the keys hidden under the planter by the gate. He returned the bed thinking I'd still want it. Good on him."

They'd returned to an apartment bare of anything but a nine by nine-foot bed, made up in pale gray sheets, a silvery spread, and scattered with red petals from the knockout rose in the planter so heavy it took a football player to tilt it on its side to regain the keys. X-avier Hopkins had the heart of a romantic.

They wasted no time making love on its wide surface, not as gently as their first time and not as frantically as the night of the wedding, but something wonderfully in between. Still, he managed to loosen her hair from her braid and fan it out over the spread, where it mingled with the red rose petals. "When I bought this bed, I imagined you here exactly like this."

He'd believed that steadfastly while she still thought she despised him. A great tenderness enveloped her. Though they'd finished having sex, for the time being, she raised her head to his and gave him a long kiss, full of warmth and future promise.

"I must have done something right." He grinned in his usual charming way.

"Yes, you believed in us when I didn't. I could use a shower." Finding a bar of forgotten soap in the bathroom, they cleansed each other with their hands in all the most intimate places and let the warm water sluice over them as they brought each other to climax again.

One of the spare sheets that matched the bed served as a towel, and the mattress did double duty as a table that would have seated six when they ate their takeout Chinese on its surface with the plastic utensils and chopsticks included in the bag. Her phone rang as they fed each other pot stickers. Stacy.

Oh dear, she'd promised to call, and the watch lying on top of her duffel bag read nine. Typical of Billodeaux family gatherings, the exhausted children slept in the nursery by now, the ponies were curried and fed, and the adults sat outside enjoying one of the last pleasant evenings before the heat took over and the mosquitoes hatched. Stacy wanted to know, of course. They all did.

"Mom said I shouldn't bother because you'd either be at Jude's crying your eyes out or having makeup sex with Jock."

She heard her mom's muffled, "Stacy!", but that did not prevent Stacy from asking which was it.

"We are now engaged," and sitting here naked with a sheet thrown over us eating Chinese dumplings. She didn't turn on FaceTime but did punch speakerphone. They heard the cheers in the background, the shouts of congratulations. They'd all waited for the word. Right now, she was at Jock's place. Tomorrow, she'd vacate her bedroom in Jude's apartment and stay here until they decided on a wedding date and place.

"Destination wedding—Australia next May," Stacy, who could be bossy, suggested.

Over the mass of paper cartons between them, Jock shook his head at her. "No, I don't think so, Stace. We'll let you know when we've decided. Tell Dre I'll have her car back before ten as promised. I had to remove Jock from an airplane right before takeoff. We're both pretty wrung out now. Talk to y'all tomorrow. Bye."

"After we get my Aviator back, I say we go for a license and whatever else we need and book one of the wedding chapels here for this coming weekend."

Her turn to shake her head. "Oh, you don't know my family well yet."

"They'll want the big affair like Josee and Trinity."

"No, it's not that. I'll be able to have any kind of wedding I want, and all that fuss isn't my style. Stacy did have the big deal, too. Annie was married at the ranch, and Xo had her reception there. The important thing is that all of them want to be there. I missed Annie's wedding because I was in Australia. I may never live that down."

His green eyes sparkled. "I was thinking just that—I'd like to get married at the ranch. Throw some snags on the barbie and have a load of beer in the Esky."

Again, she shook her head. "No sausage, more likely a whole pig, but beer and Brownlowe wine, certainly."

"Next month, then?"

Again, she had to disillusion him. She cupped his strong jaw with her hands. "It does take longer than that to put even a simple wedding together. You don't know the rhythm of American football yet. In July, you'll have summer training camp with two a days and come home exhausted. August, four exhibition games, two home, two away that will keep you running. Then in September, the regular season starts. Training all but one day a week preparing for the game on Sunday and often travel in between. Maybe a bye week in October and a little time off over Christmas. That's when Annie and Matt worked their wedding into the schedule. No honeymoon trips until the season is over."

"There must be a way we could do it sooner."

"I appreciate your eagerness. I'll talk to my mom and see what she has to say. She plans events all the time."

"She likes me. She'll come through for us."

"If she can, but don't count on anything happening this year."

They slept, were up early to retrieve Jock's vehicle, and then over to Jude's place to collect her things. She'd hoped her crabby sister hadn't gotten home from the ranch yet, but her car sat in its usual space. Jock wisely opted to wait outside. After a chewing out about throwing away her own ambitions for a man, Lori filled her suitcase and lugged it downstairs. She parked the Lexus in front of Matt's house and left the keys with the maid.

A quick call to her coach at Tulane that she'd be coming in late won her a few more hours with Jock. They spent the time at Stanley of New Orleans having a meal and a heart to heart talk over a Breakfast Seafood Platter with its soft-shelled crab, oysters, shrimp, poached eggs, Canadian bacon and hollandaise on an English muffin for him, and the more modest Eggs Acadiana, a variation of eggs Benedict, for her. The lecture from Jude had brought some interesting questions to light about marrying in haste.

She took the issue head-on. "You do know I'll be going back to Australia to train with Maisie until the Olympics. The Sinners nearly always make the playoffs in January and sometimes go on to the Super Bowl in February. I might not be here for seven months, which would mean delaying a wedding even longer." She waited for his protest—my wife doesn't need to win an Olympic medal that Jude predicted.

"No worries." Jock pulled the legs off the soft-shelled crab and crunched them. "All the more reason to get married now. Later, we spend the summers here in Melbourne, where it's winter and vice versa. We'll work it out." He downed an oyster, cut into his poached eggs, and ate them European style.

"Children?"

"Yes, whenever you want them."

"And if I don't."

That stopped him with a bit of dripping yolk and English muffin halfway to his mouth. A sticking point, then. She tested him. "It would be the biggest disappointment of my life because they'd be fine little rippers—but you hinted you wanted children back at Brownlowe when you thought I didn't."

"You remember that? I never said so directly, only that I thought you wouldn't want them."

"I could tell by the disappointed tone of your voice. Lori, I remember every second of those few days we had together before the great misunderstanding and the Grand Gesture."

"I do, too. They were special and wonderful and made your betrayal worse."

"There was no betrayal."

He might have noticed the tears beginning to form, sheening her dark eyes and making vision difficult, because he switched suddenly to jovial. "Righty-O. We need to get you to work. Dean said no practice today. I'll see about retrieving the furniture. If you don't like it, we'll choose other things later." He scraped up the last of the shrimp on his plate and called for the bill while she finished her eggs.

He dropped her off with a cheery hooroo and picked her up later, his grin wider than ever. "It's settled. I talked to Mama Nell. She told me to call her that. If you are willing, we can get married on the Fourth of July at the big bash your family hosts every year. I understand the pigs and the fireworks are already on order. Put up a few tents for shade and maybe for dancing. Morning service at the Episcopal church in town, just family and close friends, then it's a big pig roast picnic after the ceremony. Unless you want something else."

She should have recalled that he did work fast to get what he wanted. "I've always loved our Independence Day celebration."

"Yes, even better to get married on the day America stuck it to the Poms—and turned Australia into a penal colony, or we might not have met."

"Interesting way to think about it. But there are flowers and dresses and bridesmaids and groomsmen and…"

"Mama Nell said to wait for Josee to get back from the honeymoon because she has an idea we all might like."

Chapter Twenty-Six

Or not.

The family gathered in the den at the ranch as the largest place to accommodate them. Lori and Jock shared the sofa with the honeymooners, Jock taking up most of the space. Everyone else sprawled in the recliners or sat on the floor or in Teddy and Jesse's case, brought their own wheelchairs.

Some of it came naturally to Lorena's great relief. All her brothers and sisters with their spouses if married and Jock's two brothers were to be in the wedding party, twenty-two in all, though they lacked one bridesmaid. She called and asked Maisie to walk with Mick Brown. Edie pouted and held out for Nick Brown as her escort, which left T-Rex lacking a partner. Mama Nell suggested Dre.

"Oh, sure, put me with the unwed mother because Edie has a thing about Australian men."

"Hey, I escorted her when she was pregnant. It's a dear thing to do," Trinity said and got a loving glance from his bride.

"Maybe I don't want to be dear."

Mama Nell put it to rights swiftly. "Otherwise, you'd be walking with your sister, Rex."

"Like me," Mack groused. "Why do I always get paired with Jude? She's so short we look ridiculous."

"Because she can guarantee your behavior during

the ceremony. Perhaps not afterward." Her mother gave the distinct impression that Lorena wasn't the only one to observe him sneaking off with one of the model bridesmaids at Trinity's wedding. "Rex, I thought you and Dre were friends now. She's very pretty since she gave up the Goth look, and your friends won't be there anyway."

"Okay, okay. But when Mack or Edie gets married, I escort someone else."

"Wait for me to be dragged to the altar, and you'll wait a long time," Mack said.

"I should be finished with college by the time Nick finishes med school," Edie reminded them. "You never know what might happen."

Josee spoke up. "Lori, you know how women always say they never wear a bridesmaid's dress again, though I did try to choose one that had future use. Would you consider having us wear the pale pink dresses from my wedding? Yours could be shortened a trifle for Dre, and wouldn't you look wonderful in the gown I modeled in front of the Monument to the Immigrants on the River Walk with its diaphanous layers of fine white cotton. I can speak to the designer about selling it or a loan."

Just like that, Josee had taken care of her number one worry, but she had more to contribute. "Now I'm thinking about the men. Far too hot outside in July for tuxedos. What would you think about white linen suits with pink shirts and pink carnation boutonnieres, classic, cheap, fragrant, and available all year round. We can use them in the bridesmaids' bouquets filled out with greens and other flowers, but gardenias for the bride in her bouquet and in her dark hair.

"Her loose dark hair," Jock said.

But T-Rex groaned again. "A pink shirt and a white suit. We'll look like gay Huey Longs."

He sat on the floor in front of Jock, who clapped him on the back and said, "A real man can wear that combo and not give a bloody damn. I certainly don't. Whatever Lorena wants."

Across the room over by the vast fireplace, Xochi shot Lori a look that said, "Pink, I told you so."

"Hey, I've already got mine in the closet. I know I'm only the DJ, so I'll pair it with a lavender shirt," X-avier, who had offered to handle all the music, declared. T-Rex seemed less upset about the choice after that, with X being considered the coolest of the bunch.

"If it's settled, the larger members of our group, I'm talking about you Sinners, will need to get your tailors on it right away. Not likely to be any in your size. Trin, Teddy, and Rex can probably find something in stock. How about your brothers, Jock?"

"Not as big as me, but I'll get them started on it."

"See how well this is going." Josee beamed.

Lorena could only nod, but she had some details to add. "Oh, oh, Maisie will need a maternity gown, and you'll need a dress of your own. If it doesn't hurt anyone's feelings, I'd like Maisie to be matron of honor, and Mick can stand up for Jock."

"Shucks, I had my heart set on being your man of honor," Trinity said, seemingly content with his sister's choice of a groom at last. He got an elbow from his wife sitting beside him.

"I'm never best man," Mack sulked.

"Because you aren't," said Trinity, possibly the only one in the room who could get away with the remark without starting a physical fight.

"You know this would have been easier without the men here," Lorena said, eyeing her closest brothers.

Mama Nell wrapped things up for a wedding on the Fourth of July. "We're almost done, I think—a cake from Pommier's Bakery. No problem. If you are happy with the Fourth menu—roasted pork, potato salad, slaw, baked beans, rice dressing, French bread, and vegetable and tropical fruit trays, the usual watermelon for dessert along with the cake—we're set for the food. Let Mariah supply the champagne because she will insist, but we'll get some Aussie beers and Brownlowe wines as well as the soft drinks. Any objections?"

Jock raised a hand. "Only one. If you want Vegemite, I'll have to ask my brothers to bring some. I'm nearly out." He watched the appalled faces before letting his grin shine. "Gotcha!"

Chapter Twenty-Seven

Somehow, all had come together. Josee, if anything, was more of a persuasive martinet than bossy Stacy. Lorena stood crammed into a rather small room at the Episcopal church with her mother and all the bridesmaids. She wore the designer gown with its many fine layers of diaphanous cotton, making up a full skirt that hid white sandals with a low heel more practical for dancing and traipsing around the ranch—no veil, hair down to please Jock. White gardenias pinned into it filled the area with their strong scent. Josee's mother, the noted photographer, Stevie Riley, had captured the whole procedure and gone to take her place with the rest of the guests until the procession.

Ten a.m. approached. Any minute now, her dad would come for her while her mom slipped into the pew beside Mawmaw Nadine's wheelchair. X ran through his church music repertoire. Was there nothing the man couldn't do? Forced to take piano and organ lessons by his granny to help out at church when old Mrs. Proctor didn't feel up to it, he'd said. He paused for the signal to play the wedding march as the men took their place at the altar and awaited the bride and her attendants. In less than an hour since they'd opted not to include a communion, she'd be Mrs. Jock Brown, cutting the wedding cake and dancing under the huge white tents erected on the lawn at home.

Still able to rock a white suit as well as the younger men, her father appeared at the door. He beckoned to her mother, whispered in her ear, and left. Mama Nell dressed her face in a reassuring smile. "It seems the groom has been delayed. We're sure he'll be here any minute now."

Clutched around her bouquet, Lori's hands went cold. "Did he say what the problem was?" While she'd stayed over at the ranch last night, Jock told her he had a few details to take care of in New Orleans. He'd already turned the platinum and diamond wedding band over to Mick for safekeeping as his brothers and Maisie's family stayed with the Billodeauxs.

"Hmmm, no. His brothers tried to reach him, but his phone keeps going to voice mail. Maybe in his rush, he got caught in one of the speed traps on the way here."

"That's possible," Lorena admitted, but the cold spread from her fingers toward her heart. What if this embarrassment was payback for her rejection of his Grand Gesture in front of his teammates, and he'd played her the last six weeks leading up to the wedding? Could that be why he'd wanted to marry in such haste—to have his revenge served hot? Yet he'd signed his contract and couldn't possibly be on his way to Australia now.

Another knock at the door and X peered into the room full of dismayed bridesmaids and one tense bride. "I heard the word. You want me to run through my music again or let the guests wait in silence?"

"X, do you suppose…"

"No, the Jock man wouldn't do you that way no matter how much you hurt him. Put that right out your mind. I never seen a guy so gone over a woman. Well, maybe Trinity. I'll run through the songs again, maybe get them singing along. Give me a sign when he gets here."

She repeated to herself, "I believe, I believe," but didn't voice it out loud. Another fifteen minutes passed. Out in the church, X led the congregation in "This Little Light of Mine."

"Everyone join in now!"

A slight tap on the door signaled Fr. John's entrance. "Does anyone wish counseling in my office?"

"No, I believe he'll be here soon," she said with all the confidence she could muster.

"Humph," Jude muttered.

"I told her not to get mixed up with a footy player," Maisie asserted, making Lorena wish she'd chosen one of the others for matron of honor. Perhaps Xochi, who touched her arm and sent warmth coursing to her heart.

Quarter to eleven. The music stopped again. Mama Nell opened the door. "I'll check with the men."

Before she could do so, Mawmaw's voice rang out loud and clear in the void and echoed off the high ceiling of the sanctuary. "Let's get this Hadacol parade on the road. The meringue on my bread pudding will deflate in the heat."

Chuckles relieved some of the tension, but not hers. By now, the ceremony should have ended. Believe, believe in him.

"On second thought, I'll phone the ranch and ask Brinsley to pass around drinks and snacks. Dinner will be later than we expected." Bless her mom for stating the obvious, but in a way that still held a shred of hope.

Eleven o'clock. Josee came to her side and hugged

her shoulders. "Honey, I think it's time to call this game. Let's get in those limos and go have a great Fourth of July party."

"No. I'll wait. You can leave if you want." Believe.

Xo was again at her elbow, sending her strength. "We won't go until you do."

Five after eleven. Sirens sounded outside the church.

Oh, God. Had he in been an accident? Or had he gotten a ticket, disputed it, and ended up in handcuffs. She'd much rather the latter.

The opening bars of the wedding march sounded. Her dad appeared in the doorway. "He's here."

"What happened?"

"I don't know. He said everything went shithouse on him."

Maisie cackled. "Now that's a good Aussie word. I guess we'll find out later."

In some disarray, the bridesmaids found their discarded bouquets, checked their makeup suffering from being in a crowded room, and formed up to walk down the aisle. Going two by two, they parted at the altar, filling rows on either side of the church. Behind them, Lorena sought out the sight of her groom wearing a rumpled white linen suit and red in the face, but still head and shoulders above the rest. A state trooper stood in the rear with a satisfied smile on his face, a duty well done, but what duty?

"Dearly beloved, we are gathered here today…" Fr. John intoned as she and Jock stood before him. She pushed any questions aside until the brief ceremony ended. It took longer to load the wedding party into the fleet of stretch limousines hired for the occasion, but they had a state police escort to the ranch. Again, she wondered what kind of trouble her groom had gotten into on the way to his wedding.

Ensconced into the plush interior of the vehicle, Jock reached over to grasp the bottle of champagne. "Sparkling wine," he said. He opened the bottle without spilling a drop, put it to his lips, and drank heartily.

"First, let me say you are the most bonzer bride an Aussie could have, Lorena. Second, allow me to explain why I ran so late. I had some details to work out with Luca. It took longer than I expected to get what I needed, so I thought I'd better change into the suit before driving to the church. I was well on the road when I realized I'd left my phone in my other slacks, but I thought, no worries. I won't be that late. Halfway here, the Aviator ran out of petrol in the area that's all piney woods, palmettos, and deep ditches filled to the brim with black water. That's on me. Rushing, I forgot to fill the tank. You'd think someone would stop to help a bloke in a white suit and pink shirt. Plenty of gawkers, no offers."

He paused to drink some more. "Finally, Officer Rogers came along and offered me a ride, siren and all. We got fifteen minutes on the road, and I realized I'd left my laptop in the Ute."

"Give me that bottle," Lorena said. She took a swig and handed it back. "You could have bought another if it got stolen."

"But I couldn't replace what's in it. That set us back, but here I am, a married man who provided his own police escort to the reception."

A weak round of applause sounded. Dean took the bottle and drank. "I only hope you don't forget the plays as much as you've forgotten today."

"I won't be getting hitched again. No worries." Jock eyed his new wife. "I thought I'd get to the church, and you'd be gone."

"No, I believed you'd come. But what would you have done if I had left?" She noticed the relief on his face when she'd said she believed in him and felt warm to her core without Xochi's help.

"Thrown Fr. John into the squad car and taken him to the ranch to do the ceremony."

"I think you would have."

"Bloody oath on that."

The motorcade made its turn through the ranch gates, where the majority of the guests waited and showered them with dried rose petals from the little net bags on every table. Facing the mob of famished well-wishers with a smile, Lorena said, "As Mawmaw would say, let's get this Hadacol parade on the road and feed these people."

The newly wedded made their way to the first of the white tents to cut the cake and keep another vow not to smash it in each other's face. As soon as Stevie captured that moment, Brinsley presented a small key to Mama Nell. "I am afraid the fruit and relish trays are depleted, but the roasted pigs are secured in the barbecue pavilion along with the rest of the feast. I took the liberty of putting a lock on the building."

"I don't know what we ever did without you." She received a formal nod in reply.

Nell handed the key to her husband, who summoned a contingent of groomsmen to heave the heavy pigs to the table while the caterers followed with the rest of the meal kept hot or well-chilled depending on the dish. Carefully apportioned pieces of Mawmaw Nadine's bread pudding sat at each place for the bridal party. Though the dessert had acquired beads of gold on the meringue, it suffered no other damage. Lori and her groom, followed by their attendants, queued up to the tables in front of the mass of guests Jock referred to as a Sinners Hall of Fame and their families, very close to the truth.

X invited them to dance the heavy meal off in the other tent supplied with a hard floor—but first, the bride and groom wished to present their gifts to each other. Since T-Rex had been so unhappy with his partner and his outfit, Lori gave him the honor of bringing around the vehicle hidden in the barn.

"My Predator," Jock shouted with affection.

"Not yours, but one like it. Dad pulled lots of strings to get one here, and his automobile dealer custom painted it in black and red because you're a Sinner now."

"That I am for as long as they'll have me. Same goes for you. Now, part of the reason I was late for my own wedding." He signaled X to cue up his laptop and project a few pictures, the first being no more than a foundation for a small building. "It's a barn. Next photo."

Luca Lowe appeared holding the halters of two large red horses with white stockings. Her father burst out, "I know them! Sired by my Lazy Boy's frozen sperm a few years ago. Lazy Sheila and Lazy Bloke. The Bloke never had the speed and didn't like to run, ended up a gelding, but Sheila would make a fine broodmare for the line."

"Too much information," Mama Nell told her

husband, but the Aussies in the audience hooted with laughter. Not many of them since footy season was well underway, and no Magpies could attend.

"Exactly right for me, a horse that doesn't like to run. I'm told the mare has more spirit. The previous owner will board them for us until we get back to Oz."

"Oh, you gave me something you hate, and I love it. I think I'm going to cry." Lori dabbed at her eyes to keep them from leaking.

"I'll learn to ride eventually. Here's the last one."

The final shot displayed a wooden sign next to a shaded stream. It read Platypus Preserve. "This creek runs behind my house at Brownlowe. The folks at the Healesville Sanctuary are checking the conditions and might place some platypuses there. They've had a few rescued since the fires."

"Something we both love." She did cry now while the audience applauded.

X dove right in before things became more maudlin. "Let's start the dancing—dragon boat races at three and fireworks at nine. A light dinner will be served at six. In between, enjoy the pool, the volleyball and basketball courts, riding in the corral, and all the other ranch amenities."

Once the formal dancing ended, the bridal party slipped into the house to change into cooler and more activity-oriented clothes. Lorena killed at sand volleyball, and Jock's vessel took the dragon boat prize. Second dinner was comprised of leftovers, but no one complained. As darkness fell, her dad, Trinity, and anyone else who could afford to lose a finger, if careless, rowed across the bayou to set off the fireworks arranged in a long row down a sugar cane field road. As the display went off one at a time with a boom and plenty of crackling to light up the sky and reflect in the water, the crowd oohed and aahed.

Lorena and Jock, with his arm locked around her waist, stood next to Matt, balancing his two sons on his broad shoulders, and Dre with her little boy, legs dangling around her neck and fingers gripping her blonde hair. Short Annie stayed nearby for comforting in case any of the boys became frightened, but so far, so good. Between bursts of sparks and loud blasts of sound, Matt said to Jock, "I had no family left until I married into this one and made it my own. You can't go wrong with the Billodeauxs."

"I've got my brothers and knew I wanted Lorena at first sight."

"Not as fast a decision on my part as y'all know." She leaned into her husband's chest.

"I'd read about these people, this place, and kept thinking that's what I want. I believed I could have it all. Almost didn't work out."

"But now, I *believe* you are stuck with my family and me forever."

"No worries there. None at all."

A word about the author...

Once a librarian, now a writer of romance, Lynn Shurr grew up in Pennsylvania Dutch country. She attended a state college and earned a very impractical B.A. in English Literature. Her first job out of school really was working as a cashier in a burger joint. Moving from one humble job to another, she traveled to North Carolina, then Germany, then California where she buckled down and studied for an M.A. in Librarianship.

New degree in hand, she found her first reference job in the Heart of Cajun Country, Lafayette, Louisiana. For her, the old saying, "Once you've tasted bayou water, you will always stay here" came true. She raised three children not far from the Bayou Teche and lives there still with her astronomer husband.

When not writing, Lynn likes to paint, cheer for the New Orleans Saints and LSU Tigers, and take long road trips nearly anywhere. Her love of the bayou country, its history and customs, often shows in the background for her books.

You may contact Lynn at www.lynnshurr.com or visit her blog—lynnshurr.blogspot.com. She welcomes your comments.

Thank you for purchasing
this publication of The Wild Rose Press, Inc.

For questions or more information
contact us at
info@thewildrosepress.com.

The Wild Rose Press, Inc.
www.thewildrosepress.com

www.ingramcontent.com/pod-product-compliance
Lightning Source LLC
Chambersburg PA
CBHW051534260626
47170CB00003B/929